Cruel Captor

VENGEFUL VILLAINS: BOOK THREE

KRISTEN LUCIANI

Cruel Captor © 2022 by Kristen Luciani

This book is a work of fiction. Names, characters, places and incidents are the product of the author's imagination or are used fictitiously. Any resemblance to actual events, locales or persons, living or dead is purely coincidental.

Except for the original material written by the author, all songs, song titles, and lyrics mentioned in this novel are the property of the respective songwriters and copyright holders.

All rights reserved. The unauthorized reproduction or distribution of this copyrighted work is illegal. This book or any portion thereof may not be reproduced, scanned, distributed, or used in any manner whatsoever, via the Internet, electronic, or print, without the express written permission of the author, except for the use of brief quotations in a book review.

For more information, or information regarding subsidiary rights, please contact Kristen Luciani at kluciani@gmail.com.

Cover Design: Book Cover Couture

Editing: Allusion Graphics

Photo Credit: Rafa Catala

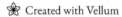 Created with Vellum

Prologue
KONSTANTIN

"Gotta be honest," my brother Gregor says before tipping back his shot of vodka. "You look like you're about to walk death row, not make a toast to your blushing bride-to-be."

I clench my fingers around my glass and swirl it under my nose. The complex scent of tobacco, white pepper, and wheat crackers teases my nostrils. I shoot the clear liquid, the aftertaste bittersweet.

Just like my engagement.

Sure, the first few days were great. Lots of champagne. Even more screwing.

But it's been a month. Something is off. And it's not just her panties.

I grab the bottle neck of the Jewel of Russia Ultra Black Label I've been guzzling for the past half an hour and pour myself another shot. "She's fucking around."

Gregor almost spits out his drink. "Get the hell out of here. How'd you find out?"

"I just know."

"Wait." He puts his glass down and walks over to me. "You don't have proof?"

"I don't need proof. I know her. She's made excuses to stay back from the last three business trips I've taken. Seychelles, Paris, Croatia. Made up some crap about photoshoots she needed to do instead. It's bullshit."

"She's a supermodel. Maybe you're being a little bit paranoid?"

I grit my teeth. "Don't question me. Not about this. It's over."

The truth is, since I slid that five-carat diamond ring onto Mischa's finger, the noose around my neck tugged tighter and tighter. I mean, Christ, within the first three months of dating, she had her wedding gown picked out and the destination venue secured. She was on the hunt for a husband and I was her prey.

Maybe I let my guard down for the first time in my life because she's hot as hell and fucks like a rabbit in heat. Before Mischa, I was one of the most eligible bachelors in the country, dating every A-lister who crossed my path.

I swore I'd never settle down. One and done was always my MO.

I should have stuck with that plan.

"You've got a whole dining room full of people, including Mom and Dad, who are here to celebrate your engagement. Don't you think that maybe you should talk to Mischa before blowing your future to shit?" Gregor shrugs. "I'm just saying you might be overreacting. Getting cold feet because you've never bothered to learn the first names of the girls you took home, and now here you are, ready to be shackled to one forever?"

I narrow my eyes and slam my glass on the polished wood bar. "Save the psychoanalysis for someone who gives a shit." My cell phone pings. I grab it from my pocket and stare at the text notification on the screen.

The sender is unknown.

My brow furrows.

"What is it?" Gregor asks.

But I don't answer. I push past my brother and storm into the hallway of the country club. I stalk past the dining room where my mother holds court surrounded by the social climbers aching to rub elbows with the elite.

My father is nowhere in sight.

I clutch the phone, my pulse slamming against my throat as I stalk down the corridor. Normally, I wouldn't give a damn if he showed up at all since he's an arrogant, vindictive, self-absorbed prick who cares more about money and power than he does his own blood.

I stop in front of a closed door at the end of the hall. Dad's bodyguard, Igor, stands in front of it with his hands folded in front of his massive body.

"Where is he?" I say through clenched teeth.

"He is in a meeting," Igor answers in a deep, menacing voice. "He cannot be disturbed."

"The fuck he can't," I growl, kicking the door in with the ball of my foot.

The lighting in the room is dim. Two figures jump out of the shadows.

"Konstantin!" my mother calls out, running toward me. "What on Earth–?"

Her next words are swallowed by a loud gasp.

I walk through the doorway, very aware of the disbelieving eyes boring into me.

Mischa grabs her dress to cover herself, her hair tangled in that "just got fucked" kind of way. She stammers something but the blood rushes between my ears, drowning it all out.

And my father. The bastard doesn't even bother to hide. The look on his face screams "I won."

Because he could never accept second place.

He always has to be the best, the richest, the most powerful, the most sought-after. For the past few months, the spotlight has been on me and Mischa, not him. He hated that I was seen as the power player, that I was all over the Internet and in the newspapers with a gorgeous supermodel on my arm.

"You gold-digging whore." I take a step into the room, firing a glare at Mischa. "It's never enough for you, is it? I gave you everything."

"No, you didn't," she snaps. "This isn't about money and you know it." Mischa's cheeks turn bright red. She backs away from the open door and darts into the bathroom at the back of the room. The door slams shut.

My father sneers. "Come on, Konstantin. She knows who really holds the power position in this family. Are you really surprised she chose me over you?"

"You selfish bastard," I hiss, inching toward him. "You just incinerated your entire fucking life and I'm gonna be the one to piss on the ashes."

CHAPTER 1
Konstantin

"I don't give a fuck who's after you." The corners of my lips twist like I've just tasted poison. "But I'd personally rather see you alive, stripped of every fucking penny and humiliated in front of the whole world, than dead and off the hook for all the hell you've caused our family."

"Mikhail," my father says, using my birth name. His voice shakes. I bet the sins of his past bounce between his temples right now like a fierce game of pinball. "I'm your blood. You can't let them do this to me. You're the only one who can save me and your mother."

I steeple my fingers, leaning forward so that my elbows rest on the top of my desk. The lines etched into my father's worn face are deeper than they were a few months ago when he blew up my life by publicly humiliating me. He's paraded Mischa around for the past three months, proving himself to be the evil prick he is. Streaks of purple stain the bags under his clear blue eyes. For years, his gaze held nothing but disdain and disgust when he looked at me. Now there's only desperation.

And fear.

"Fuck you. You think you can come in here and use Mom as your pawn? She got out, remember? Nobody is gonna lay a finger on her now that she's divorced you," I sneer. "And now that Mischa knows what a pathetic piece of conniving shit you really are, she's out, too."

"I'm sorry." His lip trembles. He probably figured I hadn't heard about their breakup. But nobody breaks news faster than the Internet. "I really never meant for that to happen—"

I shoot up from my chair, fury swirling through my insides. "You fucked her. My fiancée. On the night of our engagement party, and Christ only knows how many times before that. Do you expect me to believe your dick just accidentally slipped inside of her?" I walk around to the front of the desk. My pulse throbs against my throat as I hover over him. "You couldn't stand to be on the sidelines. You hated that the spotlight was on me, that I was the power player for once. You jealous, vindictive fuck."

All because he could never accept second place.

My father always has to be the best, the richest, the most powerful, the most sought-after. And in his eyes, I was always a threat to him. When Mischa and I were engaged, the focus had been on us, not him. He hated that I was all over the Internet and in the newspapers with a gorgeous supermodel on my arm. Just like he hated to see my arms business take off without his influence.

He jumps up from his chair. His spine stiffens, teeth gritting. And his tone shifts like I just flicked a switch. Suddenly he's shed his groveling, remorseful skin. Now he's back to his true form, a venomous, blood-sucking snake.

"I came here to ask for your help. After everything I've done to build you up, how dare you deny me protection," he hisses. His voice rises. A deep red flush floods his face. The anger bubbling just under the surface is about to spew.

Good. I hope he gives himself a stroke. I'd love nothing more than to see him dead.

"Do I really need to list out the reasons?"

"You're my son. You owe me!" He balls his fists. Spit flies from the corners of his mouth.

"I don't owe you a goddamn thing. You ruined your marriage and destroyed our family because you always needed to one-up me. And now you come here crying for protection because you made a bad choice that slapped a target on your head?" I dip my head lower, forcing his eyes upward.

Oh, yeah, he's gonna look up to *me* now.

"Why the fuck should I sacrifice what I've built to help you after you've done nothing but tear me down?" I ask.

"Because, you little bastard, if you don't, Viktor Malikov will come for you, too," he growls.

Hold the fucking phone.

"Why would he come for *me*?" I fist the front of my father's shirt, tugging the fabric tight in my fingers. "He's your partner. I have nothing to do with him or the Brotherhood 7."

My father's face pales. "Because I went against Viktor and the Brotherhood and ordered a hit on Olek Moroz instead of the real target."

"You what?" My jaw tightens. "Who fucking paid you to take out the head of the Ukrainian mafia?"

"Arseny Siderov," he says, struggling against me. "But he disappeared after the hit on Moroz. Viktor wants my blood, the Ukranians want my head, and Siderov won't expose himself to save me, motherfucker that he is."

"You betrayed Viktor. Why the hell wouldn't Siderov think you'd do the same to him?"

"I know. I fucked up. Viktor found out I went against his order and that I'm working with someone outside of the Brotherhood 7. I have too much to lose, Mikhail. I need your help. Get me out of the country. Find me a place to lay low while I figure out a way to handle Malikov. If they get to me first, I'll... we'll lose everything."

I stare at him for a long minute before letting go of his shirt. I give him a hard shove and he stumbles into the chair behind him.

"You've already lost everything, old man. And it's sad that you don't even realize it. Now get the fuck out of my office."

His eyes narrow. "You ungrateful bastard. You'd be nowhere without me. You didn't build a goddamn thing on your own. You needed my money, my influence, my network!" An angry flush creeps up the sides of his neck. "And Mischa knew who really held the power in this family. She knew you could never give her what I could, that you could never compete with me."

"Mischa is a gold-digging whore with a pussy you could park cars in. Good fucking riddance to her." I inch closer to my father. "And to you."

He straightens his shirt and stalks toward the door of my office. He grabs the handle and twists it before looking back at me one final time. "This isn't over. You'll never—"

A sea of bullets with machine gun force blasts through the windows of my office, drowning out his next words. His body jerks left and right as the shots rip through his flesh. I dive to the floor and pull myself toward my desk. With one swift motion, I grab the loaded 9mm taped to the underside.

Another hail of bullets follows. Picture frames crash to the floor, liquor bottles explode, glasses shatter. Minutes stretch into what feels like hours before the shooting finally stops. I creep around the side of the desk. The door hangs off its hinges, bullets wedged into the wood.

And my father lies facedown on the floor next to it.

I point the gun at the space where the windows used to be in case the assailant decides to do a post mortem. I crouch low to the floor as I creep toward my father's body. A pool of blood spreads underneath him, the back of his blue shirt torn up by bullets. His breaths are short, sharp, and labored. Blood runs down the side of his head, his hair matted and stained bright red.

I should feel something besides relief, but I don't. The Devil is about to die, and he can rest in Hell for all I give a damn.

His hand shakes as he raises it, short wheezes shuddering his chest. "Y-you'll never win." A thick cough rattles his body, blood spilling from the sides of his mouth. He struggles for breath, his face pale white. He's got seconds, if that.

I dip my head lower so he doesn't miss my next words before his eyes glaze over. "I just did."

NINE MONTHS LATER

"Mikhail Federov." A deep voice rumbles behind me, lancing my toxic thoughts. "How does it feel to be Enemy Number One on the Brotherhood 7's hit list?"

I slowly turn away from the bar at Tatiana, one of the most famous underground Russian mafia social clubs. My hand grips my glass...a shot of the most expensive vodka available on a tab I can't even pay.

"You've got the wrong guy," I growl through clenched teeth. "Mikhail Federov is dead."

The tall, dark-haired man nods. He slides into the empty space between me and the woman standing to my right. "I heard the news. Fortunately, I'm not a man who takes things at face-value. And since your arms trafficking business went into the shitter after your father was gunned down, it makes sense that you'd want to start over with a new identity."

Went into the shitter. That's a fucking understatement if I ever heard one. Nobody would work with me after my father fell prey to Viktor Malikov because all my clients figured I'd have the same target slapped on my ass. And guilt by association slaps the same target on their asses.

"Who the fuck are you?"

"I'm the guy who's going to make you whole again." He hails the bartender and orders Yorsch, a combination of beer and vodka.

I gulp down the rest of my vodka and slam the glass on the bar. "Fuck off. Whatever you think you know, trust me. You don't. And if you don't get the hell away from me, I'll put a knife in your throat."

"The people who put that hit on your father?" He leans his head close to mine. The stench of cigars mixed with Yorsch on his breath makes my stomach twist. Well, all that and the words he just spoke. "They're the ones who crushed your business. Nobody wants to work with you because they know you have a target on your head. That's why you 'killed' Mikhail and became Konstantin."

"Mikhail had a target on his head," I say. "Konstantin Romanov doesn't."

"Konstantin Romanov has an opportunity to take back everything he lost...if he has the right partner." The man pauses to take a long gulp of the cocktail the bartender just placed in front of him. He sweeps his tongue over his lips to lick off the foam left by his drink.

"I don't need a partner. I have the Malikovs just where I want them."

"That's what your father told me when I made him an offer to betray the Brotherhood 7." The man's eyes narrow. "And then he got his ass shot up. Do you know why? He was sloppy. And Viktor Malikov found out he'd betrayed the Brotherhood. That's what happens when you don't do things yourself. You know exactly what I'm talking about, don't you?"

I draw in a sharp breath. My plans to get revenge on the Malikovs crapped out the second I hired that asshat ex-con Hank Wheeler to heist two truckloads of weapons to crush their distribution plans. My goal was to steal their weapons and make them desperate enough to come crawling to me for help. But everything went sideways and I learned a hard lesson — if you want things done right, do them your damn self. Don't leave business up to fucking ex-con hillbillies.

"Arseny fucking Siderov." I grit my teeth. "You're the man who paid my father to assassinate the head of the Ukranian mafia instead of hitting the real target."

"The one and only. And I'm here to make you an offer, Mikhail. One you can't afford to refuse."

I drum my fingertips on the bar. "I'm in the Malikov's inner circle with my hands in their pie. Why the hell do I need you?"

"Because you deserve the whole pie and you know I can help you get it."

"You fucked over my father. He did what you wanted and you fell off the face of the Earth when he needed your protection."

"Your father came to you and you did the same thing." Arseny's gaze challenges me. "Why?"

"That's none of your goddamn business." The skin on the back of my neck prickles. This conversation is about as invasive as a colonoscopy without anesthesia, and it needs to end before I follow through on my threat and slice his fucking throat with my stiletto knife.

"Let's just say we both have reasons for making the Malikovs pay for their sins. We can take them down together, Mikhail."

I look at the crowd of faces mingling at the bar. Laughing, talking, drinking, having a grand fucking time while I sit here, plotting where I'm gonna find my next payday since business has stalled with the Malikovs. I'm burning through cash faster than I can make it, and to keep up my image as an elite arms dealer who works out of Moscow, I need money. Fast.

"My father was a scumbag prick who didn't deserve protection from his crimes against the Brotherhood 7," I say. "But you're a bigger scumbag prick for not protecting your partner. So for the last time, take your offer and stick it up your ass."

Arseny chuckles and drains the last bit of Yorsch. "Stubborn bastard. Must run in the blood, yes?" He places his empty glass on the bar. "Consider my offer, Mikhail. I won't beg you."

"If you don't walk away now, you definitely will beg...for me not to bludgeon you with a tire iron. The Malikov empire is mine, and anyone who tries to grab what belongs to me will die, slowly, painfully, and brutally." A red haze clouds my vision, my glare fixed on Arseny's smug expression. "And as the man who caused this shit storm for me and my family, you're Enemy Number One."

"Your ambition is admirable." Arseny's eyes narrow. "It would be a real shame for you to die because of it."

CHAPTER 2

Konstantin

SIX MONTHS LATER

I look down at my watch. Eight o'clock, sharp.

My chest tightens. It's time.

The bill of my baseball cap hangs low over my face. Sunglasses hide my eyes.

A jingling bell over the door tells me she's here, ready to start her morning routine.

Tori Malikov pushes open the door of the Coffee Bean Café on Collins Avenue in Miami Beach.

I don't need to look up to confirm it's her. A familiar perfumed scent wafts under my nose, along with the rush of balmy sea air blown into the café as she walks inside.

I tap my fingers against the glass of orange juice in front of me. Drops of water stream down the sides and over my fingers, hitting the wicker placemat. I count to ten, anger bubbling in my chest.

It's stupid and illogical, but scars are scars. And in my sick and twisted mind, self-torment is a constant reminder to never go down this dead-end road again.

So I come back here, day after day. To watch, to obsess, and to plot my revenge.

Early morning sun streams through the clear glass windows lining the perimeter of the café, heating the area despite the cool air pumping through the place. The hairs on the back of my neck spring to life, even before I raise my gaze.

I fight the urge to look but my eyes finally win the battle. They sweep over Tori, drinking in all five-foot-eight inches of her toned, bronze body. My gaze sweeps over her outfit — the low-slung jean shorts with frayed edges that barely skim the globes of her ass, the tight yellow tank top that rides up high enough for me to catch a glimpse of the lotus flower tattoo just above her left hip. Her long hair is swept up into a messy ponytail, tortoiseshell glasses resting on her pert nose.

Blood rushes between my temples. I can't get over it...over her, even months later.

Seeing Tori for the first time was like taking a cement fist to the gut because not only is she part of the enemy camp, she's also the spitting image of Mischa. I thought I'd buried that part of my past forever, but I know it's karma.

Every time I look at her, my asshole father flicks me in the balls from the grave. It's a constant reminder that he'll always have one up on me. I wrap my fingers tight around a straw, snapping the bamboo in two.

"Good morning, sweetie," one of the servers says to her.

"It's actually a great morning," Tori replies with a wink. "A fabulous one, actually."

"So does that mean it's a mimosa morning?"

"Absolutely. Maybe even two." She winks again at the girl.

The server grabs a menu from the hostess stand. "Just in case you decide to change it up today," she says cheerfully. The server waves her hand over at a table set up in the corner of the restaurant. It faces the window and gives a glimpse of the beach beyond the road.

Tori places her laptop bag on the chair across from the one overlooking Collins Avenue. She bends over and, giving me a glimpse of her perfect ass, pulls a laptop sleeve from her bag. A minute later, she sits in front of a rose gold-colored MacBook Air, her back to the wall. She pushes her glasses up higher on her nose and pops in a pair of AirPods. Then the typing begins.

A self-satisfied smile tugs at her full pink lips. She looks happy, settled, and relaxed.

I feel the exact opposite.

My gut clenches, memories of my father's snide, arrogant-as-fuck voice popping between my ears like bullets.

"You could never keep her satisfied, Konstantin."

Rage swirls through my body from my fingertips to my toes.

"She knows who holds the real power in this family. And now, so does the rest of the world."

Motherfucker. He always hangs over my damn shoulder, whispering in my ear, taunting me like the evil, vindictive bastard he was when he was alive.

"Here you go, love. A short stack with a side of well-done bacon." My bright-eyed blonde server sets the plates down in front of me. "Can I get you more juice? More coffee? Or maybe... something else?" She flutters her long eyelashes at me and puffs out her chest. Her fake tits practically pop out of the deep V-neck she's wearing.

A few months ago, I'd have taken her up on her not-so-subtle offer for "something else." But I've barely looked at another woman since Tori Malikov got caught in my crosshairs.

"Thanks, but I'm good."

I ignore her deflated expression. The truth is, I'm not good at all.

After my father was killed, I got sucked into a vicious shit storm otherwise known as my father's toxic legacy. I've been trying to claw my way out ever since. Sinking my teeth into the growing Malikov arms empire was my strategic play. The plan was to punish the guilty and steal back what those bastards took from me and my brother.

But things went sideways and never really straightened out again.

Manipulating the Malikovs was the easy part. And just when I was about to go in for the kill, Tori showed up on the scene and turned my world inside out because of who she reminded me of. I lost focus and my plans changed.

I take a deep breath, the smell of crisp bacon filling my lungs. I grab a thick, semi-charred slice, just the way I like it. My stomach grumbles louder as I raise it to my lips, the grease coating my tongue after that first bite.

Stalkers have to eat, too.

I grab the small pitcher of maple syrup and pour a generous amount over the stack of pancakes until they're saturated. I put down the pitcher and rub my sticky fingertips down the side of my sweaty glass. The thought of Tori lying naked on my bed, drizzled in bacon grease and maple syrup, grabs hold of my tortured mind.

No, goddammit.

I fucking hate her.

Like a vacuum cleaner, I inhale half the stack and all of the bacon within the first two minutes of getting my food. But I never take my eyes off of her.

Tori takes a long sip of the tall orange mimosa her server delivered to the table before returning her attention to the laptop screen. She pauses for a minute, cracking her knuckles as she peers at the screen. Then, a lightbulb switches on, and her fingers take off like horses at the Kentucky Derby.

They move with lightning speed over the keyboard. I stare at her hands out of the corner of my eye. Interestingly, she only uses the middle finger on her left hand and the thumb, index, and middle fingers on her right hand.

My server wordlessly grabs my plates a few minutes later. She's definitely pissed at the rejection. But if she knew where my attention was really focused and why, I think she'd be damn happy I spared her.

Tori doesn't look up again until her server shows up at her table with mimosa number two about twenty minutes later. She takes off her glasses and puts them on the table next to the laptop before stretching her arms overhead. Her cheeks flush pink and a smile stretches across her face.

I want to know why she's so fucking happy.

And then I want to crush that happiness as payback for her father crushing mine.

I take a swig of my orange juice and pick up the book next to my glass now that the empty plates are gone. I've always been a David Baldacci fan but today, *The 6:20 Man* is just a prop. I can't focus on anything but Tori.

My cell phone buzzes on the table. I grab it when I see my brother Gregor's name flash across the screen. "Hey, what's going on?"

"Where are you? I stopped by your place, but your car was gone." He snickers. "Did you make it home last night?"

Last night.

Yeah, I camped out at China Bistro at a corner table, scarfing sushi and guzzling sake while Tori and two other women had a late dinner. Without the cap and sunglasses, it was tricky not to be spotted. I'd met her friends a couple of times before. They're the girlfriends of Luka and Nik Malikov, Tori's brothers.

My enemies.

I grit my teeth. Nik's girlfriend is part of the reason why my original plan ran so far out of control, not that anyone knows the truth about it. She, her dipshit, money-grubbing Uncle Hank, and her idiot brother fucked everything up really good. I should have blasted that fucking warehouse with all of them in it.

But that wouldn't have gotten me the revenge I crave.

No. I decided Gregor and I would be in this for the long game.

A few more weeks. That's when I play my final hand.

I don't have much more time than that.

My younger brother doesn't know that my plans have changed. And he also doesn't know about my borderline-unhealthy obsession with Tori, so I adjust my story.

"I had a late dinner at China Bistro. I took off early this morning to catch some waves before breakfast." Lies. So many fucking lies.

"Okay." He pauses. "Are we gonna talk about 'the thing'?"

"I told you. I have it under control." My voice is low but abrupt. I hope he gets the message that I don't want to talk about "the thing" right now. Or ever.

"I know, but shit hasn't exactly gone well for us lately. One more slip-up and–"

"No more slip-ups," I growl. "This is on me to handle. If you want something done right, do it your damn self."

"Great, so when's that gonna happen?" Gregor asks. "We need allies. The Ukranians want blood. *Our* fucking blood, bro. You need to make a deal with the Malikovs. Cement our business relationship with them. Figure out a way to get to their associates. We have nobody right now, and those guys have a goddamn army behind them."

"You don't have to remind me," I snap, a little louder than I wanted to. A couple of people at nearby tables give me curious looks. My jaw twitches. They can't see my death glare from behind my sunglasses. Too bad. "Luka's wedding. That's when I'll make my move."

"You think that's the right place?"

"They'll all be drunk and celebrating the happy couple. All of their partners will be there, too. It's perfect."

When I stab the End Call button on the phone a few seconds later, I turn my head to stare hard at Tori for the last time.

The Malikovs don't have any idea who I really am. They definitely don't suspect that I'm about to torch their organization *and* their lives.

To them, I'm a trusted partner who's helping rebuild their weapons empire.

They don't know that I'm about to steal that empire right out from under them.

And that I'm taking Tori along with it.

CHAPTER 3
Viktorya

ONE MONTH LATER

Dark, piercing eyes rake over my body, violating me from across the dining room. I clutch the stem of the crystal champagne flute a bit tighter as the man's gaze completes its erotic assault. His lips curl upward and my pulse hammers hard against my throat.

I need to get out of here.

I thank the bartender and turn to leave the bar, my lips pulled into a tight line. My God, I need such a shower after that violent eye fucking.

"*Malyshka,*" my mother Irina's syrupy smooth voice murmurs as she places a freshly manicured hand on my arm. "Have you seen the way Konstantin Romanov has watched your every move tonight? I think you should go over and have your brothers introduce you."

"Thanks, but I already know who and what he is," I say, shaking off her fingers. "And it's not anyone I care to know."

"Viktorya," Mom says, forgetting her pet name for me and using my full one. Her tone switches from sweet to stern almost instantaneously, which tells me she has an agenda.

As always.

"You're twenty-five years old. Natasha is barely twenty-two and now she's married," Mom continues, her brows furrowing in disapproval. "And Kenzie will be the same age when she marries Nikolai. What are you waiting for?"

"Look, Mom, I'm not the least bit interested in any of the so-called eligible bachelors in this room. So Natasha is married, great for her. Her husband is a bratva boss who has a perpetual target on his head. That also puts a target on her head." I take a breath and guzzle my champagne. "I don't want that life for myself."

Mom lets out a frustrated sigh. "We don't mix with outsiders. You've always resisted your world, but you need to learn to stick with your own."

"Living every day wondering if my husband is going to get shot up like Sonny from *The Godfather* is a horrible existence. And it's only worse if I have to worry about myself being in that situation." I slant Konstantin a glance over my shoulder. A chill slips down my spine when I see that his gaze is still locked on me. I roll my eyes and look back at my mother. "Thanks, but no thanks. I'm holding out for a hero."

"You're too idealistic for your own good. And you're still part of this family. As long as you have the Malikov name, what makes you think you don't have that target slapped on your own head?" Mom snips. "I'm only trying to protect you. Being with a man in our world gives you that protection."

"Lest you forget, two of my brothers kidnapped their women. Their relationships literally began with revenge plots, guns, knives, and God only knows what else." I cock my head to the side. "Are you going to tell me that's romantic? A great story to reminisce over with the grandkids?"

"They did what they needed to do in the name of family loyalty. But look what happened. Out of the bitter, comes the sweet. They fell in love."

"Forgive me if I don't want to be kidnapped by a rival and

develop a sick and twisted case of Stockholm syndrome to kick off my happily ever after," I scoff.

"I don't appreciate your tone, Viktorya," Mom says. Her blue eyes ice over. "I am just concerned about your future."

"Don't be. I am perfectly fine by myself. I don't need anything or anyone."

"It will be a very lonely life for you. You're going to sit in the Coffee Bean Café every day for the rest of your life building websites and watching your life pass you right by." Mom takes the glass of white wine that the bartender hands her. Her lips curl downward in disapproval.

"I'm sorry that my occupation doesn't impress you, Mom." I place my empty flute on the bar and grab a full one.

And I'm sorry that you feel the need to marry me off so that you can feel better about the fact that you couldn't save Valentina from her own hell.

I leave that last part out. But deep down, I know it's true. My younger sister Val disappeared on the day of her wedding, an arranged marriage to a bottom-feeding scumbag named Dmitri Stepanov. Mom had no idea about the arrangement, and not only lost her baby girl that day but her oldest son and husband at the hand of an unknown enemy who shot up the place.

Anger bubbles in my chest. She doesn't give a damn about my future. Mom has always been about appearances. Of course, she wants me to get together with a rich, well-connected guy who can shower me with luxuries. It'd give her own social score a huge boost.

My clutch bag vibrates. I place my flute on the bar and tug the zipper. It always takes a few attempts to get the bag open because the zipper gets caught on the fabric lining. One of my two phones buzzes with an incoming call.

I glance down at the screen after I pull it out.

Sheila Ackerman.

My agent.

I hold up the phone. "I have to take this. It's work."

"Always work," she mutters, sipping her wine. "You can't marry your laptop, Viktorya."

Mom turns away and walks over to a nearby group of women. It doesn't take long for them to gush over her dress, her makeup, her hair, and every other bit of her perfectly groomed façade.

I swallow a snort and drain the rest of the champagne in my glass. I leave the empty flute on the bar. An unwelcome shiver ripples through me as I hurriedly walk through the clusters of guests at my brother Luka's wedding reception. I'd like to blame the sensation on the chilled air pumping throughout the exquisitely decorated dining hall. But that'd be a big, fat lie.

It's *him*.

And I hate myself for letting that admission creep into my mind.

I force my eyes forward, never allowing them to sneak another peek at the man whose heated gaze singes my skin like wildfire.

Konstantin Romanov may look like a *GQ* model, but underneath his Prada tuxedo, he's a dirty, sleazy thug.

Sexy as fuck, yes.

But still a derelict.

Because that's the kind of people my family associates with — criminals and killers. Sure, a lot of them have some redeeming qualities, but at their core? They're all the same breed.

Despite the inner battle waging in my mind, I peek in his direction.

Tiny tingles dance over my skin when our eyes tussle. I grit my teeth.

No way, no how, *never*.

I grasp the brass doorknob and pull open the dark wood door before stepping into the hallway. Glittering chandeliers cast a romantic glow over the spacious area. The walls are a pale ivory; slate blue sofas and mahogany coffee tables line the perimeter. Vases of white calla lilies — Natasha's favorite flower — accent every table. The effect is chic and sophisticated.

But the reality? A lot of glitz and glam slapped over even more blood. It's like putting lipstick on a slaughtered pig. My family has plenty of enemies who'd love nothing more than to destroy us. We can't hide from that perpetual threat.

Targets. We all have matching ones slapped on our backs.

Everyone is guilty by association.

So why would I want an even bigger target on mine by associating with the likes of Konstantin?

Is it so bad that I want to break away from it all?

I'm not stupid. I know there will always be risks to me because of my family name. But I've been the victim once and I never intend to go through that again. And since Malikov weddings seem to attract devastation, I came prepared. I graze the outline of the stiletto knife hidden under the fabric of my black bridesmaid gown. It presses against my upper thigh, held tight by a lace garter.

There is plenty of security lurking around the Ritz-Carlton Key Biscayne, but I'm not taking any chances.

I walk toward the side door at the far end of the hallway. I'm not sure what's so important that Sheila needed to call me at eight o'clock on a Saturday night, but curiosity grabbed hold when I saw her name on the screen. Although, the need to escape my mother was reason enough to take the call. Any call. From anyone. Literally.

I push open the heavy mahogany door and take a few steps outside. Thick green palm fronds billow overhead. The balmy Bay breeze whispers against my skin, fluttering the leaves on the tropical plants surrounding the courtyard. I take a deep breath, dragging in the sweet, salty air before dialing Sheila's number.

She answers on the first ring.

"Hi, Sheila. I saw you called?"

"Oh, Savannah, darling. I have amazing news for you. I just heard from the producers at Netflix and they want to option your latest book for a new feature film. Isn't that amazing?"

I gasp. "Are you serious?"

"Yes. It is incredible. Your last series did so well, it captured their attention. And since this new book took off like a rocket, they made an offer."

"But it's only been a month since the release," I say, holding a hand against my forehead.

"It has been several years, darling. Several years of solid best-selling books that readers adore. This last one was the icing on the cake. They know you're a star, and they want to bring your story to life. Congratulations," she gushes.

I sink onto a black wrought iron bench, gripping it for balance. Tears spring to my eyes.

Holy shit, I did it.

Well, actually, Savannah Rose did it. My super-secret author alter ego. Not even my agent Shelia knows my real identity.

"The producers will arrange a meeting for us over the next week or so. We'll need to fly out to Los Gatos, California, to discuss the terms of the contract."

I nod my head. "Of course." Then reality pummels me.

Wait.

Nobody knows my secret.

People recognize Viktorya Malikov.

But they don't have any idea who Savannah Rose is.

I can't go traipsing around California as my romance author pen name. One picture uploaded to the Internet would expose my true identity. Not a single Netflix producer would option a small-town romance from the daughter of a notorious mobster and the sister of a brutal bratva boss — the same boss who also happens to be a convicted felon — no matter how many copies the book sold.

My author career would go up in smoke if the world knew who really wrote those stories.

I live under a microscope in a very dark and dangerous world.

I want normal. What I know is utter chaos.

And I've made a lot of money over the past few years creating alternate worlds I'd love to get lost in forever. As a bestselling author, I get to build my ideal heroes and escape into lives I know I can never have.

Nobody knows about my guilty pleasure, though. My family thinks I build websites, so they don't question the reason why I'm always on my laptop, and why I spend hours every day at the Coffee Bean Café in Miami Beach.

Writing started out as my therapy. Only my younger sister Val knows about my secret pen name. Only she could understand why I need to lose myself in the small-town romance tales I spin. She was the only one I could tell when my breakout book landed me on the *New York Times* and *USA Today* bestseller lists. Val gets my reasons for doing what I do because she hates her life, too.

Now she's gone. My best friend is on the run because our father made choices that could have killed her, ones that might still kill her.

Chaos. It's the epicenter of our sick and twisted universe.

"I'll be in touch next week, sweetie," Sheila says. "We'll review the details over a few bottles of Veuve Cliquot. Go and enjoy the rest of your night."

"Sounds terrific." I stand up from the bench, my knees wobbling like overcooked spaghetti. "Thanks again, Sheila."

I click to end the call, my hand falling to my side in defeat, like it's holding a lead weight. "You have got to be fucking kidding me. How the hell is this real life?" Venturing deeper into the darkened courtyard, I bend down to grab a flat, smooth stone and hurl it into the Bay with a loud groan.

A loud, slamming noise jars me. I spin around when I hear footsteps approach me from behind.

I squint in the darkness. My breath hitches as Konstantin Romanov walks into the courtyard. His dark eyes glitter in the moonlight, his broad chest casting a shadow over me as he closes the space between us.

"Tori Malikov," he says in a deep, gravelly voice. "I've waited a long time to meet you...and to get you alone."

"Don't waste your time." Hairs on the back of my neck spring to attention. Belly flutters erupt, the strong scent of his cologne, Chanel Bleu, wafting under my nose despite the alarm bells ringing between my ears. "I don't mix business with pleasure. You're my brothers' business and I have no interest in the pleasure part."

"I'm not interested in pleasure, Tori," Konstantin says, pulling out a gun and holding it in his outstretched hand. "Just pain. Your pain."

"What the *fuck*?" I yelp, trying to process his words as I jump away from him. "You're supposed to be my brother's business partner."

"People aren't always who they say they are," he says in a low, menacing tone. "Be very careful who you trust."

My shoulders slump, and with one quick motion, I grab the knife from under my skirt and barrel toward Konstantin. I duck around his gun-toting arm and jab his other side with the tip of the blade. He doesn't even flinch. He just grabs me by the hair and pulls me toward him. My back slams hard against his chest. He reaches in front of me and closes his strong hand around my throat, choking my scream.

I gasp like a fish out of water as his grip tightens and my vision blurs. I slice at his hand with my knife, barely making contact as my limbs go slack from lack of oxygen. He sticks the barrel of the gun to my temple with his free hand.

"I have men on each one of your brothers right now who are willing to die in order to kill off the Malikov Bratva. Say a word, make a sound, do a goddamn thing, and they're all dead. You want their blood on your hands?"

"I will kill you if you harm one single hair on their heads," I rasp, using my last stifled breaths.

Konstantin dips his head, his lips so close to mine. "Not if I kill you first."

My body buckles. Then blackness swallows me whole.

CHAPTER 4
Konstantin

What the hell did I just do? Declaring war on the Malikov Bratva by kidnapping their princess was *not* my fucking plan.

I hoist Tori's limp body into my arms, wincing as I carry her over to the Ford Expedition that just screeched to a stop next to the courtyard. Each step I take cripples me more, but I don't slow down. I can't. Time isn't on my side right now, and if I don't get the hell out of here, the Malikov army will attack, wedding reception or not.

I grit my teeth, my entire right side throbbing. I graze the knife wound and bring my red-stained fingertips in front of my face. Damn, she drove that stiletto blade deep enough where I'll need to perform emergency surgery on myself as soon as we get the hell out of the line of fire.

Here's hoping I don't bleed out before that happens.

Lev, my head of security, jumps out of the driver's seat and pulls open the back door.

"Boss, uh, you didn't tell me we had to get rid of a body," he says, bringing a hand to the back of his neck. "I thought the plan was just to head to the airfield."

I glare at him. "We're not getting rid of anyone. She's not

dead. But she is coming with us." I slide her across the pebbled leather seat and jump into the back seat next to her. "Get in the truck. And toss me some zip ties."

Lev hands me two black ties over the seat. "You're bleeding."

"No shit. Now go," I yell.

Lev slams his foot on the gas. The truck lurches forward while I secure Tori's wrists and ankles. Putting just enough pressure on Tori's carotid artery made her black out long enough for me to get her into the truck. The feisty Malikov princess stirs next to me. With her tied up, there's no risk I'll be impaled with any more surprise weapons. She already got me once.

I don't believe in giving second chances.

Lev maneuvers the truck around the circular driveway of the Ritz-Carlton as he heads for the exit. Luckily, nobody saw me put her in the back of the truck since we were near the courtyard and away from the main reception area. The tires squeal against the pavement when he swings the steering wheel around the fountain in the center of the entrance. I peer out of the back window just in time to see Nik Malikov run out the front door of the resort. He stops short when he sees our truck and immediately pulls out a cell phone.

"Malikov's got security at the entrance," I say. "We need to get past them."

Lev nods. "Yes, boss." He slows down as we get closer to the iron gates. A blacked-out Range Rover sits on the left, partially hidden by a large bush. I lower my window.

Crack! Pop! Bang!

Tori lets out a weak moan, shifting on the seat next to me.

"Drive," I yell at Lev.

She tries to raise herself up but falls back to the black leather seat when she realizes she has no use of her hands. "You fucking bastard," she rasps. "What did you do? Who are you shooting at?"

"I didn't shoot anyone."

Lev makes a sharp right and we take off down the private road.

"Liar. You're a dirty fucking liar." Tori slithers back just enough to kick her feet out at me. One of her sharp heels connects with my stab wound. I yelp. A searing pain explodes down my side. "Fuck you, asshole. You're not getting away with this," she screams.

"If you're not careful, the next time I put my hand around your throat, you won't wake up." I groan, holding my hand against my side.

"Is that a threat, asshole?" She kicks at me again. This time, I block the heel with the palm of my hand. Bad idea. The spiky fucking thing tears into my skin.

"I don't make threats. Just promises." I reach over and grab the zip tie holding her ankles together with my good hand. Then I pull off her shoes with my injured one. She kicks and thrashes, but I finally get them off. I toss them to the floor and shove her feet away.

This is bad. Really fucking bad.

"Do you have any idea what I'm going to do to you, fucker?" Tori says through clenched teeth. Her voice is scathing. She spews pure venom, wide awake like she wasn't just strangled to the point of unconsciousness only a few minutes ago. "I don't need a knife for it, either. And guess what else? I only make promises, too."

I slowly turn, locking in on her fierce blue-eyed glare. My chest tightens like there's a balloon in the center, slowly filling with air, squeezing my lungs together until they're damn near ready to pop. Long, blonde hair pools under her head. Her tan face flushes deep red, contrasting with her crystal blue eyes, the only ones that can spark a flame deep inside of me.

She represents everything I hate and everyone I want to punish.

I'd been so blinded by rage that my intentions went to complete shit.

I worked hard for months to get in close with Luka and Nik Malikov after the idiots I hired fucked everything up. They trust me now.

I turn my head, peering out the back window.

At least they did before tonight.

Not that it matters. Right now, I have something more valuable than a fraction of their empire. I have something that will make me whole again...something I will be very happy to punish if she gets out of line.

Lev speeds down the private resort road that leads to the 913. He doesn't speak another word and thank fuck for that. I have enough shit bouncing between my ears right now. I don't need anyone else questioning me.

Tori was never part of my quest for revenge.

Viktor Malikov killed my father, and even though the world is better without that piece of shit contaminating it, he blew apart my arms empire as a result. I'd broken away from my father's organization and he resented me ever since I became a worthy competitor. He wanted the world to see him bring me to my knees. He thought he accomplished that when he fucked my fiancée Mischa. But it wasn't until he was dead and buried that my livelihood crumbled. Nobody wanted to do business with anyone who was at the end of a Malikov's gun barrel. My trusted associates and clients didn't care that I set fire to my father's toxic legacy and built up my own. As long as I was a Federov, I was still a target.

The money dried up, my network crashed and burned. I lost everything.

All because of Viktor Malikov.

Even though Viktor is dead now, he still owes me. And I'm gonna take every penny and every shred of power I can grab, starting with Tori.

A piercing yell rattles my eardrums. I twist my head away from the window, facing her. Tori launches her body toward me, drilling me in the throat with her skull. The force of her body knocks me into the door. Lev slams on the brakes when another car zooms past, cutting us off. I lose my balance and reach out to grab the side of the door. My fingers grasp the door handle just as he guns the motor. The door flies open, and I grab onto the "oh, shit" bar to keep myself from falling out of the damn truck.

Tori cheers, kicking me harder and harder. "Drop dead, asshole! Faster, Lev. Let's see if this dickhead can fly."

"Lev," I shout, rushing wind from the Bay muffling my voice. "Pull the fuck over."

I hold on tight until the truck slows down enough for me to grab the door handle and slam it closed. I collapse onto the seat for a second to catch my breath before I lunge for her, covering her entire body with my own.

I fist her hair, then lean my chest into her, our breathless pants intermingling in the tense air. Her heart races, the vibration in time with my own. A familiar crackle of electricity courses through my insides. I breathe her in, immediately intoxicated by her sultry and seductive scent.

No. Not fucking again.

I recoil and pull away.

It's my father again, flicking me in the balls from the goddamn grave.

"You could never satisfy her, Konstantin."

I hate him.

"She doesn't want you. She only settled for you until she was able to get the real prize."

I fucking hate him.

My pulse slams against my throat. "Don't forget," I growl. "I still have a gun. And if you don't want to find out firsthand what kinds of things I'll do with that gun, then shut the hell up and lie there." I drag the barrel of my gun down the side of her face before pressing it against her forehead.

Lev pulls into the darkened parking lot at the Miami Executive Airfield a few minutes later. The black Gulf Stream G550 is lit up and ready to fly. Lev jumps out of the driver's seat and opens the back door. I grab Tori by the ankles and pull her toward me until I can snake an arm around her and throw her over my shoulder…the shoulder on the opposite side of my stab wound, obviously. She slams her fists against my back and her knees into my gut, screaming louder with every step.

"Nobody's gonna hear you, sweetheart. Save your energy. You're gonna need it when I punish you for that stunt you pulled in the car."

"Don't you dare threaten me. Who the fuck do you think you are?" she bellows.

I carry her up the short flight of stairs leading into the main cabin of the plane and throw her into a leather recliner. My lips curl into a smile. "Your fucking master."

Tori's tongue drips malice, her expression pure shock.

Good. I figured out exactly how to shut her up without shoving my dick in her mouth.

Although, that may factor into her punishment later tonight.

"Hey, what the hell is with all this noise?"

My brother Gregor pushes open the curtain that separates the kitchen and bathroom from the rest of the plane. His favorite flight attendant adjusts her tight white blouse behind him, her blonde hair sexed up like she's just been fucked hard. Gregor follows my gaze. He flashes a mischievous smirk at me and waggles his eyebrows.

"I waited a long time for you guys to show up. I got bored." His eyebrows fly upward and he points to my blood-soaked shirt. "Kosta, what the fuck happened?"

"Let's just say the wedding wasn't all wine and roses," I mutter.

"Let me off this fucking plane right now," Tori yells from the recliner, her back to my brother. She shakes her bound wrists in the air and slams her back against the chair.

Gregor furrows his brow and pushes past me, heading for Tori. "You said you were going to the wedding to arrange a deal. Does all that mean they rejected the terms?"

"No, although that's another problem we probably need to talk about." I nod toward Tori. "I decided to take a wedding favor on my way out. She got a little overexcited when she pulled a knife on me."

"She stabbed *you*?" His voice rises. "You, the guy who has battled with the dregs of the Earth and never once gotten plugged? You let her jam a knife into you?"

I glower at him.

"That's right. He pulled a gun on me and I charged the motherfucker. I got him good, too," Tori yells. "Not such a tough guy after all, huh? Guess you underestimated me, *sweetheart*."

A twisted mix of anger and lust floods my insides. Anger, because she's right. I expected her to crumble at the sight of my gun, to fall apart at the mention of hurting her precious family. Lust, because she ignored my threats and fought me. Hard. And that made me fucking hot, much as I hate to admit it to myself.

"You are fucking finished," Tori shouts. "Dead. Destroyed. Over!"

Gregor pushes past me, grabs the back of Tori's chair, and spins it around to get a look. His mouth drops open. "Who the hell is this, anyway?"

"Tori Malikov."

"Holy fuck, Kosta. She looks just like–"

"Yeah. I know she does."

He pushes his hair back, still gaping at Tori. "And you took *her*? From the wedding? You fucking asshole. You were supposed to get in close so we could sandbag them."

"I got sidetracked."

"Sidetracked?" he yells, pacing the small aisle. "Are you fucking serious right now? What happened to sticking with the damn plan?"

I grab him by the collar of his shirt and yank him toward me. "Don't ever question me again," I growl, right in his face. "I'm calling the shots, not you."

"Great, so I'm just supposed to ignore the fact that–"

"Not another word," I say through clenched teeth.

"You just let your fucking bruised ego dictate our future when you declared war on the fucking Malikov Bratva."

"There's no war if one side disappears completely." I lean in close, poking a finger into his chest. "Now get this plane in the air and as far the fuck away from Miami as we can get so we can make that happen."

Crack! Pop! Bang!

Gregor peers out the window. "What the fuck is happening?"

I grit my teeth. "Sonofabitch."

They found us.

But I'll be damned if I let them take another thing from me, including Tori.

CHAPTER 5
Viktorya

"Nik! Luka! I'm in here!" I yell just as the plane door closes. The engine roars, tires squealing on the tarmac.

"They can't hear you and they can't save you. I've already told you once. If you try anything stupid, your entire family will be killed." Konstantin's eyes glitter with evil as he pulls the seat belt tight around me before snapping it in place. "Starting with Nikolai."

I grit my teeth. "Bastard." Nik and Val have always been my closest siblings. And since Nik and I are the last ones who were with Val before the ambush on my family at her wedding, we both share a lot of guilt over her disappearance. This fucker can't possibly know any of that, but he already picked up on one of my hot buttons.

Nobody threatens the people I love.

Gunshots pepper the side of the plane, the popping sounds farther and farther away as the plane taxis.

Konstantin peers out the small window, then whips his head toward the cockpit. "G, are you jerking off in there? Get the goddamn wheels up."

Boom!

I yelp at the explosion. The sound reverberates between the walls of the main cabin. My eardrums rattle. A whoosh of air follows.

"G, they got the tire," Konstantin yells.

"Thanks, Captain Obvious," Gregor calls back.

"You obviously underestimated all of the Malikovs tonight," I snap. "You just committed the worst betrayal of their trust. Do you really think you can get away with it? If you do, then you're stupider than you look."

More bullets plug the windows, ricocheting off the tempered glass.

"Fucking armored plane," I grumble.

"I don't take chances."

"You did with me. And look where that got you. *Skewered*." My lips twist into a grimace. "I hope you bleed out before we land."

Konstantin sinks into a chair diagonal to me and pulls his own seat belt over his broad chest. I narrow my eyes at the large black phoenix that covers his whole hand...not the one I jammed my shoe heel into. A fleeting thought enters my mind.

Does he think he's already risen from the ashes, or does he believe himself to be on his way out of them? Either way, this guy's on a total ego trip.

He winces the slightest bit as the seat belt grazes his bloody side and I smile. He's in pain. Good.

The plane speeds up, the sound of gunshots fading in the distance. Inertia forces me back against my seat as the wheels lift and we take off. To where, who the hell even knows?

"Just because they couldn't stop the plane doesn't mean they'll stop looking for me. And *you*. And we both know what will happen when they find us."

"I'll give them a little credit. They tailed us to the airfield quicker than I thought they would. But it doesn't matter. It's too late for your entire family."

"They can just contact the FAA and find out the flight path

for this plane and its final destination. They'll find me and they'll peel the skin from your bones afterward, you sick fuck." I clench and unclench my fingers around one of the arms of my recliner. My nails dig into the soft beige leather, my fists itching to pummel the hell out of Konstantin's gorgeous and demonic face.

My heart sinks deeper into my gut. I may talk a big game and I can definitely play it, but this scenario isn't ideal. I don't need a weapon. I can destroy anyone with my bare hands. But these damn zip ties are cockblocking me right now. If I could get them off, I'd rush for the cockpit and snap Gregor's neck off his body.

How I can even write sweet, small-town romances when my mind always edges toward dark, dirty, and violent never ceases to amaze me. Talk about writing the exact opposite of what I know and where I excel. And it's obviously the reason I have an alter-ego pen name…you don't get much sweeter than Savannah Rose.

"Thanks for the warning, but I'm not dying tonight. Not when I have so much to look forward to." The plane levels off a few minutes later. He unbuckles himself and creeps toward me, not the least bit fazed by his angry-looking wounds. He drags a fingertip down the front of my chest, tugging the neckline of my gown down. A zap of electricity shocks my skin as his finger grazes the peaks of my breasts. My breath hitches under his penetrating stare.

He looks at me like I'm a sizzling steak and he's a man on death row about to devour his last meal.

I should feel repulsed. Infuriated. Completely disgusted.

Instead, tiny tingles of anticipation ignite in my core, firing out to the tips of my toes and the ends of my hair. Goosebumps pebble my skin in the wake of his touch.

I feel like I've just plunged into some alternate, erotic reality.

He just kidnapped me and threatened to kill my family. He's a liar, a devious scumbag who played us for idiots.

My mind screams, "Death to Konstantin!"

But my body clearly has another plan, one that's much more carnal.

I suck in a breath, sitting straight up in my recliner. "Take your hand off of me."

"Why? You don't like it?"

It sounds more like a challenge than a question.

Maybe because he knew the answer before he even spoke the words.

He leans in close. His deep voice hums against my ear, making my pulse churn. My eyes flutter closed for a split second. Suddenly, I'm pulled into my own fantasy world. With a galloping heart, tiny butterflies swarm my belly. Delicious chills slip down my spine.

His devious net has me pulled tight, holding me prisoner.

My eyes fly open, breaking the erotic spell.

I press my back against the recliner. His alcohol-tinged breath melts my skin. Desire slithers and snakes around my limbs, weaving like an unrelenting, out-of-control vine.

Blood rushes between my ears.

I don't think.

I just attack.

With a sudden twist of my head, I capture his ear between my teeth and clamp down on the lobe.

"Fuck," he shouts, pulling away.

I keep him close and bite down with all my might. He flails and tugs his head away from me. But it's useless. I fucking have him and I'm not letting go. The sharp taste of metal hits my tongue. A warm trickle of his blood drizzles down the side of my mouth. It spills onto the top of my breast, a deep red splatter that pops against my skin.

When I finally let him go, I spit at his polished, black leather shoes. Bile rises in the back of my throat but I refuse to gag. I will not show him any bit of weakness.

"You bitch," he bellows.

I smile, pretty damn sure that the evidence of my bitchery stains my lips and teeth blood-red. "You're damn right I am. If you didn't want to play with fire, you shouldn't have lit the match."

"Lev, get me the first-aid kit." Konstantin glares down at me.

"Looks like you have quite a bit of work to do...so much blood you've spilled," I say with a toothy grin. "I don't really think you know what more you're in for. I've already bitten off your ear, stabbed you in the side, and lanced you with my shoe. You give new meaning to the words 'glutton for punishment.'"

The flight attendant rushes up the aisle with a white box.

She claps a hand over her mouth when Konstantin pulls his hand away from his frayed ear lobe. "Oh my God." Then she turns to me. Her eyes pop open so wide, I think they might just pop out of her skull. "Jesus, you people are crazy!" She darts back behind the curtain.

I roll my eyes. "She could have at least offered me some water."

Konstantin grabs a bottle from the table in front of him. He twists off the top and holds it up to my lips. I take a gulp, swish it around in my mouth, and spit it at him.

He doesn't even flinch. But he shoves the bottle back between my lips and forces my head backward so that water flows down the sides of my mouth. I gurgle and kick out my legs. He just chuckles like the asshole he is.

He finally pulls the almost-empty bottle away. The soaked fabric of my dress clings to me like a second skin. A cool rush of air from the vent above chills me to the bone.

"Forget my brothers peeling the skin from your body. I'm going to enjoy doing that myself."

"Big goals for a girl with no use of her hands."

"I managed to get some things done without my hands, if you remember," I snap. "You have no idea what I'm capable of."

"No, but I look forward to finding out." Konstantin flips the box open and tosses it on the table in front of his chair. A grimace scrunches up his face when he slides off his tuxedo jacket. His jaw tenses, and I quirk my lips into a self-satisfied smirk. Because I put that look on his face.

He works the buttons on his shirt. Slowly, methodically, and maddeningly.

I try to tear my eyes away as the white shirt opens to reveal his thick, muscled pecs. But an invisible force keeps my head pointed in his direction, my gaze focused on the black swirls of ink covering his smooth, bronze skin. A happy trail of hair snakes down toward his navel, stopping at the waistband of his black pants.

Sweet Lord, I want to lick those abs...

I suck in a gulp of oxygen and nearly choke.

He slides the shirt off his broad shoulders, his dark eyes holding me captive. After cleaning the stab wound with alcohol — he didn't even hiss when it touched his skin — he threads a needle and stitches up the gash in his side. He slaps some gauze over it, securing it with surgical tape. Then he sits in his chair and patches up his slashed hand. And for the finale, he slaps a Band-Aid over his jagged earlobe.

"Sorry to disappoint you," he says. "Doesn't look like I'm gonna bleed out after all."

"Too bad." I crack each of my knuckles. Not easy while my wrists are slapped together, but I manage. It's a bad habit that I do every time I feel "stuck" when I'm writing a scene. But this time, the habit doesn't kick in because I don't know what to write...I'm honestly not sure how this story will end.

It's also because I don't know how to handle my body's reaction to this man.

"You shouldn't do that. It'll give you premature arthritis. And you need your fingers to type."

My eyes widen. "How do you know that?"

He slowly lifts an eyebrow, the corner of his lip quirking into a sinister grin. "I told you I'd been waiting to get you alone for a long time. Waiting..." He leans forward in the seat. "And watching your every move for just the right time to strike."

"How long did you plan this?"

"From the second I saw you, Tori." He reclines in the chair, smirking when he catches my wayward eyes accidentally sweeping over his chest.

"You sick bastard." I sputter the words, completely unnerved and hating myself for being so caught off-guard. But more than that, I hate the tingles that dance down my spine under his half-hooded gaze, and the very disturbing story they tell.

He snatched me from my brother's wedding, almost strangled me to death, tied me up, and threw me onto his plane, for fuck's sake.

Fear, panic, anxiety, disgust, hatred.

Those are all reasonable emotions to have in this situation.

But the desire that bubbles in my veins when his devious and devilish gaze assaults me freaks me the hell out, if I'm being honest.

All my life I rejected men like the ones in my family because I craved normal.

Now, like a lead weight to the gut, the realization hits me.

What if chaos *is* my normal? It's the reason I write the love stories that I do, to live differently than I'm forced to live. Chaos may not be what I want, but it might be what I need.

A rush of rage floods my insides.

Surviving it is another story.

I just hope I'm around to see the ending...and that The End doesn't mean it's my own ending.

CHAPTER 6
Konstantin

It's hard to think when Tori's ass is so close to my mouth. She is slung over my shoulder like a bag of cement. Dead weight. My palms tingle, itching to brand those plump cheeks as I tighten my grip around her legs. I want to make her scream, to cry, to beg. She needs to feel pain. And I'm going to be the one who delivers it.

Shockingly, she doesn't fight me this time. I carried her off the plane when we landed at the private airfield in Sarasota, then carried her out of Gregor's Escalade once we drove onto the private peninsula on Siesta Key where I live, and now, she's still ass-up as we walk up the stairs to one of my spare bedrooms.

In a house I can barely afford to rent, thanks to her father.

A little over a year ago, before my entire organization was crushed, I owned a home just like this. Bigger, actually. I had everything before Viktor Malikov put a hit on my father. Now I can barely scrape by. I steal from Peter to pay Paul, and so far, nobody has caught on. I created an image that would attract the right partners for my arms dealing business, and it's fucking expensive as hell.

But now that I have Tori, all of that is going to change.

I want more. I need more. And she's going to get it for me.

We get to the top of the stairs and I take a left down the long hallway, kicking open one of the bedroom doors in the guest wing. The space is massive, the room draped in white with splashes of bold-colored art on each wall. Oversized windows overlook the bay. A large, king-size bed sits in the middle of the white, marble tile floor. I stop next to it and drop her onto the mattress.

She lands in the center of the white comforter, her light eyes firing a lethal glare in my direction. "Just so you know, I'm flipping you off in my mind."

"That all you're doing?"

Her jaw tenses. "Actually, I've just moved on to impaling your asshole with a fire poker. No fucking lube."

"I'd be stupid to think anything different."

I stare down at her wiggling on top of the mattress. She's not gonna lie here quietly. This girl is a hellraiser. The second I leave, she'll find a way to escape. She's damn resourceful, that's for sure. I bring a hand to the Band-Aid on my chewed-up earlobe. My eyes dart left and right. This half-assed plan came together fast, long after I left my house here for the wedding.

I need to do a quick sweep of the place to make sure she can't find any weapons…or make one herself like fucking MacGyver.

Twenty minutes later, I've confiscated all the potentially deadly devices from the drawers. Pins, scissors, pens, a screwdriver. All of it is stuffed into my pants pockets now. I grab the skeleton key on top of the en suite bathroom doorway and lock the door. Then I grab the key above the doorway of the bedroom and hold it in front of her.

"This is your freedom. I'm taking it with me," I hiss. "There are cameras set up everywhere in this house. And hitmen crawling all over the Ritz-Carlton Key Biscayne just waiting for me to call and give them the word to blast the shit out of whoever didn't tail us to the airfield. I'm sure dear old Mom is still hanging around by the bar along with all of the girlfriends and newlywed wives. I'll get every last one of them. Lie here until I get back."

"Or what?" she yells. "You'll make me suffer?"

"I'm going to make you suffer regardless." I yank the landline phone cord out of the wall and grab the portable phone as I pass the nightstand on my way to the door. "And I'll be watching."

"Fuck you," she bellows.

I walk to the door and motion over Lev who stands against the wall right outside of the door. "Come in here and give me a hand for a minute."

He walks in and, between the two of us, we cut the zip ties from Tori's wrists and wrestle her arms behind her back, zip-tying them again while she twists and curses.

"Keep an eye and an ear on her. Call me if she pulls anything," I tell him as we leave the room without a look back.

Lev nods and I stalk past him, headed for the stairs. Gregor paces the foyer in the center hall, stopping short when he sees me walking down the stairs.

"You fucking asshole," he says through clenched teeth. "Are you gonna explain what the fuck you were thinking by taking her?"

"I don't have to explain a goddamn thing to you," I growl. "But if you have something to say, keep it to yourself until we're behind closed doors."

I push past him and storm into my office. Gregor follows and slams the door shut before his anger spews.

"You were supposed to go to the wedding to make another weapons deal. We supply, they distribute, everyone wins. That was the plan. Build our empire back up using their network and resources."

"I came up with a better way to get what we want." I give him a cool stare, waiting for the inevitable explosion.

"You said you had a plan to take down their empire, so I went along with it. You lured people out of the Malikov organization, paid rats for information, launched attacks on them and their businesses that went completely sideways, and in the end, we're still holding our dicks because none of it worked. The plan's fucking failed."

"Because we didn't do the work ourselves. If you want something done right," I say. "You don't leave it to the king of the dipshits and his court of fucking jesters."

"And now you've made it personal with the girl." Gregor's lips twist. "Tell me, when did the plan to slowly and secretly dismantle their empire turn into a kidnapping?"

"I found a use for the girl."

"And dragging her onto our plane tied up like a fucking string of Christmas lights was the way you figured you'd spring it on me?" he scoffs.

"I knew you'd have issues with it."

"Come the fuck on, Kosta. How could I not have issues when we both know you didn't snatch her for revenge. You took her because she's a goddamn mirror image of Mischa. So you could have a toy to torture and torment because after all this time, you still haven't gotten over what happened."

Blood rushes between my temples, rattling my eardrums. Flashes of red color my vision. I grab my brother by the shirt and slam his back against the office door.

"What can I say, Konstantin? She needed a bigger dick. Yours couldn't satisfy her."

I fist the fabric tighter. "This isn't about him."

"The fuck it's not. This is about taking control back after Dad stole it from you in front of the whole world."

"This is about retribution." My throat tightens, my voice thick with fury. "Malikov killed our father. He killed our livelihood."

"Yeah, *after* Dad killed your ego, your arms business, and then took a torch to our whole family," Gregor says, closing his hands around my wrists. "Viktor Malikov isn't the guy you're pissed at. And Tori can't help you break free of the hell Mischa put you through. Using this stranger to fight Dad's ghost won't help you move on. This isn't fucking therapy, Kosta. This is trouble, for both of us."

"I don't need your dime-store psychoanalysis, G. She's gonna help us get back what's rightfully ours."

"How? You can't keep her forever. If you think she'll help you, you're crazier than a shithouse rat. I don't understand how the hell you let her get close enough to do all that to you," he says, waving his hand in my direction. "You never miss. You never lose. You always have your eyes open. But with her, it wasn't enough. She wants to kill you, bro. And judging by what she's already done, I think you're seriously fucked."

I let go of Gregor's shirt and back away from him before sinking into the chair behind my desk. I sit back against the smooth black leather. "They will do anything to get her back."

"Yeah, so you're gonna ask for ransom?"

"Ransom is a one-time payment." I steeple my fingers. "I have bigger plans than that."

"Am I going to hear these plans before you actually execute them? Since you seem to be flying by the fucking seat of your pants." Gregor straightens his shirt and collapses into a chair across from me.

I swing my chair around so that it faces the bar behind me. I stand up, fill two highball glasses with ice, and twist open a bottle of Jewel of Russia Ultra Black Label. I pour the clear liquid over the ice and turn to hand one to my brother. "It's simple…I'm going to marry her."

Gregor takes the glass and pauses before taking a sip. "Are you fucking kidding me?"

I hold the glass under my nose. I breathe in the scent of tobacco, wheat, and pepper. That flavor combination usually calms me, but tonight, it fills me with a voracious hunger. Hairs on the back of my neck prickle, lust courses through my veins. The image of Tori thrashing around on the bed in that tight dress…the high slit exposing her long, toned legs, the ones I want to bury my head between…

I tilt my head back and shoot the vodka, then slam the glass on the top of my desk. "I'm not kidding. She is the key to their kingdom who will unlock everything that we need."

My future. My fortune. *My wife.*

Mine. All of it will be mine.

"If you survive the fucking engagement," Gregor mutters. "And trust me, if you get iced by your bride-to-be, I'm the hell out of here. I'll go find a job as a bartender on a Caribbean island and fuck Hawaiian Tropic models all day. Screw guns. I'll work for pesos...or just sex."

"Pesos are Mexican currency." I flash a smirk.

"Whatever, Kosta." He guzzles his vodka. "I'll be your best man for better, but not for fucking worse."

"Good to know my only brother has my back."

He holds out his glass and I fill it. "You're gonna need a lot more than me to protect your ass against Tori Malikov. I mean, forget her brothers and their beef with you. She's the one to watch out for. And I like my ears intact. Just saying."

A quarter of the bottle of vodka remains by the time Gregor leaves my office and staggers into the living room to crash. I cap the bottle, gulp down what's left in my glass, and put the glasses on the bar.

Then I grab a burner phone out of my desk drawer. I can't take the risk that any of the Malikovs use my signal to track my location. It's also why I shut down all network connectivity to the house. Nobody will find us. So, ignoring the time, I dial Nik's number.

"Who is this?" he growls.

"You know exactly who it is, Nik. Don't bother trying to track me. This will be over before you get a signal. All you need to know right now is that I'm keeping Tori. *Forever.* In a week, we're gonna be married and I'll collect everything your father stole from my family. So fuck you. Fuck you all."

I stab the End button before he has a chance to respond. Then I shut off Wi-Fi and Bluetooth, take the SIM card out of the phone, and crush it, just to be safe. They won't ever be able to contact me now.

I'm not taking any more chances with the Malikovs. They'll go to the ends of the Earth to find Tori so I need to protect myself and my plans by keeping them far away from this house.

I open the door to my office and furrow my brow. The foyer lights are off. They're on an automatic timer that shuts off at two a.m. I grab onto the banister and stagger up the stairs. My brain is thick with cobwebs, but my cock is still very much alert.

I give Lev a nod when I reach Tori's door. "Thanks for hanging around," I say, giving him a clap on the back.

He looks into the room and shakes his head. "Be careful with that one, boss. She's brutal."

"Nothing I can't handle."

"Guess we'll see in the morning." He snickers and walks down the stairs.

"I should fire you for that," I call to him.

"But you won't because I'm irreplaceable."

"Nobody is irreplaceable. Always remember that. And everyone has a price. You'd better hope nobody ever figures out yours, or else I'll put a bullet in your skull." I rake a hand through my hair. "You should crash here tonight. It's late."

Lev nods. "Only if you're buying breakfast."

"Might be lunch. I don't know if G or I'll make it up in time."

"Lunch works. Lots of possibilities."

I turn toward the open doorway. Tori's bare feet hang over the side of the bed, her legs wide open.

Fuck yeah. So many possibilities.

I inch toward her. All the vodka numbed the stinging pain of my wounds. Well, at least the physical ones. But tonight I won't go there.

Her body is still, eyes closed, her hair spread out under her head. She actually looks angelic. So fucking different than the demon princess she turns into when she's awake.

My eyes drop to her tits. The dress hugs them tight, pushing them up to the edge of the neckline. I reach out a hand, my fingertips sizzling once they hit the curve of her hips. I slide my palm up her torso, my thumb skimming the side of one lush breast. My cock jerks, straining against my pants.

I want to strip her out of this dress.

Scratch that, I want to tear it off of her with my teeth.

Her eyes fly open and a startled gasp escapes her lips. "Don't touch me."

"When your eyes and body have been begging for it all night? Why should I stop?"

Her eyes glitter with hatred, but she doesn't shift away from me.

Because she wants this. She wants me, no matter what lies she spews.

That only makes me want to break her more. Not because she looks like Mischa, but because she's a threat to something I want. And the only way to get it all is to bring this vixen to her knees.

With one swift tug, I pull her off the mattress by the neckline of her dress. Her cheeks flush with anger, chin tilted in defiance. Streaks of blood still stain her lips and fuck me if that doesn't get me hot because I am just as twisted as she thinks. Probably more.

I flip her around, my arm snaked around her lush tits to hold her in place. I thrust my hard cock against the curves of her ass. Her back is flush against my chest, her heart humming against my palm. I sweep my tongue over the outer shell of her ear before latching onto her earlobe with my teeth. Enough to shock her, but not enough to take a bite. I will devour her like she's my last meal. But right now, I only want a taste.

She shudders in my grasp, her breaths catching like she has no idea what to expect next.

And she doesn't. Not at all.

My queen thinks she holds the crown, that she controls the throne.

She doesn't realize the villain is about to become her king.

CHAPTER 7
Viktorya

I just woke up to a nightmare.

And it's about to become his, too.

His heartbeat hammers against my back, heavy pants hot against the back of my neck. I grit my teeth, the heat pooling between my legs a complete betrayal of my body. Konstantin presses his muscled bicep against my breasts, killing my ability to drag in a single, deep breath. Tiny sparks explode over my bare skin in the wake of his rough touch and again, I wonder...who really is darker and more twisted?

Konstantin for inflicting this torment or me for secretly craving it?

He thrusts hard against me, and I swallow a low moan. I'm no virgin but just the sensation of his thick, hard shaft rubbing against my ass has my pussy sizzling because she's a traitorous fucking whore.

I don't want this. I don't want him.

My bound hands are wedged between his cock and my ass. I have no alternative but to fight and only one choice of weapon. I open my palms so his cock rubs against them, then cup what I think are his balls. He moans and I smirk. Fucking guy. He thinks I'm playing along with his sick game.

I wrench my hand, gripping the family jewels through his tuxedo pants. I dig in my long fingernails as much as possible, squeezing whatever I can to get him the fuck off of me.

He shoves me forward onto the mattress, his tortured groans shattering the silence. I peek over my shoulder. He drops to one knee, his gorgeous face wrenched with pain. I can't help it. A giggle slips from my lips, and after a few seconds of watching him, it turns into full-fledged laughter.

I flip myself over to lie faceup on the bed, a wide smile stretched across my mouth. "Oh, that was fun."

I hook my feet on the side of the bed frame and use them to slide my body to the side of the mattress. I need to see the look on his face. I want to see the defeat etched into his chiseled features, the mortification that Mr. Badass Arms Dealer Thug himself was stripped of his manhood by *me*. If he's gonna try to cage me, he'd better get used to my venomous bite.

I shimmy closer to the edge of the mattress until my bare feet hit the cool tile below. Using every bit of strength, I pull myself to a seated position.

"That's a really good look for you, *sweetheart*. On your knees. I love it." I cock my head to the side and flash a toothy grin. "Have you had enough yet? Or are you thirsty for more?"

I'd clap with glee if my wrists weren't tied together.

Since he still doesn't speak, I kill the silence for both of us. "I told you I didn't need a weapon. You obviously didn't take me seriously. But look at you now, hunched over like a little bitch." He raises his murderous gaze toward me and I lift an eyebrow, a smirk curling my lips. "I won't stop. I will only hit you harder and harder. Maybe you'll come to that realization before you die. Or maybe you're just too pretty to be smart about your safety. We can't have everything, right?"

Konstantin's eyes take on a demonic glow and he stands up, a sinister smile spreading across his face. Like he isn't hurt at all. Motherfucker.

"Did you really think you could hurt me, Tori?"

My mouth drops open. But I'd *had* him by the balls. Literally.

He takes a few steps toward me. "I thought you were smart."

My toes curl under his heated stare. I clench and unclench my useless fingers. He reaches out and pushes me backward onto the mattress.

"I think it's my turn to make you suffer."

His low growl makes my insides hum with hunger. Hunger, not disdain.

Oh, holy hell, what is wrong with me? Why did my legs just fall open? Why is my heart pounding so hard? And why is my goddamn pussy tingling like a bunch of Fourth of July sparklers?

Konstantin hovers over me. He drags his good hand down the front of my chest. His fingers tug at the neckline of my gown, exposing my lacy strapless bra. Heaving breaths quake my shoulders.

He shoves the gown up to my hips and presses himself between my quivering thighs. I gasp, his cock thick and hard against my pussy. Only a thin scrap of black lace covers the fact that I am dripping wet for this lunatic.

Which I guess makes me a lunatic, too.

"Stop," I rasp, even though my mind screams, *"Fuck, yes!"*

"Do you really mean that?" He hikes my gown up higher. Goosebumps pebble my skin in the wake of his fingertips. His eyes rake over my mostly bare body, his tongue sweeping over his lips. "I bet you don't."

"I do." My belly quivers and clenches.

"I want what I want, Tori." He wraps his fingers around the neckline of the flimsy fabric and tugs hard. His hand injury doesn't seem to faze him at all. "To expose you, to take you, to own you."

"Never." I flounder under him, helpless to stop what comes next. My hands press against the small of my back, my ankles locked together. I can't kick. I can't punch. *I can't escape.*

So many emotions assault me in these dark, heated seconds... angst, fury, anticipation, longing, excitement. They attack me like a hive full of killer bees, each one stinging me with the realization that who I am and what I want are the exact opposite of what I've always thought. For Christ's sake, I write gooey-chewy love stories with honorable, upstanding heroes and smart and sassy heroines who melt for their chivalrous soulmates.

There is nothing honorable, upstanding, or chivalrous about this man. He's dangerous, vengeful, and evil. There's nothing remotely heroic about him.

He reaches a hand around my back and slithers it under the part of my dress that's still intact. His fingers slide over the bra hook, and with a flick of his fingers, unlatches it. He pulls it off of me. A cool whoosh of air hits my breasts. He dips his head low, his tongue dragging a determined path around each one of my nipples, so hard they could cut glass.

Oh God, oh God, oh God...

He swirls his tongue around one at a time, taking each one in his teeth and giving it a hard-enough tug to elicit a gasp from my lips.

"You can't lie to me. Your body gives you away," he murmurs, suckling my nipple. His wrapped hand kneads my other breast. So focused, so demanding. The bandages are rough against my skin, creating friction that makes his oral invasion even more irresistible.

"Leave me alone." I squeeze my eyes shut and swallow the moan dancing on the tip of my tongue. I don't like this. I don't like him!

His hands slide down the sides of my torso, the demanding touch singeing my skin like he's holding a match against it. It taunts me, threatening to set my entire body aflame. Shivers slip down my spine when his fingers loop into the sides of my lacy thong. With one swift tug, he tears them off of me. My body shudders with uncontrollable force.

How can this be happening to me? And why do I crave this sicko so deeply?

My eyes fly open just in time to see him hold the shreds of my panties up to his nose. He breathes them in, then lets them fall from his fingers.

"You fucking liar," he growls, falling to his knees in front of me. "You can't fool me. I know what you want. And I'm going to make you beg me for it."

He grabs my legs and pulls me toward the edge of the bed. "This is how I win. How I will always win." Then he flips me over, my ass bare and in the air. A sizzling sting follows when his hand smacks against my prickled flesh.

He brands my ass over and over with his good hand, each slap making my pussy scream louder and louder for release. The heat radiating through me...damn, it's enough to make me spontaneously combust. Desire rages through me. My mind spins like a top, drowning in a sea of pent-up lust. Any bit of self-control I have left is like a lifeboat just out of my reach as I struggle to remain afloat. I pant and wheeze when his hand finally rests on my sensitive flesh, my heart ready to explode out of my chest.

Holy shit, this is so opposite of any sex scene I've ever written.

I try not to make a sound, but the cry I'm so desperate to choke back finally erupts from my chest.

"That cunt is dripping over my fingers. Do you know why?" He leans into me, pressing himself against my back. I don't bother with a ball grab again since it was fucking useless the first time. "Because you want what's forbidden. Your body craves what it shouldn't. You have a weakness, Tori."

"I don't. I can't," I sputter, squirming against him. My face mashes against the comforter, muffling my moans.

"You do. And you will. But not now...*later*."

"Later, my ass. I'm getting the hell out of here, you psychopath. Do you hear me? You can't keep me," I snap.

"I can do whatever the fuck I want."

My belly flips, the heat generated by his dirty mouth raging through me like an inferno.

"Fuck you," I choke out. "Figure out another way to get your revenge on my family."

"I already have." He weaves his fingers into my hair, tugging my head backward.

He flips me over again and I clench my teeth. "I'm not a goddamn flapjack."

"I just don't want you to miss a single word of my plan." He hovers over me with a sadistic grin spreading across his face.

I swallow hard, his lips so close to mine. Close enough that I can bite them. My breath hitches, pulse hammering against my throat at his nearness.

"I'm going to marry you, Tori."

CHAPTER 8
Konstantin

Words spew from her mouth like the most poisonous venom. "You are out of your goddamn mind if you think I'm going to marry you," she shouts. "I'm nobody's trophy, and I'd rather die than be someone's pawn."

"Someone *will* die if you resist. I promise you that."

Her face screws up in defiance. Her lips curl into a grimace. Hatred sparks in her blue eyes. She is all passion, from the ends of her hair to the tips of her toes. White-hot and deadly emotion is what drives her. It commands her every word and action. I can use that. I can use *her*.

My brain clouds with lust. I can't stop my hands from sliding down the length of her flushed body. Her skin sizzles under the pads of my fingers. And despite her rage, she doesn't shove me away or shake off my hand.

Weakness. She has one, a very fucking big one. And I'm gonna expose it like a raw nerve. She's mine, whether she knows it or not.

A strangled gasp escapes her lips when I graze her inner thighs.

I can break her. I can make her lose control. And she hates that I have that power.

Her legs quiver in my grip. "You can't have me."

"I already do." I push her legs open and thrust against her

pussy because I can't help myself. Even through my clothes, I need to feel the effect I have on her. And she doesn't disappoint. When her back arches the smallest bit and she meets my thrusts, I know I have her.

Tori Malikov is a viper of the deadliest kind but she's equally addictive. The fire that glows down deep inside of her can singe my insides like no other woman ever could.

She-devil may look exactly like my ex-fiancée, but the similarity ends there. Mischa was cold, vapid, and emotionless. Gorgeous but flat, like a week-old Coca-Cola. There were no bubbles. No excitement. No ferocity.

Nothing like Tori.

When I first spotted the Malikov princess at a dinner hosted by her brother Luka, a rush of fury consumed me. I was choked by toxic memories — the shock of walking in on my father fucking Mischa during our engagement party, the humiliation of her choosing him...my nemesis...over me. It was the ultimate victory he never let me forget until the day he died.

My original plan had been to play the long game and use the Malikovs to rebuild my fortune.

But Tori changed all of that. When I brushed against her that night, a spark shot through my insides like I'd just stuck my wet finger into an electrical socket.

She became the long game.

I was drawn to her like a moth to a flame.

Fuck, I crave that flame. I want to make it rage.

And I will drag it out of her so that she melts in my hands like ice.

"My brothers will never agree. They'll never hand me over to you." She speaks through clenched teeth. But not because she's angry.

Because she can't control her body when I'm near.

It's a wasted effort. I already know the effect I have on her.

I dip my head low so that our foreheads touch. "You're in *my* bed right now. I don't ask for permission, and I sure as fuck don't beg for forgiveness. Your brothers don't have a choice." I lean closer so that we're lip to lip. "I won. And they lost."

I slide my hand around her back, slipping one finger between her ass cheeks. A tiny moan slips from her mouth when my finger circles her tight hole.

Weak. She is so fucking weak.

Dirty, filthy sex to Tori is like blood to a vampire.

"You can't control me," she rasps. "I w-will never be your w-wife."

I push one digit inside of her, working her clit with my other hand. Her body shudders like a sudden shock of electricity just jolted her.

"You can't even speak because of what my hands are doing to you right now."

"M-my brothers will find me. A-and they'll kill you." She yelps when I press a second finger into her asshole. I stand over her writhing body, desire burning a hole in my pants. Thrusting forward and backward, her cries get louder and more desperate.

Mine. She is all mine. Too fucking stubborn to realize it, though.

She will, soon enough.

The head of my dick tingles with hunger. I want more than anything to tear off my pants and sink into her wet pussy, but I don't.

Because her loss of control is my gain.

And I will never lose my own control ever fucking again.

"Tell me you're mine," I hiss, working my fingers harder. Her walls tighten and quiver. Her juices drown my fingers with every push and pull. "I want to hear you say it."

"N-never." Her cries turn into full-fledged screams. "Oh my God, oh my God!"

"If you want to come, tell me what I want to hear."

"F-fuck you!" Her legs lock around my arm, her ass thrusting against my other hand. Her body is in a complete frenzy. She's close, so fucking close to unraveling. And she's exactly where I want her, on the brink of her complete undoing.

And that's exactly where I'm gonna leave her until she learns to obey me.

I abruptly pull my hands away. Her eyes fly open. She struggles to raise her upper body off the mattress. Only her shoulders make it off the bed. Her mouth drops wide open in shock.

"What the hell are you doing?"

"You didn't tell me what I wanted to hear."

"Because it's never going to be true."

I narrow my eyes. "I always get what I want. And I want you."

"Well, I don't want you."

I hold up the fingers that just fucked her pussy and drag them over her lips. "Open your mouth," I growl.

She doesn't. Shocker.

I shove them inside, taking a big gamble that she won't bite them off. "I want you to taste the truth, Tori. Taste what my fingers did to you. To your ass, to your pussy. You can't lie to me. You may hate me right now, but you love what I do to you and how I make you feel. Your body gives it all away, all the secrets you're so desperate to keep."

I pull my fingers out of her mouth before she sinks her teeth into them...because I'm not up for more stitches. Taking a step backward, I drink in every inch of her tan, toned body. A shiver ripples through her. Her lush breasts heave, nipples so hard they could stab me, pussy lips glistening...taunting me.

"There's nothing special about you," she says. "Any man could have gotten that reaction from me."

"I don't believe any man has ever done those things to you." I snake my arms around her back and pull her toward me. "I don't think you've ever let a man get close enough to make you feel the way I can. The way I *do*."

Her blue eyes flash. "You don't know me at all."

"I know plenty." I lean my head into her neck, whispering against her smooth skin. Her head falls backward, inviting my lips to do more. "You spend every day at the Coffee Bean Café in Miami Beach. Most days, you start with coffee. But on some days, you get a mimosa. You're glued to your MacBook Air. You never leave your house without that laptop. And you only type with a few fingers on each hand. You crack your knuckles when you're stuck. You talk to yourself when you think nobody is watching. But I always do." My pulse throbs. The scent of her perfume teases my nostrils, completely fucking with my head and the plan.

The plan.

Don't forget the plan.

"You wear glasses unless you're going to the gym. You work out hard. You push yourself to the limit and never stop until you're finished. You're fierce. Driven. And you've taken down more heavy bags with your kicks and punches than anyone else at that gym."

"Fucking crazy stalker," she gasps. "And big deal. You watched me. You don't know who the hell you're dealing with. And you definitely can't imagine what I'll do to you once I get out of these damn zip ties."

"You think I'm afraid of a little pain?" I growl against her ear. I nip on her lobe and she hisses in a sharp breath. "Pain doesn't scare me. And neither do you."

"You kidnapped me to get revenge on my family. And you haven't been able to keep your hands — or your cock — away from me since then." She pauses, breathless. "So who's the liar now, Konstantin?"

I don't answer.

Because for as big of a liar as Tori is, I'm just as fucked.

CHAPTER 9
Viktorya

"Fuck me, Konstantin. I need to feel your cock deep inside of me."

"Tell me where." His eyes are dark with lust, his voice a low growl that makes my skin tingle as his mouth hums against my skin.

"In my pussy, in my ass," I rasp. "Everywhere."

"Beg me." His cock bobs between my legs, the head grazing my slit.

I don't want to beg. Begging makes me look weak. But it's the only way. This evil sex god will torture and torment me to the point of frustrated tears if I don't. "Please make me come."

"I'm the only one who can make you feel this way." He drops to his knees in front of me, his breath hot against my prickled flesh. I cry out as he captures my clit between his lips and suckles it. "And I'm the only one who ever will."

My eyes fly open. I awaken with a strangled gasp, fingers and toes prickling with the sensation of pins and needles. Sweat pebbles my skin, the oversized white T-shirt Konstantin put on me last night clinging to me in wet patches.

"What in the fresh hell was I dreaming?" I mumble.

But it didn't seem like a dream. My God, it all felt so real.

A loop of X-rated fantasies captured my unconscious mind as I slept fitfully on the plush comforter. Erotic images of me and Konstantin wallpaper my mind. My pussy tingles as they flash across my eyes.

No, no, no. This has to be a symptom of post-traumatic stress. Wild, salacious dreams. Helplessness manifesting itself in the most insane scenarios.

Sweat drizzles down the sides of my face.

That doesn't make a damn bit of sense.

But neither does the alternative...that my mind secretly desires the man who stole my life away.

With a pounding heart, I turn my face into the pillow to wipe away the perspiration. Memories of Konstantin unleashing his carnal assault on me last night pop between my ears like bullets. A delicious and very unwelcome shiver slips over my flushed skin.

God help me, I want more.

I slam my head against the pillow, a groan of frustration shattering the silence.

Wait, what in the actual fuck?

I gulp down oxygen and count to ten.

Okay, Tor. Let's calm the hell down. Forget Konstantin. Forget his hands. Forget his cock. Forget his gorgeous and demonic face. Forget it all and focus on getting the hell away from him.

Bits and pieces of my dark tryst with Konstantin explode between my temples. They are jagged pieces of an erotic puzzle that begs to be assembled. Blood bubbles in my veins, lust flooding my body with hunger and yearning.

All because of him.

My captor.

My enemy.

But for all I order myself to forget, the need to tell my twisted story grabs hold like a noose around my neck. My mind is a jumble of words, emotions, and sensations. But I have zero ability to release them.

I thrash around on the mattress, craving his dirty promises

and rough touch. Then I remember the security cameras. He's watching. He's always watching. Isn't that what he told me?

A low moan slips from my mouth. I let my legs fall open just enough so my pussy can wink at him. My belly flutters, a rush of desire consuming me. I'd finger-fuck myself if my hands weren't plastered against my back and bound by this damn zip tie.

And he'd love every second of it. Might even join in.

I slam my heels on the bed. Dammit, I should be plotting a way out of this prison, not a new novel.

I love the books I write. The angst, the buildup, the first kiss, the first "I love yous."

But writing those kinds of stories doesn't turn my mind inside out and back again. They don't drive me crazy with yearning for a bad boy with a filthy mouth who treats me like his whore. They don't make every cell sizzle with the need for his hands, his tongue, and his dick.

I want to write a new kind of story, the kind I swore I'd never want to star in.

My fingertips tingle like they know exactly what I need. A keyboard, a pen. But if I'm being honest, it might actually be therapy, because wanting Konstantin like I do makes me think I'm a bigger headcase than he is. He represents everything wrong with my world, everything evil and manipulative and dangerous. Konstantin Romanov is everything I despise. Everything I vowed to avoid.

But yet here I am, counting the seconds before my sexy-as-fuck captor appears in that doorway and launches me into the stratosphere like no other man ever has.

He truly is the Devil, dangling the forbidden in front of my face and bringing it close enough for me to taste.

And then he ruined me for anyone else.

A swift knock on the door jolts me. Sparks of anticipation dance around in my core. The door opens, and an older woman pops her head inside the room. I recoil when I see her kind face, sparkling brown eyes, and dark hair wrapped in a tight bun on top of her head.

Shock paralyzes my ability to speak. But a whisper of cool air between my legs reminds me that my girl parts are still on full display. I slam my legs shut.

"Good morning," the woman says. She walks in with a tray. "Konstantin asked me to bring you something to eat and drink. You must be hungry."

"And you must be Mother Enabler," I scoff with a roll of my eyes.

Her brows furrow, her lips turning downward into a frown. "Oh no, dear. I'm not his mother. I'm his housekeeper and cook, Isabella."

One of my eyebrows shoots up. "Still an enabler," I mutter. "I'm a hostage tied up in his house, half-naked. And you show up without even blinking. There's something very freaking wrong with this picture, *Isabella*. Makes me wonder just how many girls he's kidnapped in the past."

"If it makes you feel better, you're the first." She smiles. Her light brown eyes crinkle in the corners.

"That just made my day," I say sarcastically. "The first and only one privileged to be targeted by that sick bastard."

Isabella walks over to the nightstand and sets the tray on top. My stomach growls, the smells wafting under my nose reminding me that I haven't eaten since yesterday afternoon. Konstantin snatched me before dinner was served, and I'd been starving at the reception. But after the trauma of almost being choked to death and flown to some obscure location, I guess I just forgot about my lack of sustenance.

I sweep my eyes over the silver tray. A fluffy egg white omelet filled with vegetables, a stack of whole wheat toast, and a bowl of fresh mango chunks.

I love mango.

My teeth clench. Fucking asshole. Of course he knows that.

There is a steaming mug of coffee, cream, sugar, and two tall, crystal champagne flutes.

Mimosas.

There's a scribbled note written in blue ink underneath one of them. I pull myself closer so I can read it since I can't very well pick it up with my hands tied behind my back.

Squinting, I finally make out the words.

I figured today might be a two-mimosa morning.

Fuck him. It might even be a three-mimosa morning.

A smile tugs at my lips, despite the wildly crazy circumstances that brought me here. He's watched me sip the drinks at the café, but he has no idea of my tradition. He knows I only drink them on certain days, and that's true. Book release days.

When I first started publishing my stories, I'd drink a mimosa to calm myself down. There's a lot of panic involved with putting something so deeply personal out into the world. Even if nobody on Earth knows it was me, Tori Malikov, there's still a harsh element of rejection that goes into seeing a bad review. When anyone reads my words — words that poured out of my mind, heart, and soul — and trashes them, it stings worse than a hive full of wasps ever could.

I give Isabella a long look as she stirs my coffee. She knew exactly how much of the cream and sugar to dump into it.

Jesus, either he has a photographic memory, or he took pretty copious notes.

"What would you like to try first?" Isabella asks, picking up a fork and knife. "The mango is delicious. So sweet and ripe–"

I quirk an eyebrow, interrupting her ode to the mango. "How about we talk about why you're so calm about the idea of feeding a prisoner? You know this makes you an accessory to a pretty major crime, right?"

Isabella laughs softly. "My dear, if you only knew what my life has been like, you'd know that being an accessory to a crime is the least of my worries."

"Aiding and abetting is pretty major in the eyes of the law," I say. "And then there's the real judge and jury...my brothers. Are you really so loyal to Konstantin that you're willing to risk your life when they find me? Because they will."

"Konstantin has his reasons for bringing you here," she says after a long minute of silence. "I don't question him."

"Really? So when he told you that he had a woman tied up in his bed who needed breakfast this morning, you didn't have *anything* to say about it?"

She shrugs. "It's not my place. I do as he asks and he takes care of me and my son Julian. He's always been so good to us. I have no reason to challenge him."

Huh. Sounds like Isabella's had a few too many morning mimosas. That, or Konstantin has completely brainwashed her.

My stomach growls again. Sounds like it's fed up that I keep using my mouth for everything other than eating. Pun intended.

"Okay," I say. "Well, do you even care that your golden boy is a killer?"

Isabella furrows her brow. "I'm sorry?"

"He threatened to kill my family if I tried to escape."

Isabella is quiet for a second. She places a napkin on my lap. "Then I'd say you should probably stay put, dear."

My jaw drops. Did I wake up in the middle of some kind of fucking alternate reality? Who talks like this and just blindly obeys orders, no matter how crazy they are?

"Oh my God, you're as twisted as he is," I mutter.

"Might you want a sip of a mimosa now? Looks like you can use one."

"You should have just brought the whole bottle of champagne. I'd guzzle the whole damn thing down to blunt the bite of this insanity."

The bubbly liquid hits my tongue, and for a split second, I try to forget the hell I've been plunged into. Isabella doesn't move the glass from my lips. She tilts it back just enough that I don't wear the mimosa while I gulp it down.

I don't get the same effect from this sunny cocktail that I

normally do on a release day. On release days, I celebrate glowing reviews and out-of-control sales numbers. Today, I celebrate the fact that I'm still breathing.

But when Konstantin finds out that I have no intention of lying around here, half-naked on my back, eagerly waiting for him to launch another deliciously erotic attack on my body in the name of revenge, he'll try to make damn sure that my celebration comes to a very sudden, and very painful, end.

Yes, he'll *try*. And he'll fail. Epically. Because, like every other typical dumbass guy, he never learns the errors of his ways.

And it'll be up to me to teach him.

CHAPTER 10
Konstantin

I take a long gulp of coffee, the scorching liquid sizzling the sides of my throat. But I barely feel the heat. My eyes are locked on the video feed streaming on my eighty-inch plasma screen.

Tori's frenzied body flounders on the mattress. Her long, toned legs part, desperate-sounding moans tumbling from her lips. Sounds like she's getting fucked.

My cock strains against my jeans. I lean closer to the screen, my eyes tracing every move her body makes. Who is she dreaming about? Who has her so damn hot?

"I want you," she murmurs. *"Your hands, your lips, your tongue. Make love to me, Jake... Now. Make me feel so good, like only you can..."*

I stab the Stop button on the remote control, gaping at the screen before I hurl the remote at the wall.

Who in the fuck is Jake?

I never saw her with a guy who wasn't one of her brothers for the entire time I followed her around Miami. No boyfriends, no friends with benefits, no one-night stands. Nobody who claimed her attention.

A rush of ire bubbles deep in my gut. I jump up from the

couch and stalk toward the window that overlooks the glittering waves of Sarasota Bay. It's calm, the exact opposite of me right now.

Whoever this Jake guy is, I will find him, hang him on a cross, and use a mandolin to slice the skin off his body. And then I'll nail his hands and feet to the wood before setting fire to the bastard.

A sharp sting of unwarranted rejection pierces my heart. Again.

"You could never keep her satisfied the way I can."

"She wants a winner. And that will never be you, Kosta."

"I have an empire — power, control, influence. You have nothing. You are nothing."

"Sonofabitch," I yell, hurling the coffee cup against the window. The mug bounces off the tempered glass and crashes against the tile floor. Thick chunks of white porcelain scatter, the steaming coffee spreading across the white marble.

This is about retribution. This is about claiming my fair share of the Malikov empire. This is not about that whore Mischa, or my rat bastard father.

I bring a hand to the back of my neck and squeeze the stress knot lodged at the base.

It's always about him, though, even though he's been gone for close to two years.

That dick flicker is always hanging over me like a black cloud. He wants to see me fail. He wants me to crumble, to lose everything he swore I'd never build without his help. To him, it would be karma for not saving his life when he came to my office that day, for watching him get shot up while looking on with not even the smallest bit of remorse.

As if I'd ever show the fucker any bit of mercy after a lifetime of his abuse. He thought he was better than me, but who's calling the shots now? Who has everything he wants within his reach? Who's not lying in a grave six feet under because he was too much of a cocky and conniving thief to realize that, for as much power as he had, he wasn't immune to his own karma?

I suck in a breath.

Fuck Jake.

She can dream about whoever she wants. I don't own her mind.

But I fucking own her body.

I ball my hands into tight fists, seriously considering punching a hole in the middle of my flat-screen.

No. I need to keep the control I've grabbed back. Taking her from her family, bringing her here, making her submit to me... that was all in the name of control. Nothing else.

I press my fists against my closed eyes to keep the grainy surveillance camera images of Tori moaning on the bed from looping through my head, and kick one of the pieces of porcelain across the floor with my shoe.

She's going to be my wife. I can't fuck her knowing she's dreaming about another man.

I stalk out of my office and up the stairs to Tori's bedroom. The door is closed. I kick it open. Isabella jumps up from her chair and turns away from Tori, a startled look on her face when she sees me in the doorway.

Tori just glares at me. Piercing blue eyes, hot with rage, lance me with all the fire I know lies behind them. "What the fuck do you want?" she snaps.

Isabella gets up and places the fork and knife on the tray. She looks between us and backs away. "I'll be downstairs in the kitchen," she says before quickly making a beeline for the door.

I shove the door and it slams shut with a loud bang. Tori sits with her back against the headboard. Her blonde hair hangs over her shoulders, sleep-tousled like someone was tugging it all night while fucking her.

My throat tightens. Because in her mind, someone was.

Jake.

"I'd flip you off for sending Isabella away, but you wouldn't see it since my hands are tied behind my back, you sadistic fuck."

I close the distance between us, the muscles in my legs tensing with every step I take. I reach for her throat and close my fingers around it, leaning in close. "Who the hell is Jake?"

Her eyes pop open wide. "Wh-what?"

I give her neck a little squeeze. "No wife of mine–"

"No wife of yours," she interrupts, her voice hoarse. "That is exactly right. I am no wife of yours, and I never will be. So whoever I dream about fucking is my business."

My hand moves to the neckline of the T-shirt she's wearing. I fist the cotton and pull her close against me. Her pouty lips beckon, begging me to devour them. Or at least they do in my dark mind.

"If you don't tell me who he is, I will find him and slaughter him like he's goddamn livestock."

"That's a vivid image," she rasps. "I guess Jake had better grow eyes in the back of his head, yeah? Now that you're onto him?"

"You think I'm joking?" I let go of the shirt and bring my hands to her tits. I knead them hard. "I don't share. You are mine, Tori. Everything you are. It's mine forever."

"I think you need to call Isabella and ask her for your meds because you are clearly off of them." Her eyes blaze with challenge.

I stare at her, my jaw twitching. Words escape me. The only thing I can focus on is the rush of need that crashes over me in those seconds. I wasn't kidding when I said I'd kill Jake. Any man who interferes with my plan is a threat. Anyone who commands her focus is dead.

"You can't control me. My mind is mine alone," she whispers. Pink spots flood her cheeks. "You'll never have all of me, no matter what you do."

I pull away from her, then reach into the back pocket of my jeans for a stiletto knife. I click the button, and the gleaming steel blade pops out. "Is that what you think?"

"That's what I know." Her voice shakes the tiniest bit, eyes still glued to the sharp tip of the knife.

I hold up the blade to her eyes, then lightly drag the serrated edge down the side of her face. She sits against the headboard of the bed, paralyzed with fear, shock...maybe both.

With my free hand, I push the T-shirt up to her tits, exposing her flat belly and bare pussy. I bring the blade to her flushed skin. She shivers against the steel touch. I gently graze her flesh with the edge of the blade, my eyes glued to hers. They're usually shielded, protecting her inner-most thoughts. But right now, I can see right into her soul — what she wants, what she needs, what she craves.

I can taste the angst and the panic...but it's the desire that overpowers everything else. It charges me, electrifies me.

I see it all, Tori. You can't protect yourself from me anymore.

The blade hovers between her quivering thighs for long seconds. She drags in a sharp breath when the steel presses against the inside of her leg. Apprehension mixed with anticipation. Lust versus terror.

With a sudden and deft flick of my wrist, I slash the zip tie holding her ankles together. She gasps when the knife whizzes through the plastic. Her ankles fall open, and she wiggles her toes, her mouth parted in disbelief.

Like, am I really that fucking crazy?

And yeah, I guess I am.

This is a big leap of faith. Removing her binds means she can use her feet and legs against me. But I want to prove a point, and I'm willing to take the risk because I'd much rather have her legs wrapped tight around me for this next part.

I lean toward her and snake an arm around her back, guiding her down to the mattress. Then I loop my arms under her legs and pull her ass to the edge of the mattress. Her pussy lips glisten, because for all of the anger bottled up inside of Tori, she aches for a release. And she wants me to give it to her.

I sweep my tongue over the sensitive skin of her inner thighs before sliding it down her wet slit. She yelps, her body tensing as I take her clit between my lips. I suck it hard. My dick throbs harder as she thrashes left and right. Control seeps from her body, cries for more slipping from her mouth.

My tongue pushes into her pussy, thrusting between her walls. She raises her hips, fucking my mouth like the dirty whore she wants to be for me. The tang of her juices hits my lips. My dick tingles, blood rushing to my groin. It strains against my jeans, desperate to sink inside of her perfect pussy.

Tori's legs clench tight around me, her body begging me to delve deep. I let go of her legs, letting them fall open onto the mattress. The heady scent of lust and sex clouds my mind. It hangs heavy in the air, so thick I can chew on it. In this carnal bubble of ours, the only thing that matters is making her come so hard, she forgets everything and everyone.

Except me.

I reach one hand around to her ass. I grip one cheek hard before skimming the rim of her asshole. Her pussy responds as soon as my finger presses into her ass. Her walls quiver, sweet juices fill my mouth. She writhes and screams as I finger-fuck her ass. My mouth works her pussy, tugging at her clit with my tongue and teeth. Her body flails and jerks under the command of my tongue and hand. She tightens her legs around me.

"Oh my God! So...fucking...good!"

That's it. I have her. Every bit of her.

I am her undoing, whether or not she realizes it.

I pull my finger out of her ass and my mouth away from her pussy.

Her eyes fly open and she lets out a sharp gasp.

"Why did you stop? Again!"

"You didn't deserve to finish."

"Is this how you get off? By toying with me? You think getting me all crazy hot is going to make me beg for your cock? Newsflash, it'll never happen." Her eyes flare with disgust. But she doesn't kick me away.

My heart pounds against my ribcage, still working overtime from the adrenaline coursing through me. That sweet cunt is like the most potent drug. Instantly addictive. And it takes everything in me to drag myself away from it.

Nobody else can have this effect on her body. And nobody else will.

"Just because you know how to tongue fuck me doesn't mean I'm going to melt in a puddle at your feet," she spews when I don't answer.

"No, but making you come harder than you ever have makes your body battle with your mind. You want me, you crave me, and you hate yourself for it. And you also hate that I'll use all of that against you."

She scoffs. "You're a psycho lunatic who thinks he can get me to submit. But that won't ever happen. You may need that to stroke your big-ass ego, but you'll have to find another sucker because you can't break me."

I dip my head closer to hers. I slide my fingers down the side of her face. "I don't need to break you, Tori. You're already broken. But you do need me to piece you back together. And that's what you hate most."

I stand up and back away from the bed, convinced that she won't be thinking about Jake Whoever-the-fuck-he-is any longer.

But she never answers me. Stunned into silence, because she knows, deep down, it's the truth.

I force myself to turn away from her. As I rake a hand through my hair, the realization pummels me like a brick to the temple.

Because for as much as I wanted this woman to give me back the control I'd lost, all she does is pull it farther out of my grasp.

That makes us both fucked.

And equally broken.

CHAPTER 11
Konstantin

"Julian's been tracking the Malikovs since you snatched Tori and told them about your grand plan to marry her and take over their organization. Our guys on the inside told him that they brought in the senior member of Red Ladro to help find her. Alek Severinov." Gregor's lips press into a tight line. "Remember? Your buddy who now wants to put an ice pick through your skull for duping him?"

"Yeah, I remember. He can be pissed at me, but he'd have never been able to figure out the truth about who I am." I scrub a hand down the front of my face and take a sip of vodka. "Konstantin Romanov is an elite arms dealer from Moscow. He flies under the radar and keeps a tight circle. Nobody knows that Mikhail Federov is his evil alter ego, and my real identity."

"Yeah, well, after your weapons empire got torched to ash after Dad's murder, you didn't really have a choice about changing your name to Mom's maiden one."

"I'd have never gotten close to them as a Federov. Someone would have connected the dots about Dad's murder if I'd have shown up as myself. If not the Malikovs, then Severinov. Red Ladro has a network like a hive mind. The world is a damn small place, G. Viktor knew our father fucked him over and was ready to sell secrets to Arseny Siderov."

"Viktor is dead now."

"Who knows what Viktor told his sons about his work? I wasn't gonna take that chance." Water droplets drizzle down the sides of the glass as the ice melts. "I'm not worried. They won't find us. Our Sarasota place is off the grid. I have all network and GPS signals scrambled so they can't be traced. No hacker can break into that fortress. All the email accounts I used to get to Alek are shut down. Same with the ones I used to contact Luka and Nik while we worked together. Everything is inactive. Like they never existed. The phones and SIM cards, shattered. No trace."

"People still talk," Gregor says in a low voice even though the door to my office is closed. "And we still need to do business, which means you can be tracked. You know they'll pay a shit ton for any information about Tori. Like you said, Red Ladro has a massive underground network."

"Yeah, and Severinov only found me because I wanted him to. They're looking for Konstantin Romanov. They're not looking for Julian Costas. He's the front man who finds the clients and makes the deals."

Julian is Isabella's son and our other business partner. After Isabella's husband was killed in a car accident twelve years ago, they both moved into my parents' house. We grew up together and he's like another brother to us. He's a little hotheaded, but nothing I can't handle. He works hard and pulls his weight.

And soon enough, Tori and I will be married. According to the contracts I'm having drawn up, I'll take ownership of half the Malikov empire. Nik and Luka will do anything to keep their sister safe, so there's no doubt they'll meet my demands.

Gregor picks up his glass and sloshes his drink around. Ice cubes clink against the crystal. "I want you to tell me something. The truth, Kosta."

I hate when he starts a sentence with words like that.

"How long did you lie to me about working with the Malikovs to build our arms business back up before you decided to snatch Tori?" His blue eyes darken, fingers tightening around his glass. "I want to know how long she's been part of your plan."

With a sigh, I sit back against the pebbled cordovan leather chair. "Look, things didn't go the way I wanted when I plotted this whole thing out. It all went to hell from the beginning when I recruited that asshat Hank Wheeler to boost those trucks. And then after he completely fucked everything up, I had to come up with another plan. So I became Nik Malikov's trusted supplier for gun parts to steal back everything we lost, under the guise that we were going to be 'partners.' But that put me at their mercy. The money came in too slow, and without a really solid stake in their business, I'd never have the influence or power to grow our own network."

"And you didn't think I deserved to know any of that? You went off the rails, Kosta. You slapped targets on our backs–"

"There have always been targets on our backs," I growl. "I changed the plan so we'd have leverage to take control of what was ours. What the Brotherhood stole when they killed our father. Our network, our reputation, our supply chain. They destroyed it all. There was no other way to grab our share of that empire unless I had something that was important to them. Like Tori."

"And you really think they're gonna go along with this wedding? You think they'll accept your demands?"

"I've watched this family for a long time. I know what they've lost. Not only Viktor and his oldest son, but a daughter. She disappeared on the day she was arranged to marry Dmitri Stepanov, and for all they know, she's dead." I pick up a pen from my desk and twirl it around my fingers. "There is no way they'll risk the same thing happening to Tori."

"Not that you'd ever kill her." Gregor lifts an eyebrow.

"I will do whatever I need to do to get what I deserve." My lips pull into a tight line. "We've lost a lot, too. And from now on, I call the shots. Nobody else."

"And what happens if push comes to shove and her brothers revolt?" Gregor narrows his eyes. "Are you gonna be able to pull the trigger, Kosta? Are you going to do right by your family? Or satisfy your cock?"

I fling the pen at him and he ducks out of the way before it hits him. It lands on the floor with a clatter. "I don't answer to you, G. You answer to *me*."

"I'm not your fucking peon. I'm your partner." Gregor pushes his chair back. The legs scrape against the floor with a fingernail-blackboard squeak. "And as your partner, I'm telling you to stop thinking with your dick before we lose anything else."

He grabs his jacket and pulls it on.

"Where are you going?" I ask, flipping on my computer.

"Out for a drink, and then maybe a fuck." Gregor slants me a glance. "Wanna come? You need both. You're wound like a damn top."

"I'm good. And remember, someone is always watching. Keep your eyes open, G."

"Always," he says before walking out of the office. The door slams shut. I recline in my chair, letting out a deep sigh.

Retribution. It's always been my goal.

I can't ever get the revenge I want on Viktor for killing my father and my livelihood. But I can take back what he made off of my family and our connections. My father helped him create an empire, after all. I'm simply taking my fair share. And Tori is how I will get it.

I watch the security feed streaming from the cameras in her room. She lies on her side, her legs stacked, eyes closed. Her lips move but no sound comes out.

Looks like she's dreaming.

I zoom in to get a closer look. A single tear streams down her cheek. Her shoulders quiver.

Or having a nightmare.

I switch off the monitor and walk upstairs. The downstairs

area is quiet and dark. Julian and Gregor are gone, and Isa is probably sleeping.

The lies I just spewed to my brother loop through my mind as I take the stairs two at a time.

It's business. Only business.

Yeah, bullshit.

I'll do anything I need to, to get what I want.

That's the only part that *is* true. And not the truth that Gregor wants to hear. Definitely not the one I want to admit.

I pick up the pace when I hear her soft whimpers. Tori is more the type to inflict tears than shed them herself, so something is haunting her mind, much like my own demons haunt mine. Something nudges me closer and closer until I stand over her shaking body. This is the most vulnerable I've seen her since she lay unconscious in the back seat of my truck.

I reach over to stroke the back of her head. Her soft hair slides between my fingers. Even in her fitful sleep, she captivates me. I want to know what could devastate her to the point where she cries in her sleep.

With a loud gasp, her eyes fly open. "No! Please, no!"

I pull my hand away like she's just erupted into flames.

"What are you doing here?" she yelps. "Spying on me while I sleep?"

"I heard you crying. I came to find out if you were okay." Without thinking, I swipe her tears away with my thumb. "You had a nightmare."

"Don't touch me." She jerks her head away from my fingers. "I'm fine now. And spare me the bullshit that you actually care one bit about me or what I was dreaming about."

My spine stiffens, but was I really so delusional to think she'd just melt into my arms? "I wouldn't have come if I wasn't concerned."

"Well, bottle up your concern for someone who gives a shit. You can just fuck right off now."

Rage bubbles in my chest. I shouldn't have come in here. I should have stayed away from her...far fucking away.

The hold she has on me tightens like a noose. My pulse slams against my throat because even though she is pure venom, I only crave her more.

Every bit of her — heart, mind, and soul.

But her cold words lance my chest, the rejection biting.

"Remember where you are, Tori," I growl. "And what I can and will do to you if you push me."

I storm out of the room and slam the door shut so hard, one of the pieces of framed art on the wall in the hallway crashes to the tile floor, the glass in the frame shattering. I sidestep the shards, flames roaring inside of me like an inferno. Gregor's challenge screams out in my mind. I clench my fist and pound a dent in the drywall outside my room.

Don't worry, G. When push comes to shove, you bet your fucking ass I will pull the trigger.

CHAPTER 12
Viktorya

Minutes stretch into hours. I barely sleep another wink after being yanked from that horrifying nightmare.

Val is gone. Possibly dead. All because of a business deal gone very wrong.

She was sold as property to the highest bidder, and then disappeared into thin air on the day of her wedding.

My baby sister.

This fucking life.

I fought so hard against the same fate for myself, defying my father at every turn. Because of me, he gambled with Val's freedom and lost.

Guilt clenches my heart. It could have been me whose life was signed over to Dmitri Stepanov. But Val never spoke out against our father. She accepted the consequences of our father's actions and never said a word to any of us. She kept his dirty secret. Val did what was expected of her. She played the role of the dutiful mafia daughter. And she suffered alone in silence.

Maybe she's still suffering.

For all I know, she's someone else's captive now.

Scared. Alone. Desperate.

Not much of a difference than my current situation, if I'm being honest.

I wiggle my fingers to circulate the blood. My wrists get a reprieve every once in a while when Konstantin lets me use the bathroom. He watches like a hawk with the door open to make sure I don't try to bludgeon him with the toilet brush since there isn't anything else in that room I could use as a weapon. As creative as I am in lethal weaponry, even I can't come up with a halfway-decent torture device.

I squeeze my eyes shut. Memories of my nightmare about Val come rushing back like a raging wave. Screams pop between my ears like exploding bullets.

It's Val's wedding day. She looks gorgeous and angelic in her white floor-length dress. But she's sad...crying. I try to talk to her, to ask her what's wrong, but no sounds come out of her mouth in response.

It's like someone stole her voice.

An eruption of gunfire follows. Seconds later, blossoms of blood stain the front of her gown until no hint of white is visible anymore. Tears run down the sides of her perfectly made-up face, but those tears aren't clear now.

They're bright red.

She waves her hands in the air, more bloodstains splattering her skin and gown like exploding paint balls. Her body jerks left and right as if it's being stabbed with invisible blades. Val's lips move in a frenzy, her eyes brimming with panic and fear. Still, I can't hear her words.

Her warning.

She knew this was her fate.

Maybe she was trying to warn me against my own.

I could have helped. I could have saved her.

Anger ripples through me, growling deep in my gut.

Why didn't she tell me, dammit? Why didn't she trust me?

Tears sting my eyes.

God, I miss her so much.

For a second, when I saw Konstantin standing over me last night with a concerned look in his normally cold eyes, I had a sudden urge to tell him what had haunted my dreams. The soft touch of his hand massaging the back of my head softened me. In that fleeting moment, the wall between us crumbled and I forgot he was responsible for stealing my freedom the way Dmitri had almost stolen Val's.

Then I remembered and lashed out to remind him that he may have my body, but he will never have my respect or my heart.

But I lied.

Because it was my panic that drove him out of that room... panic that he's touched me on a level I swore I'd never expose to a man like him. He's exposed a layer of darkness I never knew existed down deep in my core. The dirty, filthy words and actions that undo me every time he appears in my bedroom — my prison... He has some kind of erotic superpower that makes me melt like an ice cube in the sun.

A soft knock at the door makes me jump. I sniff hard, wiping my tears by dragging my cheeks across the pillow. Isabella pokes her head into the room with a heaping tray of food, and for as miserable as I am right now, my stomach convinces me that I am more hungry than irate.

"I brought you brunch," Isabella says, nudging the door open with her hip. "There are all sorts of treats for you."

She puts the tray down on the night table next to my bed and guides me to a seated position against the headboard. I drop my eyes down to the tray, and the hint of a smile lifts my lips. "Lobster Benedict," I muse.

Isabella nods. "He said it's one of your favorites."

Yes, of course the creepy stalker knows I love lobster Benedict since I have it pretty often at the Coffee Bean Café. I check out the rest of the tray. He also knows I love chocolate ice cream with butterscotch sauce, shrimp and avocado salad, and ciabatta bread.

It's a weird combination of foods, but warmth floods my belly in spite of my circumstances.

He still cares, even after I kicked him out of here last night when he was probably at his most vulnerable. Maybe that means he'll grant me one wish. It wouldn't be freedom in the physical form, but it would help my mind process the crazy and conflicted emotions plaguing me.

"This looks incredible," I say. "But instead of food, there is something else I'd prefer."

Isabella raises her eyebrows, a confused look on her face. "Like what?"

"A notebook and a pen."

Her jaw drops. "Dear, I can tell you right now. He will never give you a pen. Not in this lifetime."

"Just please ask him," I urge. "Isabella, I need it. For my sanity. Please. He'll listen to you."

"I really think you need to eat something," she says nervously. "You can talk to me. You don't need to write anything down."

"You don't understand," I say. "There are so many things running through my mind right now because of my situation. I need to work them out, and the only way I can do it is to write. You have to do this for me. I swear I'll eat. Just ask."

"Okay." She backs away from the bed. "But he'll say no. I know him. He'll never agree to it."

"Tell him I will do anything."

The words are out of my mouth before I can swallow them down.

No matter what he wants.

I bite down on my lower lip as I replay the words in my mind. It *is* all for the story, though.

Or is that just another one of my many lies?

Because deep down, I meant every word.

Some writers suffer from lack of inspiration, but Konstantin Romanov has given me material that could last for years. A shiver ripples through me, so many scenes looping through my brain, the taboo type of scene I've never written before. I need to see them written on paper to see if they elicit the same response reading them, if they are as thick with emotion as they are in my twisted reality.

Isabella hurries out the door. Barely a few minutes pass before Konstantin strides into the bedroom. All thoughts of food and my very empty stomach dissipate. I realize I'm still starving, just for a very different kind of sustenance.

It looks like he's just stepped out of the shower. His bronze skin glistens with droplets of water, thick, dark hair slicked back save for a single strand of hair that hangs sexily over his right eye, covering the single freckle that sits underneath it. His jaw tightens as our gazes tussle.

I swallow hard, unable to keep my eyes from navigating a path down the length of his bare torso. Swirls of black ink cover his thick chest, hiding a few scars left behind from his obviously violent past, a dark one I know nothing about, but one I want to somehow understand.

My tongue tingles with the need to trace the outline of his ripped muscles, including the deep V leading into the waistband of his low-slung shorts.

I lose myself in thoughts of what I'd do to his god-like form if I wasn't bound together by plastic zip ties, and almost forget why I had him summoned in the first place.

Konstantin folds his arms over his chest. My gaze falls to the phoenix that adorns his right hand and again, I wonder about the significance of the design.

As a writer, I pay close attention to details that give depth and dimension to my characters. People aren't all perfect, and that's one of the things that makes them relatable. They have flaws — physical and emotional — and that's what makes readers root for them. It's not fun to cheer for a hero or heroine who is perfect. There's no intrigue, no obstacle to overcome. Perfect characters make for extremely boring reads.

Take me, for example. I was snatched and have been tied up for days as this man's captive, and instead of thinking of creative ways I could use a pen to escape my hell, I want to write about all of the filthy hot things he does to me because they...*he*...makes me feel like his dirty little whore, and *I love that*.

Hello, headcase! I am head over heels in complete lust for my devious, sexy-as-fuck kidnapper.

If that's not fodder for a dark romance, I don't know what is.

See why I need the pen? The paper is optional. Hell, I'd write on my own skin if a pen is all he'll afford me.

I've never felt so inspired to write a character during my entire author career. Figuring out what made Konstantin into such an arrogant and brutal monster, and why I fit into his plans to take over the world, are mysteries I want to uncover.

"You didn't eat," he says in a flat tone.

I force my eyes away from the happy trail of hair that leads into the waistband of his shorts. "I was surprised to get the tray. I figured after last night you'd have starved me."

"If you were dead, I couldn't punish you."

His ice-blue eyes narrow, darkening with pent-up anger. Meanwhile, my skin tingles with anticipation at the mere mention of the word *punish*.

Speaking of punishment...

"Isa said you want a pen." He lifts an eyebrow. "Do you think I'm a fucking idiot?"

"I know what you're thinking, but I swear, I just want to write. I *need* to."

"Need to?"

I shift on the mattress since my ass is almost completely numb from being in this upright position. "It's...uhhh...a hobby of mine. I keep a journal at home, and when I feel overwhelmed, I like to write in it. Helps me clear my mind." I pause. "And this is that kind of a situation."

"Why should I make you comfortable?" He takes a few steps toward me, his voice dripping with disdain. "Why should I give a damn if you feel overwhelmed?"

"Look, you caught me in a bad moment last night. Don't hold

it over my head." My throat tightens. "Besides, you can't keep me tied up forever."

"Can't I?" he growls.

He's obviously not interested in what I can do with my hands if they're freed. I roll my eyes. "Why do you need to give me such a hard time? After everything you've done to me, out of anger for something I had nothing to do with, can't you just give me this one thing?"

He's quiet for a long minute. "Are you going to write about me?"

Duh. Does he think I want to write about my cush prison cell? Or my elaborate meals? And fabulous attire?

"Why would you care? You've made it pretty clear you don't give a damn about what I say or think."

"I don't."

"Liar." Heat creeps into my cheeks, because at the mere mention of writing, all of the crazy and insane things he's done to me ravage my mind. I sweep my tongue over my lips, forcing my eyes away from the bulge in his shorts. My skin prickles under his heated stare, and if I was wearing panties, I'm pretty sure they'd have just melted off my body.

"I'll give you what you want," he says. "Under one condition. I get to read what you write."

"All of it?" I gasp.

"Every word."

"No way. These are my private thoughts. I don't share them with anyone."

"Then you already know my answer."

I grit my teeth. Motherfucker. "You've already taken my freedom. You can't take my private thoughts, too. I already told you — you'll never have all of me. No matter what your demented mind tells you."

I fully expect that he's going to tell me to go to hell at this point and just leave the room. Instead, he walks over to a desk opposite my bed and pulls open a drawer. The jingle of handcuffs makes my spine stiffen.

Jesus, the inspiration within these four walls just flows like water from a garden hose.

"So you just happen to have a pair of handcuffs laying around?" I question. Jesus, what the hell else is in those drawers?

"You never know when they might come in handy. Today is your lucky day." He whirls them around his finger as he walks over to me. He uses a key to open one of them. Then he picks up a knife from the breakfast tray, and with a flick of his hand, slices the zip tie that holds me hostage.

My hands fall to the mattress. I wiggle my fingers. The tips are cold and tingling. I bring them in front of me to stretch my shoulders and crack each knuckle to relieve the cramping. The idea of having a pen in my hand actually makes me giddy.

Before I can get too used to freedom, Konstantin takes my right hand and holds it against the bedpost because he knows I'm a lefty, like he knows I love lobster Benedict. He locks my wrist to the wood and then slips the key into his pocket.

"Does this mean you're going to give me what I want?" I ask the question, my words laced with promise.

For both of us.

He leans close to me, setting one hand on the mattress next to my left hand. I breathe in his aftershave and choke back a satisfied moan. Sandalwood with a twist of amber. He's so close, I could jut out my tongue and taste his smooth skin. I trace my free fingertips over the phoenix, never moving my gaze from his face.

Desire burns bright in those ice blue pools. I drop my head back against the headboard, my hand still on his. With a pounding heart, I let my legs fall slightly open.

He dips his head lower, his hot breath fluttering against my cheeks. I part my lips the tiniest bit. Sparks crackle in the air between us, the tension so heavy I can choke on it. He moves his free hand to the back of my head. His fingers tangle in my hair and my eyes float closed, my mouth eager for the assault to come.

Except it never does.

"If you get any bright ideas about stabbing me with the pen, you'll need to learn how to write with your toes." Konstantin tugs my hair hard. My eyes fly open, a yelp slipping from my lips.

His lips curl into a sinister smirk, the hint of a challenge alive in his eyes. "And that's not even close to the worst part of the punishment you'll suffer. Happy writing, love. I can't wait to read what you have to say."

CHAPTER 13
Konstantin

"You gave her a pen? Are you fucking nuts?" Gregor stares at me, his mouth hanging open. "Do you need me to list out all the shit she can do with it? That bitch is vicious. Why didn't you just hand her a damn machete instead?"

"She wants to write."

"Since when do you give a damn about satisfying the whims of your prisoner bride? You're only marrying her to get to her family fortune. Right?"

I grit my teeth at my brother's challenging tone. "You know that's the plan. Besides, she's not gonna be able to do anything with the pen when she's handcuffed to the bed."

"What the hell does she need to write so badly?" Gregor takes a spoonful of buttered white corn from the steaming bowl in front of him.

"She didn't say." But I have my suspicions. And based on her reaction to my request to read her words, I think I'm damn close to right. She's writing about me. About my hand, my lips, my cock. I'd bet my left nut her journal writing ain't about what a deranged psychopath I am.

It took every bit of concentration I had to focus on work since

I'd given Tori the notebook and pen she wanted. For hours, I juggled between reading contracts and watching camera feeds. My full attention has been on the words Tori was writing so furiously with that ballpoint pen, not on the weapons deals we need to close.

As soon as Julian gets back from his meeting with our next potential client, I'll have him eyeball the terms of the deals. That'll free up my eyes...and my imagination...for other things.

Isabella walks into the dining room with a pitcher of water and a bowl of sauteed spinach. She places them both on the table, her forehead pinched.

"What's wrong, Isa?" I ask.

She shakes her head, her gaze on the front door. Because of the open floor plan, the foyer is visible from where we sit in the dining room.

"Julian said he'd be home for dinner." She twists her apron in her thick fingers. "But he's late and still hasn't called. That's not like him."

"He's in a meeting right now. I'm sure he'll be back soon enough." I drum my fingertips on the table to keep them from scrolling to the camera feed on my phone so I can spy on Tori.

"Okay," she says, her gaze still locked on the door. She stands there for a second and mouths something before turning and walking back into the kitchen.

I take a spoonful of spinach and dump it on my plate before shoveling in a mouthful of food. For a split second, the scent of the seasoned porterhouse steak, mixed with her famous roasted potatoes, brings me back to the days when our dinner table had more than two place settings for me and G, back when we were actually a family. Before my father turned into the selfish and self-centered asshole I grew to hate, before my mother cut him off because he had no idea how to play the role of the loving, caring parent, or the one of a faithful, devoted husband.

That was a long, *long* time ago. So long, I think it may actually be a figment of my imagination.

My fork hovers in the air. I glare at the piece of steak at the end of it. Medium rare with a warm red center. My father loved his meat blood rare. Black and blue with a cold center.

Just like him. Fucking bastard.

My stomach knots even though it rumbles with hunger pangs.

I toss my fork on the plate where it lands with a clatter and scrub my hands down the front of my face. My mind is a fucking toxic wasteland of conflict. It has been ever since I first saw Tori. The need for revenge has taken a back seat to the fierce rush of lust that consumes me every time I walk into that room and see her stretched out on the bed.

Watching, waiting, fantasizing…plotting.

The way her body responds to me despite the venomous threats that come out of her seductive lips make me certain she's writing about me.

About *us*.

Giving her something she wants means she owes me. Hell, she's already offered me anything and everything to let her imagination run free on those blank pages.

And I will collect.

Just at the right time.

Fuck her brothers and anyone else who thinks they can stop me from taking what's mine.

As the days pass, I find it hard to think, sleep, or breathe unless I'm near Tori. That is very bad for business. I've given her the power to capture and control my thoughts…power I swore I'd never lose again. Power I've been desperate to yank back ever since my life imploded at Viktor Malikov's hand.

"What the hell is happening to you, Kosta?" Gregor interrupts my inner battle as he grabs a slice of hot Italian bread from the basket. He slices a thick square of butter and slaps it onto the doughy center. "You should be focused on what the hell you're gonna do with your piece of the Malikov empire, and how you're going to escape the torturous death her brothers are probably plotting for you. Instead, you're playing hide the goddamn salami with your bride-to-be, a woman who supposedly hates you, but can't help screaming her bloody head off every time you're behind closed doors with her."

I narrow my eyes and pick up my steak knife, holding it in the air so that the tip gleams in the overhead light.

"You think I don't know what you're doing every time you walk into that room and slam the door closed?" Gregor rolls his eyes and stuffs the bread into his mouth. "Nuh alls ah pahuh nin."

"What the fuck did you just say?" I snap.

He swallows the bread. "The walls are paper thin, dick. I hear it all."

"They aren't that thin, perv. Not unless your fucking ear is pressed against them."

"She's a screamer."

I bite back a self-satisfied smile. Fuck yeah, she is. She screams for me. *Only for me.*

"This is supposed to be about making us whole again, Kosta. Right? Isn't that the bullshit line you fed me? It was never about falling in love with the princess."

The hairs on the back of my neck spring to attention. "I'm not falling in love with anyone."

"You've changed direction too many times for me to believe it's only about retribution." Gregor throws his fork onto the table. "Don't forget we have other enemies, enemies who haven't forgotten about the many ways Dad fucked them over. Enemies who want what he took from them. Remember Olek Moroz? The head of the Ukrainian mafia? He's dead, but he's got sons and daughters. Brutal ones like your forced fiancée. Only worse. And they have lots of axes to grind…into your skull."

"I haven't forgotten anything or anyone," I growl. "I have a plan."

"You say that today. But what happens tomorrow? You decided to marry Tori to get a bigger piece of the weapons pie, but it's only gonna sic more fucking enemies on us. And we've already got plenty of our own to handle. There are two of us, Kosta. And a big fucking battle at our doorstep because you're letting your cock do your thinking."

I push back the dining room chair. The wooden legs scrape against the tile floor. I lean across the table, the knife still in my hand. Droplets of red from my steak stain the sides of the steel. I impale the thick cut of meat with the tip of the blade.

"Nobody will find us with Julian as the face of our business. And I will make sure nobody ever takes anything from us again." I lift an eyebrow. "Don't question me. Not unless you wanna be cut up like that piece of meat."

"You're a sick fuck, you know that?" Gregor says with a shake of his head. He maneuvers his fork around my hand, which is still clutching the handle of the knife, and stabs another slice of steak. "If you make it through your forced wedding without someone trying to snipe you, I'll be shocked."

Before I can open my mouth to respond, my cell phone buzzes on the table next to my glass.

Unknown number.

I never answer calls from unknown numbers. I look up at Gregor. His eyes are locked on the screen, jaw tensing. "You have to answer it."

I pick it up and stab the Accept button. "Romanov."

"Hello, Mikhail."

Blood curdles in my veins. The heavily accented voice makes my pulse hammer against my throat. I don't need to ask who it is. I've been expecting this call for a long time, ever since that night at Tatiana months ago.

"What do you want, Arseny?"

"Fucking Siderov," Gregor hisses. "You said nobody would find us here." He springs out of his chair, reaches into the waistband of his pants, and pulls out his gun before darting over to the glass panes on either side of the front door. "Where the hell are you, asshole?"

"Your brother is always willing to run into the line of fire for you," Arseny says with a deep chuckle. "Would you do the same for him? Or for your business partner, Julian?"

I jerk my head left and right. This place is off the grid. I made sure of it. And how the fuck does he know about Julian?

"Don't bother trying to guess, Mikhail," he says, interrupting the barrage of questions peppering my brain. "Just accept the fact that I know everything. I see everything. And I control everything, including you."

"You have nothing on me. And if I were you, I'd be hiding out in some fucking third-world cesspool hoping that Olek Moroz's family doesn't find me and skin me from head to toe before filleting me like a side of beef." I wrap my fingers tight around the phone. "So why don't you crawl back under your rock before someone takes a machete to your head? Because if I see it, I promise you, I'm fucking slashing."

Arseny laughs. "Last time we spoke, I made you a very generous offer that you flatly refused. I guess I just don't like taking no for an answer."

I rake a hand through my hair, fisting it tight in my fingers. "My exact words were 'fuck off.' Did you wait all this time to hear me say them again?"

"You've got some set of balls for someone who has no money and a laundry list of hired guns out for your blood, first in line being your future in-laws."

Blood turns to ice in my veins. That's why he surfaced. He knows about Tori. "Nobody has gotten to me yet."

"Except *me*." Arseny pauses. "I wanted to give you a wedding gift. I made sure to have my messenger deliver it so you would have it in time for the big day. He just left the big white box with Julian. That's why I'm calling. If you don't get to your business partner in time, my gift won't be the only thing that doesn't make it to the wedding."

CHAPTER 14
Konstantin

"That motherfucker is just waiting for us to open the door so he can blast the hell out of us." Gregor paces the front hall, rubbing the barrel of the gun against his forehead.

I stab Julian's number into my phone. After the fourth ring, I let out a frustrated yell. I should have known something was up when Isa told me he hadn't answered her calls earlier. "He's not answering. I'm going to find him. You stay here with the girls."

"That's why Arseny called you, Kosta. He knew you'd run as soon as you heard Julian was in trouble. If you leave, you're gonna walk right into his trap."

I glower at Gregor. "There's no other option. If Arseny got to him, God only knows what kind of shape he's in. I'm going and you're staying."

"You're gonna battle that asshole and his army of scumbags? Alone? This all part of the fucking plan, Kosta?"

I walk over to one of the walls on the far side of the dining room and hit a button behind the buffet table. The large abstract painting that hangs on the wall over the table slides to the right, exposing a hidden closet. I punch the code into the keypad and the door beeps before it creaks open.

"You're so ready to run, but do you even know where you're going?" Gregor calls from the front hall. He's still in position, ready to battle in case that door opens and all hell literally breaks loose on our doorstep.

"Julian had a meeting at Hyde Park Prime with Remi Kosovich tonight. That's where I'm going."

"Fuck, what if Arseny is in with Kosovich? What if Kosovich planned the meeting to lure Julian down there and start a whole shit show?"

I pull out a loaded Glock 19 and Sig Sauer P365, then stuff them into the waistband of my pants. My stiletto knife is already strapped to my ankle. I narrow my eyes at my collection, assault scenarios looping through my mind. This rescue mission is gonna require more firepower.

Fuck it.

I grab an AR-15 and load it before turning to Gregor. "Take what you need from here. As soon as I leave, lock this place down. Nobody gets in, do you understand? Nobody. I don't give a fuck who shows up at the door."

Gregor scrubs a hand down the front of his face. "I got it. I got it."

I rush past the dinner table, my gaze snagged by the steak knife I used to impale the meat. Arseny has about the same chance of staying in one piece as that porterhouse if I get my hands on him.

No fucking chance at all.

Gregor follows me to my blacked-out Audi R8. I put the guns on the floor in front of the passenger seat and slide into the leather bucket seat before pressing the ignition button. The engine roars. "You should have backup," he says, his eyebrows pulled together.

"I'm not sacrificing anyone else. He went after Julian to bait *me*."

"You're not a one-man army."

"The fuck I'm not. You should have more faith in me, G."

"I did until I saw what your fiancée did to you. Maybe you should bring Tori. She can kick some major ass. It'd be a good bonding experience for you guys before the wedding." He lets out a dry snicker.

"So damn funny. Now get the hell back inside." I flip him off and pull my door closed. Gregor disappears back into the house and I grip the steering wheel, rubbing my palms over the leather. A second later, I hit the button on the garage door opener.

Ironically, my future brother-in-law, Nik Malikov, turned my car into a bulletproof, fireproof tank when he thought we played for the same team. As the premier car restoration expert in South Florida, he knew exactly how to reinforce the windows and panels to keep me safe from explosions and a hellfire of bullets.

But nobody else knows that, including Arseny.

About ten minutes later, I pull into the parking lot of Hyde Park Prime Steakhouse. A quick look in the rearview mirror confirms there's no tail on me. Then again, sometimes they can pop out of nowhere, just like the Malikovs showing up at the airfield after I'd snatched Tori. And the time when a hail of bullets blasted through my office and killed my father.

My gut knots as I pass the valet and circle through the lot. Julian's cherry red Corvette stands out like a dick on a cake, day or night. I squint at the cars as I drive through the lot. But I don't see it anywhere. I massage the throbbing stress knot at the base of my skull.

Where the fuck could he be? Arseny wouldn't send me on a wild goose chase through the city. He wants to get me into that box, wherever the hell it is.

I pull into a parking spot near the back entrance and turn off the engine. The door is dark and out of sight, a private spot where the high-end clients enter and leave. Keeps things under the radar. We use one of the back rooms for a lot of deals. I've got a few insiders who might have seen or heard something.

My phone buzzes against my leg. I grab it. Julian's name flashes across the screen with an incoming text.

With a hammering pulse, I click on the message.

You told me to fuck off, Mikhail. You made us enemies that night.

Three gray dots appear on the screen. My throat tightens so much I can't even squeeze out one word. And I've got plenty of choice ones for that snake flooding my mind.

The gray dots disappear. Then his ominous message follows.

And you know how I handle my enemies.

I slam my fist on the steering wheel. That sonofabitch. Arseny's going into a damn meat grinder. I'm gonna fill sausage casings with his fat-ass body.

After sliding the AR-15 under the passenger-side seat, I stuff the other guns into the back of my pants. Then I push open my door and step onto the pavement. Red floods my vision like some crazy night vision filter. Blood rushes between my ears, feeding my rage. When I find Arseny Siderov, I swear he's gonna–

A strong hand clamps down on my shoulder and pulls me backward.

"So the fucking weasel finally decided to pop his head out of his hole," a menacing voice growls from behind me. "And I'm gonna be the one to blow it off."

I grab the massive hand and twist it hard before turning to see who the fuck was dumb enough to lay a finger on me.

When I stare into the icy glare of Alek Severinov, I know immediately that his wrist ain't gonna snap that easily.

"Fuck you, Sev," I growl. "If you're gonna be pissed off at anyone, be pissed at yourself for giving me direct access to your asshole buddies. You handed me over on a silver platter because you didn't dig deep enough. And now everything they have is about to be mine."

"You think you're gonna get away with kidnapping Tori Malikov? With marrying her?" He steps toward me, a few inches taller, but I've popped bigger guys without blinking an eye. "You have no fucking idea who you're dealing with, Romanov."

He thinks he can intimidate me with his size. Shit, he couldn't intimidate me if he had a gun to my temple.

Fucking idiot. He doesn't realize I have nothing to lose.

Except Tori.

The thought explodes between my ears and assaults my heart. Where in the *fuck* did that come from?

I don't give him the satisfaction of backing down. And I don't have time for dick swinging. So I gamble.

"Do you think I'm afraid of your crew, Sev? Or the Malikovs? I've got the princess. Okay? None of you fucknuts could stop me that night. Too little, too fucking late."

His jaw tightens. "You're about to open yourself up to a very big attack."

"Not if I use Tori as my shield. Her brothers would never let her get hurt. They're not about to lose another one of their own."

"They're not gonna let this wedding happen."

"And you're here because why? You their messenger boy or something?"

The massive fist cracks against my jaw before I can stop it. But I don't go down. I just laugh and wipe the drizzle of blood from the side of my mouth. "You let me get away because you didn't dig deep enough. That's on you. And now it's too late. I have Tori, and that means I have them all by the balls. Them and every last dollar of their money."

"You'll never survive long enough to get a fucking cent of it."

"Then why aren't I already dead?" I straighten up and spit at his black shoes. "I've got the prize in my bed. Handcuffed and naked. You wanna know what I'll do to her if you or any of the other guys make a move against me?"

"You're a sick fuck," Alek grunts.

"Maybe so. But I'm also the one with my hands all over the trophy. It's mine and there's nothing you or the other assholes can do about it. And you can tell them that all of this is because of their father. Viktor Malikov fucked with my family and my business. I'm just collecting on the debt. And we both know you're not gonna do a damn thing about it because that'd open up your little club, Red Ladro, to a whole world of shit."

"Viktor is dead, though. You wanna suffer the same end?"

"He took everything from my family. If he's dead, the next in line pays the price. You know how this works. Don't try to bullshit me and say you'd do things differently. I've heard the stories. I know all about your family and what you did to make them whole and what you did to Sofia Rojas's lieutenant that night in that Monaco restaurant." I step toward him, my voice dropping to a low growl. "And I'm not afraid of what you can do with a fork because I can do worse with my bare hands."

An amused look flickers across Alek's face. "You're a cocky bastard. Killing you would be fun."

"You had your chance, old man." I open my arms. "Wanna take the shot? Wanna save face with your friends in Miami for letting the wolf into their fucking barn?"

"I didn't come here to kill you, Romanov. I came here to tell you that you're not the only one after the trophy. And trust me, I want a front row seat to that battle because there's no way you come out alive."

Alek turns away and walks toward a waiting Escalade. He opens the door to the passenger seat and jumps inside.

"I'm like a cockroach, Sev," I call out. "If a nuclear bomb goes off, you can bet I'll be the only survivor."

Alek lowers the window. "Keep that attitude, Romanov. You're gonna need it if you plan on seeing the sunlight every day."

"See you at the wedding," I snap, flipping him off. The truck zooms out of the parking lot, tires squealing against the pavement. I lean back against my car and let out a long breath.

Someone else is after the trophy.

Someone else is after the trophy.

My mind trips back to the conversation with Arseny.

The wedding present.

A vibration against my leg makes my chest tighten, and I remember why I came here in the first place.

The threat to the wedding. My missing friend. And the promise of revenge.

I pull out my phone. My stomach drops into my shoes when I see Gregor's name on the screen. "What's wrong?" I say after accepting the call.

"Julian's here," Gregor says.

"Lemme talk to him."

It feels like hours pass before I hear Julian's voice. "Julian, what the hell happened tonight?"

"I had dinner with Kosovich, made the deal, and left Hyde Park. Came straight back home. I didn't see the calls because I forgot my phone at home. I realized it when I got to the restaurant and didn't have time to run home and grab it before the meeting." He pauses. "What's the story with this box?"

I ball my free hand into a fist and pound it against my forehead. "Arseny Siderov called me. Said he gave you a box with a wedding present in it. Said if I didn't get to you fast enough…"

My next words catch in the back of my throat as the puzzle pieces fly together with disturbing speed. The final picture is of a fiery hell.

Fire…

He warned me.

He fucking warned me. And Julian drove it right to them.

"The trunk," I choke out. "It's in the fucking trunk. Grab Tori and get the hell out of the house, now," I yell.

CHAPTER 15
Viktorya

My eyes fly open. The heavy door to my prison cell opens with a loud crack against the wall.

"I need to get you out of here," Gregor says, barreling into the room. He's a younger version of Konstantin with the same build, fierce blue eyes, and dark hair. The big difference is that Gregor actually smiles. He must have some degree of humanity, unlike his brother, the Devil Incarnate, who has ice water for blood and a blackened lump of tar for a heart.

Since I'm still cuffed to the bedpost because my asshole captor didn't bother to switch my binds, I'm already sitting straight up against the wooden headboard. A shooting pain erupts down the back of my neck like a blast of fire when I shift on the mattress. I grit my teeth, squinting in the dim light coming from the hallway.

"Why? What's happening?" I demand.

He doesn't answer.

"Goddammit, Kosta," he mutters when he sees my wrist dangling from the post. Then he pulls open the night table drawer and rummages around.

"You really think he's going to leave a key within my reach?" I roll my eyes. "He took it with him, genius."

Gregor fixes a dark glare on me. "Okay, *genius*, then tell me how to get you the fuck out of here since I forgot to bring my machete."

"Why do you need to get me out of here? Where's Isabella? And Konstantin? I need to get my notebook."

His hand is still lost in the mess of a drawer, jaw twitching. "Fuck, does that mouth ever stop?"

"Nope." I flash a toothy grin. "Just ask your brother."

"Julian, I need a paper clip," Gregor yells. "Get your ass up here now."

No less than ten seconds later, another guy appears in the doorway. He runs over with a paper clip that Gregor immediately stretches apart.

Isabella's son is shorter than Gregor, but still bulky and broad. His dark hair is shaved around the sides. A tattoo of an elaborate cross behind his right ear catches my attention. It dips down the side of his thick neck. With these Romanov brothers as his cronies, I get the feeling a single cross may not be enough to protect him from the hell they probably raise.

Julian's gaze sweeps over me, landing on the tops of my thighs as Gregor jimmies the lock with the end of the paper clip. I cross my ankles, very aware that I'm not wearing underwear, and the T-shirt Konstantin gave me to wear keeps riding up higher and higher.

"What the fuck is taking so long?" Julian snaps.

"Will someone please tell me what the hell is going on?" I yell.

Gregor's forehead pinches, his focus solely on the lock.

Julian's dark eyes meet mine. "Kosta thinks someone planted a bomb in the trunk of my car."

"And your car is...?" My chest tightens.

"Downstairs. In the garage." He looks at Gregor. "Come on. Do it. We don't have time for you to dick around."

"Fuck off," Gregor seethes. "I'm working on it."

A split second later, the cuff falls open. I grab my wrist and twist it around. The skin is red, scratched, and irritated from rubbing against the metal. Gregor doesn't waste a second. He grabs my wrist and yanks me out of the room behind him. Julian follows. I know he's got to be staring at my ass, but this isn't the time to be self-conscious. Let him stare at my ass all he wants. Just let me get the hell out of ground zero alive.

"Where is Isabella?" I gasp as we fly down the stairs.

"Outside. Far enough away," Julian grunts.

The front door is already open. We run through the front hall, darting toward the archway. We barely make it out of the house before the explosion erupts in the garage. Windows shatter, car alarms blare. But by some miracle, the blast stays contained and doesn't blow out the garage door. Gregor pushes me to the ground once we're down the front steps.

I roll around to my back. A groan slips from my lips as I lie on the cool, damp grass, staring blankly at the stars glittering in the blackened sky above. My lungs squeeze tight, the air knocked out of them when I landed. I run my hand down the front of my T-shirt, relieved that I'm still decent and somewhat covered.

"Oh my God," Isabella whimpers from a few feet away, her hand over her heart.

"Are you okay, Mom?" Julian asks her, placing a hand on her shoulder. She clamps her own hand over his and nods, tears shining in her brown eyes.

Gregor dove to the ground a few inches away from me. He rolls to a seated position with a few choice expletives. "Christ, look at this place."

Thick pieces of shattered window glass blanket the ground outside of the garage door. Bright orange flames dance among the plumes of smoke, but the explosion looks to be pretty tame considering other bombs I've witnessed, most recently when my brother Nik's now-fiancée Kenzie tried to blow up our South Beach restaurant, La Gioia.

That did serious damage. Almost took out my brother, Luka.

The person who crafted this explosive wasn't going for nuclear impact. But if Julian had been in that car when it went off...shit. He'd be in crispy fried pieces right now.

Gregor rushes for the garage. "Julian, help me out. We need to put out the fire before the cops come sniffing around."

I don't need to ask why. God only knows what they have stored in that garage, or throughout the house, for that matter. And oh yeah, they have a hostage, too. All the more reason to clean up the mess on their own before the authorities ask any questions.

I tug the hem of the T-shirt, pulling it over my knees to stretch it out. I crack each one of my knuckles. So satisfying. It's the little things you miss when you're held captive with your wrists bound together by plastic ties. I flex my fingers, the tips tingling to dance over a keyboard with the events of the night that have unfolded just adding to my plotline.

Jesus.

It's barely been a week. I never go a day without typing, even if it's a silly little blog post. Writing in that notebook for the past few days while being held captive has been cathartic, but not nearly the same as listening to the click of the keys as my frantic fingers furiously empty my innermost thoughts onto the laptop screen.

Writing. Laptop.

My Netflix meeting. Fuck.

My brain kicks into overdrive. I've missed almost a full week of my life. How many times has Sheila tried to contact me since the night of the wedding? She doesn't know Savannah Rose's true identity. Savannah is linked to her own publishing company with her own employee identification number and bank account. To the world, she's an actual person. Sheila has no way of finding out where I am, if I'm alive or dead. And what about the Netflix people? Are they just going to move to the next book topping the charts since Savannah's disappeared off the face of the Earth?

What about me? What about my life, my big chance? Possibly ruined because of this life I was born into.

Konstantin doesn't give a damn about any of that. All he cares about is revenge, revenge for something I had nothing to do with. So he stole me. He stole my life and my career, my hopes and my dreams.

Fury boils my blood.

But worst of all, I fucking hate myself for letting him steal my heart, too.

I clench my fists, my teeth gritted. For days, I've been caged like an animal, violated in the most erotic of ways, unable to eat, sleep, or breathe without imagining how he would feel buried inside of me. He's turned my sweet and pure aura of romantic bliss into a thick black cloud of lust, greed, and yearning.

It's like Savannah withered away like the Wicked Witch of the West after a good dousing, and only her whorey alter ego remains.

I need to get away from here. From *him*.

After only a few minutes, Gregor and Julian manage to snuff out the flames. They examine Julian's car, poking their heads around the trunk and interior, I guess to find clues about what kind of device detonated and how.

I rub my hands down the sides of my arms. A whisper of a bay breeze makes my skin prickle. With a turn of my head, I scout the long, dark road leading away from the house.

It's desolate.

I turn my head back to the garage. The guys are still futzing around with the car, not paying any bit of attention to me. A quick look behind me confirms that Isabella is more concerned with praying for God's mercy than my whereabouts. My teeth clamp down on my lower lip.

The road is long and gravelly. The tiny rocks will tear my feet to shreds if I run it without shoes.

I slant a glance behind me in the darkness. I just need to make it far enough down the road to where I can slip into the foliage and disappear. With a hammering pulse, I slowly rise to my bare feet. The T-shirt is stretched out enough that it resembles a nightshirt. The soft, faded cotton covers the good parts well enough.

Backing away from the house, I hold my breath. Isabella's eyes are closed, her mouth moving a mile a minute in what I can only imagine is prayer. Clouds of smoke stream from the garage. If the guys look fast, they may not see me right away…

Fuck it.

I have one chance to escape. I'm not going to waste time convincing myself of all the reasons why it's a good idea to make a run for it.

I flip around and dash across the lawn. The bottoms of my feet skid along the damp grass. I hold out my arms to regain my balance. I yelp, the gravel stabbing my soles once I hit the road. I kick up pebbles as I run, the sharp edges scraping my calves.

But I don't stop. My breath hitches as my feet pound against the pavement. Gregor and Julian call out my name. Footsteps thump along the ground behind me. I never look back. I run from my fate, my fears, and toward my future because I choose life, not captivity.

Tears sting my eyes as troubled thoughts about my missing sister suddenly invade my mind.

I squint in the darkness when I approach the end of the road. My legs slow, my chest heaving from the impromptu sprint to freedom. The honk of a horn startles me, flashing headlights blinding me for a split second. I yelp, jumping backward before I become roadkill. My right foot lands on something sharp. I scream, a burning pain tearing through my heel. A sob bursts from my chest. I hop around on one foot, my arms flailing until my other leg gives out.

Did Val also try to escape? *Did she fail?*

I tumble to the ground. Gravel and stones lance my flesh. The car squeals to a stop right in front of me, blocking every possible path. As if I could even drag myself to my feet. I blink fast, shielding my eyes from the harsh beams.

A tall, dark figure dressed all in black steps into my line of sight. His eyes are dark and menacing, lips twisted with malice, and his expression holds the threat of death and destruction.

With each step he takes toward me, my gut clenches tighter and tighter.

Did I?

CHAPTER 16
Konstantin

I fly through a Stop sign, taking the last turn down my private road like an Indy 500 race car driver. I cut the drive back from Hyde Park in half and managed to avoid any cops in my rush to get back here.

To get back to Tori.

Because someone else is on the hunt for my fiancée.

The sky is dark, the threatening cloud hanging over me ominous.

A chill licks the hairs on the back of my neck. Severinov confirmed my worst fear back in that parking lot. Without Tori, I have nothing.

No leverage. No network. No money.

No fucking chance.

She's literally the glue that holds my entire fucking plan together.

I stomp on the gas. The car shoots forward like a speeding bullet. I take the turns leading back to my house hard and fast, practically on two wheels. With a hammering pulse, I round the last corner that leads to my house.

"Fuck," I yell, slamming my foot on the brake when I see the taillights of a car in front of me. I lurch forward, breath hitching.

Pop! Crack! Bang!

Stray bullets pepper the front of my windshield as I barrel toward the car. The shots ricochet off the tempered glass. But I know from Nik that a steady stream of bullets focused on the same spot will fracture the glass and shatter it.

I swing my steering wheel to the right, narrowly avoiding the car. I take in the scene, the figures dressed in black that swarm the intruding car.

Where the fuck is Tori?

I dive across the front seat and push open the passenger side door, dropping to my knees. I hold out my Glock 19 and fire a hail of bullets at the first figure stupid enough to pop out from behind the other car. His body buckles, jerking left and right before he collapses facedown on the hood.

"Kosta, they've got Tori," Gregor yells from the distance.

An icy hand clenches my gut. I duck down as more gunshots explode into the air. One hits my front headlight, one blasts off my passenger side mirror. I crouch low to the ground and creep around the back, my heart jumping into my throat.

More bullets wedge themselves into the armored metal that protects my car. I pop my head around to the driver's side, point, and fire a few more shots.

"Kosta, no. St–!"

Gregor's voice. Silenced.

"You fucking bastard!" Julian yells, firing a spray of bullets at the car.

No, no, no. Please no...

Then one of the figures in black appears in my periphery. He flips around and steps into the headlight beam. My finger freezes on the trigger. I stumble backward, bile rising in my throat.

Tori's back is plastered against his chest with a gun to her temple. She struggles against him, dressed only in that damn T-shirt. The hem barely skims the middle of her thighs. My chest tightens when I see the man's hand slide up the side of her leg. White noise floods my ears.

"Take that bastard out, Kosta," Julian shouts.

Fury bubbles in my chest. His hands are on her. His gun is on her.

She doesn't belong to him.

She's mine.

I rise to my feet, the gun tight in my outstretched hand. With a quick look in my direction, I see his lips curl into a smirk. "You're not the only one who wants a piece of this pussy, *Federov*."

My eyes tangle with Tori's. A small movement catches my side view. I slant a quick look at the ground. A dark shadow creeps around the tire of the other car, visible only because of my one working headlight.

He's coming for me.

Bastard.

I'm coming for you first.

"Who the fuck are you?" I growl at the man holding Tori, my eyes still on the slow-moving shadow.

"Who I am doesn't matter. Who I work for is the more important question for you to ask, dipshit." The guy's voice is deep and raspy, with an unrecognizable accent. In the thin stream of light, I can make out the details of his face. Deep lines are etched into his jaw and forehead, his eyes beady and black.

His full lips form words I don't hear, my focus still on the shadow.

Five, four, three, two–

Tori suddenly hunches forward and drives one elbow hard into her assailant's balls. He drops to his knees with a pathetic moan, the gun in his hand forgotten. The other guy jumps up from his spot by the tire and fires. My ears ring from the deafening crack of bullets as I empty my own mag.

He goes down like a bag of cement, and I rush toward Tori. She flips around, landing a roundhouse to the guy's temple as he sputters and coughs.

"Actually, the really important question is why you were

stupid enough to think you were gonna get away with putting your disgusting hands on me?" Tori screams. She kicks him in the face with her heel, and he falls backward against the side of his car.

Julian darts out of the darkness with his gun. He runs around the car toward us, stopping when he's next to the guy hugging his groin.

"Here's a message to your fucking boss," Julian grunts, firing off two shots to his temple.

The guy collapses backward, his bloody head smacking against the gravel, the pain in his balls forgotten.

Another shadow moves on the ground about twenty feet away. I point my gun, but Julian smacks my hand away. "It's only G. He took a hit."

"I'm okay," Gregor yelps as he slowly rises to his feet. His hand covers his right shoulder, a patch of darkness spreading over his white shirt. I let out a breath, my shoulders slumping. Thank fuck.

I turn to glare at Julian. "What the fuck did you shoot that guy for?"

He narrows his eyes. "Was I supposed to let him plug you?"

"I had him. Now how the fuck are we supposed to know who sent him and these other guys?" I growl.

"He had a gun," Julian says, his words dripping with anger. "Was I supposed to watch him pop you?"

"He wasn't gonna pop anyone." I cast a look at Tori. "Not after you put him on the ground." I slide off my jacket and wrap it around her shoulders before telling her, "That was fucking stupid, by the way."

She pulls the jacket tight around her shoulders, casting a defiant look at me. "It worked."

"You got lucky."

"Maybe I'm just more skilled than you give me credit for," she shoots back, a challenge in her voice. And fuck me if it doesn't make my dick jump.

"She's lucky she didn't get herself popped," Gregor mutters as he hobbles over to us. "Your fiancée decided to make a run for it after the bomb in Julian's trunk leveled the garage."

I scrub a hand down the front of my face. With a slamming pulse, I turn away from the aftermath of the shit show the Malikovs brought to our front door.

Take a fucking breath. Count to ten. Do some-fucking-thing before you're the next bomb to explode.

"You ran?" I ask, my fists clenched tight against my sides.

Tori doesn't respond.

I twist around and bellow, "You fucking ran?"

She lifts an eyebrow, her blue eyes shooting white-hot daggers. "I did. And I'd do it again."

An imaginary noose loops around my neck, tugging hard. Sparks of ire ignite in my chest as I take a few steps toward her. "Is that so?"

She folds her arms over her chest, a mocking smirk tugging her lips upward. "Fuck, *yes*. Because you're not the one in control, *sweetheart.*"

I close the distance between us, forcing her back against the car. She slams into the side view mirror, a startled gasp escaping her mouth. I bring a hand to her throat and give it a squeeze. Her hands fly up to her neck, her fingers clamping mine.

"Tell me again who's in control," I hiss. "I must have missed it the first time."

"Tell me who you really are," she chokes out. "Why did that guy call you Federov?"

"You don't get to ask me questions after what you just did." I look beyond Tori at our captive audience. "Julian, get G to the house and patch him up. Then call Lev and tell him to get the hell over here with the cleaning crew."

They don't move.

"Now," I yell. "And make sure you keep Isabella inside with you until we're ready to leave."

"Leave?" Gregor asks. "To go where?"

"We can't stay here," I say through clenched teeth, my jaw

twitching. "They know where to find us now. How, I have no clue. But they'll be back to finish the job."

My house is at the end of the private road, far away from nosy neighbors with curious eyes and big ears. I rented it specifically for that reason. Gregor and Julian jog away from us, kicking up gravel as their feet hit the ground.

I turn my attention back to Tori. Her chin is tilted upward, her eyes a mixture of fire and ice. There's a battle in their depths, both struggling for control.

Kind of like us.

Loosening my grip around her throat, I thrust my chest against her. Her heart races alongside my own. I slide my hands down the sides of her torso and over her hips, forcing the T-shirt to her waist. Her mouth parts, her breath hot against my neck as I hover closer.

"Tell me you're sorry for running away."

"No," she rasps. "No fucking way."

With one hand still clamped on her hip, I reach around to grab her ass, squeezing the flesh hard. My palm tingles, my mind consumed by an overwhelming need to punish her for what she did.

For putting herself in danger.

And for leaving me.

I should get her inside, away from the danger I know lurks close by. But my body has other plans.

"Say it or else you know what I'll do."

"Fuck you," she hisses. Her nostrils flare, her lips twist in disdain.

I pull her away from the car to give my hand access to her ass. And then I flip her around so her chest presses into the car. Looping an arm around her waist, I jerk her backward so her ass is piked. My hand whizzes through the air, smacking hard against the plump cheek.

My cock struggles to break free of my pants more and more with each slap of my hand. It strains against the fabric. Blood rushes to my groin, faster with every yelp that slips from Tori's beautiful, venomous mouth. A mouth I can think of other uses for.

I spank her bright red until my palm numbs. She collapses against me, her chest heaving, her breaths short and sharp. But I'm not finished with her yet. I lean forward and bite her shoulder, her neck, and her earlobe. She melts farther into me, giving me back the one thing I crave.

I slide my hand over her pussy, her lips slick with need. She moans as I press my fingers deep inside of her. "Fuck," I mutter. "I need to be inside you. I need to feel that wet cunt wrapped tight around my cock."

"No..." she whimpers as I pump my fingers faster. "I hate you."

"Lies," I grunt. "You could never get this wet for me if that was the truth. You want my cock deep inside of you. You want me to fuck you like a savage. You're just afraid to admit it because that would mean you gave up complete control. To *me*."

"Never. I will never–"

I pull my hand away from her pussy and shove my fingers in her mouth so she can taste what I already know. What I've just taken from her. *"You just did."*

CHAPTER 17
Viktorya

Good God, he's right...

Seconds fly past in a carnal blur. Konstantin turns me around, lifts me into his arms, and carries me over to his car before dropping me onto the hood. My ass slams hard against the cool metal. I cry out, the blistery sting sizzling my branded cheeks.

He fists the neck of my T-shirt, forcing me closer. "You could have gotten yourself killed." His voice, shaking with anger, hums against my face.

"Get off it. You don't care about me," I hiss, my lips so close to his I can practically bite them. And my God, I want to. "You only care about money and about hurting my family. You need me for both. I'm a pawn to you. A pawn and a plaything. Nothing else."

I swallow hard. My heart thumps like an 808 drum as I watch his expression morph into his deviant sex god alter ego. The vein in his neck throbs, his lips pull tight together. But for a split second, his half-hooded gaze flickers with a mess of emotion, a jumbled mix of conflicted feelings that mirrors the one tormenting my mind.

Then, darkness swallows his fleeting vulnerability.

"You are whatever I want you to be." He releases the T-shirt and snakes an arm around my waist. His fingers rake down my spine, my skin exploding with tingles at his rough touch. "Anything I want. Whenever I want. Wherever I want."

I let out a mewl when his tongue juts out and traces the outer shell of my ear. My head falls backward, my back bucking. God, I'm weak. So damn weak. And after I swore up and down to myself that I'd never be like Natasha and Kenzie, that I'd never fall prey to the dark side.

But Konstantin knows just how to touch me, how to make my inhibitions fizzle like water dousing a lit match. And in such a short time he already knows every single one of my hot buttons, like he's some kind of sex Yoda.

Oh, yes, the Force is strong with him. *So freaking strong.*

"You're *everything*," Konstantin growls against my ear. "So don't fucking run away from me ever again."

"And what will you do if I try? Punish me again?" I murmur, gazing up at him through lowered lashes. I lean back on one elbow, anticipation scuttling down my spine. With my other hand, I reach between my legs. Choked with lust and dizzy with hunger, I rub my fingers over my throbbing clit as he watches, mesmerized. I moan, slipping my fingers into my slit. A jolt of electricity in our heated gazes crackles in the air between us.

My thighs quiver, my pussy screams for his dick.

I want him. I need him. *I have to have him.* But I won't tell him that.

"Fuck me," he mutters, unable to move his eyes from my face. A primal growl turns Konstantin — Federov, or whatever his name actually is — into a starving lion. He tugs open his belt and pants, then shoves them to his knees before lunging for me. He wraps his arms around me and pulls me against his chest, muscles rippling beneath the thin fabric of his shirt.

His mouth crushes against mine. Our teeth clash, tongues twisting and tussling as we attack each other like voracious predators desperate for a meal. We kiss like we need each other to breathe, like we would wither and die if our mouths weren't cemented together as they are.

His frenzied fingers clench and clutch and claw at me before disappearing into my hair. He tugs my head backward, giving his lips full access to my neck. I loop one of my legs around his waist, forcing him close as his mouth trails a scorching path to my breasts. He captures one nipple between his tongue and teeth, teasing the other with his hand. I squeal, the pleasure zapping me like a live wire.

"You want me?" he growls, bringing one hand to my pussy. His thumb toys with my clit, then he dips his head down between my legs so he can take it in his mouth. And then, holy fuck. His tongue flicks my nub relentlessly as my orgasm builds. Heat pools at my core when his other hand slides between my ass cheeks.

"Oh *God*," I weep as he presses a digit into the tight ring of muscle. My hands move from his hair to his back, nails raking over his skin as his mouth and fingers rocket me to a place where I know I shouldn't go, a dark, seductive place that tempts me to do bad things, dirty, sexy, hot things that I swore I'd never do with such a deviant and dangerous man because I didn't want this life. I wanted the happily ever after with the perfect, normal man.

But here I am, my body begging for every last one of them. Begging for *him*. The *chaos* that I so desperately tried to avoid.

A cool whisper of air hits my pussy once his mouth finishes its oral assault. My skin tingles, shivers skittering over the scorching trail of his retreating tongue and finger. He hovers over me, his eyes blazing with need.

"Beg me for my cock, Tori." His forehead grazes mine. "Tell me you want me to fuck you."

My heart pounds with such force, I can barely hear my own response. My mouth refuses to form words, only sounds laden with desperation. He yanks my ankles toward him, sliding me down so that my ass perches on the edge of the hood. My breath hitches. I writhe beneath him, digging my fingernails into his hips.

"I...I..."

The words lodge in my throat. Flames of passion rage, my inhibitions long since incinerated. But still I don't give him what he wants.

"Say it." He jerks his hips toward me, then pulls away. Talk about literally being the biggest cocktease ever.

I arch my back and thrust against him, grinding hard against the head of his thick cock. He can't be that resistant, for fuck's sake. He's a guy. A controlling prick of a guy, but still a guy.

"My dirty girl wants what she can't have," he taunts, moving away. "All because she won't ask for it."

My arms flail as I try to reach for him, but he only backs farther away. It's the most carnal battle of wills that I've ever experienced...or fantasized about, for that matter. The man's self-control is damn impressive. Mine, on the other hand?

Nonexistent. It has completely evaporated in the steamy night air.

"Please...oh my God, just fuck me," I yelp. "Fuck me, whoever you are, whatever your name is." Each roll of his hips torments me more until I can't take it any–

I scream out in shock, fisting his hair as he suddenly thrusts into me. His cock tears through my walls, stretching me wide. I clench my teeth as my body opens up for him. Tears spring to my eyes from the intense burn as he drives into me, over and over. So fucking good. I squeeze my eyes shut, locking my legs around him. I meet him thrust for thrust, our skin pebbled with sweat and flushed with desire as he tugs at my nipples with his tongue and teeth.

He fucks me hard with long, deep strokes. His mouth forgoes my breasts, navigating a desperate path back to mine. His lips scorch my skin, every nip and tug of his teeth sizzling my insides. Grunts of pleasure rumble in his chest and ring in my ears. My pussy sings the most gleeful tune with every delicious push and pull of his dick.

I've never felt a connection like this before, one where I don't know where he ends and I begin. Or maybe the other way around. I don't know. I can't think right now. Hell, I can barely breathe.

He presses his finger into my asshole. I cry out, consumed by a thick haze of euphoric bliss. Sinfully erotic sensations course through me, in complete command and control of my mind, body, and soul. It's like I've just been swept up in a swirling curl and hurled into the surf with nothing cushioning my plunge into the dominating waters.

I've never felt so exposed, so vulnerable, and so filled with rapture at the same time. My core ignites with a desire reserved only for him. Whoever the fuck he is.

And at this second, I don't care.

My pussy convulses, clamping tight around his cock with fierce, throbbing pulses. A sudden scream...my scream...pierces the air. White noise fills my ears, blunting the sound. Bright white flashes of light explode behind my closed eyes as I come hard all over his cock.

"Come for me," I whimper. "Come with me."

He grinds into me, a low growl of pleasure deep in his throat. His cock jerks as he climaxes, his body shuddering against me. He drops his head onto my chest, his cock still burrowed inside of me. Our ragged pants are the only audible sounds in the still air. But the mess of unanswered questions looping through my mind blares between my ears like sirens.

"I need to know the truth, Konstantin. Why do those guys want you dead?" I rasp. Not the most appropriate for post-coital pillow talk, but let's be real. Nothing about this forced engagement has been any bit romantic...and I want answers.

He slowly pulls himself off of me. The headlight casts a glow on his face as he straightens up in front of the car. His jaw tenses, neck muscles corded. "They didn't want me dead, Tor." He casts a look over my shoulder at the entrance to his private road. "They want *you* dead."

CHAPTER 18
Konstantin

The tires of my R8 squeal around the circular driveway as I come to a screeching stop in front of the house. I run around to Tori's door and fling it open. I lift her into my arms since her feet are scraped and bleeding from her failed escape.

Our gazes tangle. I've never seen her so broken down, even in the face of potential death. My heart clenches at the sight, my arms gripping her tighter.

"You know I'm not afraid of my family's enemies," she murmurs once I seat her on the ledge of the Jacuzzi tub in her bathroom.

"I can't see you being afraid of anything." I reach into the cabinet for cotton balls, a bottle of rubbing alcohol, and some Band-Aids. Once I drop to my knees in front of her, I twist off the cap of the bottle, soak the cotton with alcohol, and dab it on her injured feet.

"I know how to take care of myself. I just never wanted this life. I don't want to constantly have to look over my shoulder, wondering when the next attack will happen, and who might get hurt. Or worse."

I stop patting her scrapes with the cotton ball and look up at her.

Tori's eyebrows knit together. "It doesn't seem like I have much of a choice about that anymore."

"Your family name will always keep a target locked on your head." I tear open a few Band-Aids and place them over her cuts. "You know that."

"I figured if I detached myself, I could fly under the radar."

I lift an eyebrow. "There's nothing about you that could ever fade into any background. And you know as well as I do that when you're born into this life, there's only one way out."

The corners of her lips lift the smallest bit. "Yep. In a coffin."

I gently massage the bottom of her foot. "I'm gonna take care of those bastards. I'll find them and make sure they never get close to you again."

"My dad always swore that to my mom, but in the end, his enemies won. They got him and my brother, Dima. And my other brother Luka, a master freaking assassin, was almost killed in an attack against our family." She shakes her head. "The strongest men I knew couldn't stop those hits."

"I'm not them."

"You're exactly like them," she whispers, a pained look in her eyes. She pulls her foot away and stands up from the ledge.

I rise to my feet and let out a deep sigh as Tori hobbles out of the bathroom. She pulls on the sweatshirt and sweatpants I laid out on the bed for her. "Still no panties, hm?" she says with a pointed look at me.

"I prefer you without." I lean against the doorway of the bathroom and watch her.

"You really have that stalker thing perfected," she says with a flip of her hair.

"I had a lot of practice."

"And you don't think it's weird to admit that?"

I push off the wall and inch toward her. "I knew what I wanted the first time I saw you."

"And I knew you were exactly the kind of guy I didn't want when I first saw you."

I lift a hand and run it down the side of her face. Her eyes flutter closed, her head tipping backward. "Do you still feel that way?"

"Kosta!"

Tori gasps, her eyes popping open wide. My hand drops back to my side.

Fuck. *Perfect timing, G.*

I lift Tori into my arms, carry her down the stairs, and set her on the floor outside of my office door. Gregor is already in there pacing while Julian lounges in one of my recliners.

"How's the arm?" I ask.

"The bullet only nicked me," Gregor says in a tight voice. He cradles his arm as he stalks the length of the room. "Lev and the cleaning crew are working on the roadkill we left behind."

Unfortunately, no amount of cleaning can resurrect what was destroyed in my garage. Crates of weapons earmarked for sale, suitcases of cash we needed to sustain ourselves. It's all fucking ash now, which means the weapons deal with Kosovich has to go through fast or else we're broke.

Tori sinks into a chair near the door. She hugs her arms around herself and stares at her feet. I didn't bother to tie her up this time. I figured her injured feet and the bomb I dropped on her outside were enough to keep her from trying to escape again.

I was right.

She's a fighter, but she's not stupid enough to make another break for it.

Flashbacks of that fuckhead touching her make my blood simmer. She may be queen of the badasses, but she's my queen above all else. Nobody lays a finger on her except me. I will kill anyone who tries. No matter who, no matter where, no matter when. And based on the ambush brought to our doorstep tonight, I know that time will come sooner than later.

Guilt wrenches my gut. For all of this time, all of these months of planning my attack, I thought I was the only wolf in sheep's clothing. I never thought kidnapping the bratva princess would lead the real enemy right to their front stoop with me as the fucking welcome mat.

I also never anticipated falling for my fiancée, which stings like a bitch because the only emotion she seems to reserve for me is disdain.

"This place was supposed to be off the grid. How the hell did they find us?" Gregor snaps at me.

"The explosive must have had a GPS baked into it. Led them right to us. They couldn't find the place without help because we're on lockdown." I look at Julian. "Where are we with Kosovich?"

Julian pulls out his phone and flips through a few screens. "Still waiting for confirmation on the terms of the deal."

"We need that sale," I say. "Everything else was wiped out by that bomb. I'll get in touch with our supplier as soon as we get the green light from Kosovich. But it has to happen fast."

"Why don't you just ask your fiancée for a loan?" Gregor grumbles, pressing his fingers to his temples. He hunches over in his chair, shoulders slumped.

I narrow my eyes at my brother. "That's not how this works. This is our problem to solve. I don't need a goddamn bailout. I need partners who can deliver. Can you do that, G? Can I count on you? Or do I need to find a replacement?" I take a few steps toward Gregor, my voice dropping to a low, menacing tone. "Because if you can't do the job, I'll find someone who can."

Tori's chair legs scrape against the floor. She springs out of it like a stick was just shoved up her ass. "Wait. What do you mean... a loan?"

Gregor recoils, casting a quick look at me. "Oh, so you didn't air the family's dirty laundry after you fucked her? No pillow talk afterward?"

"What the hell is he talking about?" Tori demands, turning toward me with a murderous glare in her eyes.

"Looks like everyone is in the dark here with your master plans, Kosta," Gregor mutters.

My spine stiffens. "Shut the hell up, G, or I'll cut out your fucking tongue."

"You're supposed to be some big-time arms dealer," Tori seethes, taking a few steps toward me. "Why are you so desperate for money? What else don't I know, besides your real name?"

A quick glance around the room confirms that there are a lot of potential weapons available for Tori's use if she hears something she doesn't like.

And that time is right now.

I point to the door. "Guys, go check on the cleaners. Then pack your shit and get ready to leave."

Gregor glowers at me for a second but stomps out the door without another word. Julian follows behind. I slam the door shut, and before I can twist around, Tori gives me a swift shove.

"So it turns out that you're the goddamn liar here, not me." She shoves me again, her eyes spitting fire when I don't budge from my spot. Tori's got a lot of rage, but I have size to my advantage. "I've spent years trying to stay away from guys like you, scumbag bottom-feeders who are so crooked they can't even walk a straight line," she bellows.

"Guys like me," I sneer. "You think you live in some ivory tower in Fantasyland? You're right in the middle of the shit, sharing the same blood by exactly the same kind of guys as me."

"You're all a bunch of lying, selfish assholes. You cheat, you steal, and you kill. You're as bad as my brothers. As bad as my father was. And I bet the apple doesn't fall far from the tree, either."

With a hammering pulse, I grab her by the wrists, holding them tight behind her back. Then I pull her close. "Don't you ever fucking say that again. I'm not anything like my father."

"Oh, so that's *your* hot button, huh?" she asks. "Daddy

issues? Are you looking for his approval? What are you trying to prove, Konstantin? Or is it Mikhail? Federov? What the fuck is your name, anyway? Maybe I should just make it easy and call you Prick Bastard!"

My grip on her tightens. She struggles against me, her accusatory words pounding in my ears. "Your father and brothers drove me to this. They're the reason why you're here right now."

"Oh yeah? Humor me. How'd they screw you over? I like to compare notes with all my captors," she spews. Her face screws up into a grimace, disgust coloring her expression.

"Viktor Malikov killed my father." I back Tori against the bookcase, blocking her ability to punch, kick, or grab anything she could use to impale me.

"And that's why you took me? You thought you were going to kill me? An eye for an eye?" Her eyes pop open wide, voice rising.

"I was never gonna kill you." I grit my teeth. "And my father deserved to die. He was a lowlife, abusive sonofabitch. Self-centered and power hungry."

"Then why did you kidnap me? Sex? Is that why you decided to marry me? Were you seriously that hard up for pussy? You couldn't get laid, so you figured you'd take me as a wedding favor and tie me up so I couldn't fight you off?"

A haze of fury consumes me. "Like you even tried once you had a taste of me."

"Don't flatter yourself. I've had better."

"I seriously doubt that." Tension is thick in the air, choking me more with each stifled breath I take.

Anger mixed with lust flares in her gaze. I press my chest against her, shoving her legs open with one knee.

"I never wanted to be a victim. I won't be a fucking victim," she says through clenched teeth, shifting against the bookcase. One of the hardcovers skates on the edge of the shelf and falls off. It lands on the floor next to my foot. I kick it aside, locking Tori in place with my legs.

"I won't let you be a victim."

"You can't stop it. I'll always have a target on the back of my head, just like you said."

"And you'll fight like a hellcat to defend yourself."

"I always do. And I always will." She leans her head back against the shelves, a defeated sigh escaping her lips. "But fuck, I wish I didn't have to. God, I hate this life. I hate what I've been forced to do, who I've been forced to become. Nobody gave me a choice. My father decided our fate a long time ago, and now I'm living it."

I dip my head and look down into Tori's eyes. The flicker of sadness jolts me. She definitely shows a lot of emotion, but it's usually rage, so this new feeling stops me in my tracks.

"You know, I wasn't sad when my dad was killed," she says.

"It's hard to be sad when they completely fuck you over for the entire world to see," I say, my voice laced with fury.

"After we found out who he really was, that he'd taken so much from so many people, using them all as stepping stones to get where he was..." She pauses. "I couldn't even pretend. Not after what he did to us, especially..."

My brows furrow when her voice trails off.

"Especially what?"

"Who, not what. My younger sister Valentina. My dad arranged to marry her off to one of the biggest derelicts on the planet. My dad and brother were gunned down on the day of her wedding. Then Val disappeared. We haven't seen her since, and that was a year and a half ago. We have no idea where she is, if she's even still alive."

Tori's eyes glaze over with regret. "It should have been me. I was older. Val never even told me about the arrangement. I'd have helped her get away or do something that would have saved her from being a victim of my father's ambition. But she was gone before I could try. I couldn't save her," she whispers. "Just like I can't save myself...from you."

My fingers loosen their grip on her wrists. I pull away. "What the hell is that supposed to mean?"

"It means that getting in any deeper with you would be more dangerous to me than any of the enemies who want me dead."

She brings her hands forward and presses her palms against my chest like she's trying to push me away.

Or maybe she already has.

CHAPTER 19
Viktorya

"You're not going to tie me up for this next part?" I ask Konstantin as we pull up to the ornate entrance of the Ritz-Carlton in Sarasota an hour later. It's a weak attempt at an icebreaker since the ride here was pretty damn frigid. I'd actually have been warmer if I was touring Antarctica naked. "Aren't you afraid I'll run again?"

He slants me a glance. "Based on what almost happened tonight, if you run, it'll be at your own risk. And you already made it clear that running would be a better option for you, anyway. The door to your gilded cage is open. If you wanna fly, I won't stop you."

I recoil, my eyes widening at the sharp sting of his words. He brakes hard in front of the valet stand and I lurch forward, using my hands to brace my fall against the dashboard. Without another word, he puts the car in Park and opens his door.

There weren't many words exchanged on the way here, either. Cold or otherwise. Just a lot of tension, thick and heavy in the air. It's like a switch flipped when I told him being with him was more dangerous than any of my family's worst enemies.

I wasn't lying. But he doesn't understand the real reason why, and I didn't bother to explain. I just left the biting words hanging between us.

Now he can barely look at me.

A valet dressed in black hurries over to my door and pulls it open. I step gingerly onto the cobblestones in the flip-flops Konstantin bought me from a drug store on our way here. Pain shoots through my feet as I creep toward Konstantin where he stands at the front desk. I clutch my notebook to my chest. It's the one thing I brought from the house. Writing started out as a way to regain my sanity, but it's quickly become something much more perverse. And hotter than hell, if I'm being honest.

Over the past couple of days, the more I write, the more conflicted I become. Getting my feelings about being held captive by Konstantin onto the pages was supposed to be cathartic. I needed a way to free the emotions that went along with all of the losses I'd just suffered — the loss of my life, my career, and my self-control.

But instead, the words have turned into a dark and twisty rollercoaster ride of emotions I've never allowed myself to experience. Instead of a journal, I have the beginnings of a taboo love story weaved with threads of forbidden needs, desires, and turbulent passion that come to life in the most carnal of ways.

It's like nothing I've ever written. And it's everything I've sworn I never wanted.

The risks of falling for a man like Konstantin...Mikhail... whoever the fuck he is...are many. Not only to my family, but to me. That's why I ran tonight. Because of what he's brought out of me, what he's stripped from me, and what he might do next to assert his total control over me.

I stop next to him. He continues talking to the woman behind the desk. A pang assaults my heart. He never looks at me once.

I wonder if he'd even give a damn if I ran now, not that I could even think of darting anywhere with these busted-up feet. I shift my weight, trying not to put too much pressure on either heel. The girl behind the desk finally hands him his credit card and a set of keys. She flashes a bright smile at him and gives me the evil eye.

I swallow a snort. If she only knew what an asshole he is behind the hot-as-fuck exterior.

He picks up the black leather duffel bag at his feet and turns in the direction of the elevator bank. I roll my eyes. Not that I was looking for a piggyback ride or anything, but an acknowledgement would have been a nice gesture.

He walks fast, taking long, swift strides while I follow along like I'm dancing over hot coals. "You want to slow down, please?" I gasp, cringing with each step. "My feet are killing me."

"Mikhail," a throaty female voice calls out.

Without warning, he stops short at the sound of his name. It's so sudden, I crash into his back, nose-first. I clap a hand over my face.

He twists to the right, his shoulders squared and his jaw so tense, it could possibly crack from the pressure. "Mischa," he says, his voice tight.

"I thought that was you," she says, her high heels clicking on the tile. I peek around him to get a look and choke on a gasp.

Holy fuck...

She looks just like me.

I mean, not the way I look right this second. She's dressed in sky-high stilettos and a dress so tight, so short, and so low-cut, it's practically a glorified bathing suit. And she's got a knockout body to boot.

Not that I'm jealous over here in my ridiculously oversized sweats and raggedy flip-flops. I might as well be wearing a burlap sack.

But it's not the clothes that have me reeling. It's everything else. I gaze at her hair, her eyes, and her facial structure. My temples throb, my mouth agape. This woman is my doppelgänger. My identical freaking twin.

The woman...Mischa...catches my eye and does a double take. "Oh, my goodness," she murmurs before looking back at Konstantin. "I didn't realize you were with someone." With a quirk of her eyebrow, she smiles. "Still trying to replace me, sweetie? Well done. This one is a dead ringer."

I gasp. What in the fresh hell is that supposed to mean?

"But can she fuck you as well as I did?" she croons, her voice dripping with condescension. "She definitely has a unique...*style*." Her critical eye glances over my outfit once more. "I think you're scraping the bottom of the barrel though. You need to shoot a little higher, love."

"I figured this time around I'd try something other than a backstabbing, cocksucking whore...and this one doesn't want anyone in my same bloodline," he says, his voice unwavering.

Her blue eyes narrow. "Maybe if you were better at the fucking part, I wouldn't have looked for any other cocks to suck."

"Step the fuck off," I hiss, pushing past Konstantin and taking a few painful steps in the bitch's direction. A rush of rage loots my insides, bubbling in my chest. "He's my fiancé, you cunt. *And* he fucks like a porn star." I flash the fakest smile I can muster. "Ever thought that maybe your pussy was defective?"

A snort of laughter from Konstantin empowers me to take the final shot.

"Mine definitely isn't. And right now, it's very, *very* hungry," I continue. "So I think you should just wrap up your little trip down memory lane, piss off, and find some rich guy who'll pay you for a fuck since I can't imagine why anyone would do it for nothing after talking to you for even half a second. And that'll free me up to take advantage of what you stupidly gave up."

I reach for Konstantin's hand. He laces his fingers with mine and squeezes tight. A swarm of tingles in my belly explodes, heat and lust radiating through me.

Mischa's face twists into a mask of disdain, her cheeks stained a deep red. "So classy. Good luck with your trailer-trash bride," she snips at him before stalking away from us. It's not until she disappears through the front doors that I let go of his hand.

"We need to get upstairs right now," I say, clutching my notebook.

He doesn't respond. He just walks toward the elevators, his back stiff. I follow behind as close as possible. He holds the doors for me. I hobble through them and collapse against the mirrored wall with a deep sigh.

"How long ago were you and Mischa together?" I ask.

"We were engaged a year and a half ago," he replies abruptly.

"And then she cheated on you?"

"With my father...at our engagement party." His lips twist like he's just tasted poison.

I gasp. "Damn, I'm sorry. That sucks."

"She always thrived on drama." Konstantin shrugs and runs a hand through his hair.

"What about your father?"

The elevator dings on the ninth floor and the doors slowly slide open. I follow Konstantin down the short hallway. Cream-colored walls create a calm, peaceful space. Large brass chandeliers cast a soft glow on the terracotta-colored marble floors. But the entire effect is lost on me completely in light of the battle waging in my mind and heart.

He stops in front of a door at the end of the corridor, sticks the plastic key card into the slot, and waits for the click before he twists the knob and pushes open the door. He tosses it onto a table near the door and walks into the room.

"My father was a toxic piece of shit. He was always looking to grab as much power and control as he could. In business, in relationships, in life. Mischa's a model. She always got lots of attention, and my father hated that I was in the limelight with her and not him. He hated that I was in business for myself, and that my relationship with Mischa didn't benefit him. Most of all, he hated that I was successful despite everything he did to tear me down over the years," he says. "He might not have sold my hand in marriage, but he was an abusive fuck in his own way. He drove my mother away and destroyed our family."

He takes a few steps toward me, his face etched with anger. "I wanted him to pay for what he did to us all. So when he came to me for help when he knew Viktor was closing in on him, I sent him away. I told him I'd never help him, that he deserved to die. That's when the hit happened. Viktor had the shit blown out of my office after my father showed up there."

My breath hitches as he closes the space between us.

His eyes narrow. "I could have been killed, too. But instead, Viktor killed my business. Nobody wanted anything to do with me once my father died. It was like the same target that was on him was now painted on me and G like a fucking scarlet letter. I lost everything. Money, clients, my network. All of it. I've struggled like hell to get it back ever since then. I was forced to change my name and start over, building it all up from the ashes under a new identity."

My eyes fall to the phoenix on his hand, and suddenly the image makes perfect sense. I'm supposed to help him rise up again. "And that's why you came for me."

"No," he growls, backing me against the door. The vein in his neck throbs hard like it always does when he's about to fly into beast mode. "You weren't part of my original plan. But when it all backfired on me, I needed a different strategy. When I saw you for the first time, I knew I had to have you."

"Why?" I ask in a stifled whisper. "Because I look like Mischa? Because you were trying to replace her? Or was it something more?"

"I would never try to replace that bitch." He raises a hand and sweeps it behind my head, fisting my hair. "But you...I fucking hated you. And I wanted to hurt you because you were a reminder of everything that went so fucking badly in my life. I wanted to make you feel the same pain and anger I felt. I wanted to make you suffer because of what your father did, and for what he took."

He tugs my head backward, his face hovering over me. His eyes glow with pent-up fury.

"What about now?" A chill slips down my spine. The roots of my hair tingle from his tight grip. "Do you still want to hurt me? Do you still hate me?" My throat tightens. "Did you ever really stop?"

CHAPTER 20
Konstantin

"Do I still hate you?" I repeat, dipping my head low and forcing her to look up at me. "You ask that like you don't already know the answer."

"What can I say?" she snaps. "You're a twisted headcase, and I can't read you for shit."

"You know, flattery isn't really your forte." I slide my knee between her legs and force them open, but there's way too much fabric blocking that perfect pussy. I loosen my grip on her hair and shove the sweatpants to her ankles.

"So you're not going to answer? You're just going to fuck me again?" She gasps as I drag my fingers down her wet slit.

"Maybe it's a hate fuck," I growl. "And why does it matter? You've made it clear how you feel about me and this whole situation."

"How am I supposed to feel?" She moans when I plunge my fingers deep inside her wet heat. "You stole my life from me, plucked me right from my brother's wedding. I had plans for myself. I had a career. You took that from me, all because you hated me and wanted to make me and my family miserable."

I move my fingers in and out, faster and deeper. She writhes against my hand, her words morphing into whimpers. I work her clit with my thumb. Her pussy clamps down on my fingers, squeezing them tight and grinding her hips against mine.

"You were such a bitch the first night I saw you," I mutter, pressing my hips into hers. She cries out, her warm juices flowing over my fingers. "Full of attitude. You looked at me like I was a bug on the bottom of your designer shoe."

"Because I can't stand men like you," she gasps, reaching behind my head and grabbing fistfuls of my hair as she thrusts against me. "Arrogant, deviant bastards who only care about three things — retribution, money, and pussy. And you won't let anyone stand in the way of you sinking your claws into any of them."

"You're a dirty slut, Tori." I attack her neck with my lips. "You call me arrogant and deviant, but you fucking love what I do to you. What only I can do to you."

"No, I hate it." She grabs my belt and fumbles with the buckle. She tugs at the leather, her fingers working desperately to pull it open. "I fucking hate all of it. Everything my father was, everything my brothers are. I never wanted any of it."

"Then why are you so wet?" I grip onto her earlobe with my teeth. She finally gets my pants open and shoves them to my knees. I stroke my cock and drag the head over her pussy lips to get it lubricated. A tortured cry escapes her lips as I rub it against her clit. "Why is your body begging for my cock? Why is your mouth crying out for more?"

"Because I'm as much of a fucking headcase as you are." She throws her head back and locks one leg around my waist to draw me closer. "Men like you are evil criminals. You're dangerous."

"And yet you still want me." I let go of her and my cock, then pull away enough to grab the hem of the sweatshirt and yank it over her head. "I'm the only one who can make you lose control. You hate knowing that. But what you hate more is that I make you feel incredible."

"I do. I *so* do." She collapses back against the wall, her chest heaving. I reach around her back, unhook her bra, and toss it to the floor.

"Nobody has ever fucked you this good...and nobody ever will again." I knead one of her breasts, burying my head in the other one. With a swirl of my tongue, I capture one of her nipples, suckling it with my teeth until her sudden scream shatters the air. "Tell me I'm the only one who'll ever fuck this sweet pussy. Tell me it's mine forever."

Tori grinds her hips into me, her face flushed, eyes squeezed shut. Sweat beads on her forehead as she pants for breath. "Don't tease me," she hisses.

"Then don't disobey me." I snake an arm around her waist and pull her tight into my chest. "Tell me what I want to hear."

"Or what? You'll punish me?" Her eyes flutter open and she runs her fingertips down the front of my chest with a come-hither look that makes me want to flip her around and fuck that perfect ass of hers. "So punish me. And then fuck me like the savage you are."

I kick off my pants, my cock damn near ready to explode. She pushes me backward with her palms, taking small steps as she runs her tongue over the ink covering my pecs.

"I thought you wanted me to fuck you." I capture her wrists in one hand and hold them over her head, my free hand running down the side of her torso. Her skin prickles, goosebumps popping in the wake of my fingertips.

"That was me taking control," she murmurs.

"And this is me taking it back." I turn her around so she's facing the couch. "Get on your knees."

I wrap my hands around her hips and guide her toward the leather cushion. She sinks onto her knees and settles against the back of the couch, giving her hips a little wiggle. I grab my cock and give it a few strokes as I edge closer.

She thinks I'm gonna spank her.

My cock throbs.

I'm not.

"I want that ass in the air now," I growl, grabbing her cheeks and spreading them. I kneel behind her, massaging the globes of her ass as I lick the rim of her asshole. Her body stiffens, ass muscles twitching as I press my tongue into her dark hole.

She lets out a startled gasp at the penetration of her most forbidden place, her hips rigid as I fuck her ass with my mouth. But then she relaxes and backs her hips into my mouth just like I knew she would, giving herself to me completely. My dirty girl writhes and moans with every thrust of my tongue. Her tits bounce, her body convulsing from the erotic assault.

"Oh my God. Fuck me. Please fuck me now!"

I pull my mouth away from her ass. My dick drips with precum. I slide my hand over the tip and rub it down the sides before I rise to my feet. My cock bobs between my thighs, the tip grazing the tight rim of muscle. Her asshole winks at me as if it knows what's coming next.

Namely, *her*.

I step onto the couch for leverage. Then I lean into her back and snake one arm around her waist, freeing up my other hand to play with her clit. I slowly thrust into her ass. She yelps at the intrusion. Her stomach tightens as I plunge farther.

"Ahh," she cries out, tightening up.

"Let me in," I murmur. "Relax, babe."

With a deep breath, her muscles loosen. She takes my cock, inch by inch, until I'm buried balls deep in her heat.

"Nobody gets to fuck you like this," I hiss against her ear, my thumb and forefinger taking turns tormenting her clit. Her hips buck forward, riding my fingers while her ass squeezes my dick. Tremors rumble deep within her as the orgasm erupts. A warm, wet rush flows over my fingers, drenching me with her desire, drowning me in my own hunger.

I thrust into her ass, rolling my hips. She rides my cock hard. A tingling in my balls shoots out to the head of my dick. My cock swells with cum. I pull out, then bury myself deep, over and over, long, slow strokes that have her whole body trembling with need.

It's so taboo. So tight. So fucking perfect.

"I'm gonna come, baby," I say. "And I want you to take it all. Every fucking drop, deep in your ass." I bite her shoulder. "Is that what you want?"

"Yes," she pants. "I want it all."

With one final thrust, I explode inside of her. My body shudders from the force, my abdominal muscles tense and tight. My dick jerks, spurts of hot cum shooting deep in her ass. I bury my head in the back of her neck, one hand plastered across her tits, the other between her thighs.

She melts against me with a deep sigh. I kiss the back of her neck, then move my lips toward the sensitive spot behind her ear. I could just whisper the words taunting me from the tip of my tongue, but I don't.

I can't.

It's hard to breathe. And yet, I've never felt so alive in my life. The carnal energy flowing between us...it's electric. Everything about Tori Malikov is fiercely addictive. One touch, one taste ruined me for life. My feelings for her are more powerful than a shot of adrenaline to the heart...and potentially more deadly than a bullet to the brain.

Because for as dangerous as she thinks *I* am, falling in love with her could be fucking lethal...

For both of us.

CHAPTER 21
Viktorya

"This place reeks of sweat and sex," Gregor mutters, pushing past Julian to get into our room at the Ritz. He looks around. "Nice digs. Why do we get stuck staying at Lev's shitty apartment while you guys live it up here? Besides, I thought we were broke."

"If anyone is watching, they'd expect us to be with you. They know Lev works for me. They'd be camped out at his place, just waiting to pounce on us all. I'm not taking any chances with Tori." Konstantin shuts the door after Julian slumps inside. "And it's a regular room. Nothing crazy. We don't even have a butler."

The two brothers snicker, and it breaks the tension the tiniest bit. I watch Julian. He stands a few feet away from the guys and stares at his phone. His forehead pinches and he tugs the ends of his longish brown hair. But he doesn't speak. He barely lifts his head from the screen. His face definitely spells trouble. I glance at Konstantin and Gregor, but neither seem to notice.

I relax my back against the headboard, my legs crossed at the ankle while I re-read the last scene I wrote. I try to block out their conversation, but the lack of privacy makes it nearly impossible to focus.

Gregor glances at me, and then at Konstantin. "No more zip ties? She's not running anymore?"

"Do you see my feet?" I snip. "I can barely get to the bathroom."

Gregor looks around the room with a raised eyebrow. Heat creeps into my cheeks as I follow his gaze. The room isn't huge, but we've christened pretty much every inch of it. "Or maybe he's got you occupied doing other things to distract you from taking off again."

Konstantin smirks. I roll my eyes, flip to a new page in my notebook, and bury my head in it. My hair hangs around my face, hiding my flaming cheeks. Tingles explode in my core as I scan the dirty, sexy hot scene I just wrote for my characters. With all the heat coiling my insides at this moment, I might just spontaneously combust.

"We're here to talk about Kosovich," Konstantin says. "What I do before or after this meeting is none of your damn business."

I sneak a look up from the pages. Julian rubs the back of his head, still frowning at his phone.

"Julian, did Kosovich get back to you on the terms? Are we a go?"

Julian looks up quickly from his phone, like he's startled by Konstantin's question. "Almost. But he wants one thing before he signs."

"What?" Konstantin narrows his eyes.

"He wants to meet with you. He's hosting some gala in a couple of days, and he wants to discuss the terms with you in person."

"No fucking way," Konstantin says. "He either agrees now or the deal is off."

"No," Julian bellows. "That's not an option."

"What the fuck did you just say?" Konstantin levels him with a glare. He takes a few steps toward Julian, his fists clenched.

"Look, we need this deal to go through. I know the timing is shit with Arseny Siderov on the hunt for your ass, but that means we need Kosovich now more than ever. If we don't partner with him, who's gonna work with us, knowing he passed on our deal? You want to build this business back up, Kosta? Go to the goddamn gala."

"You're supposed to be the closer, and you couldn't get him to sign when you met him for dinner the other night. If you were so desperate to work with him, you never should have let him leave until he agreed to our terms." Konstantin stalks toward the window and yanks open the curtain.

Bright afternoon sun streams into the room. I blink fast, adjusting my eyes to the light before returning to my steamy scene. Damn, I wish I had my AirPod Pros to cancel out this noise. I'm not used to all of the sniping while I write, and I'd love to block it all out so I can get back to my dirty, deviant sexcapade story.

Julian lets out a frustrated sigh. "I know. I fucked up. But you know we need this deal. This is a second chance to get it done."

I peek up at Julian just as his disgusted gaze hits mine. "If the Malikovs find out we're broke, they're gonna barrel in here and steal back the princess with no fucks given. We need allies, or we'll get steamrolled." He flashes a pointed look at Gregor. "You know exactly what I'm talking about. The Brotherhood has too many enemies, and you won't know they're coming until it's too late."

The Brotherhood 7. That's the thread that connects all of this malice and brutality. That's what connects us all.

I look at Konstantin. His eyebrows knit together, his voice taut when he addresses Julian. "What do you know about the Brotherhood?"

Julian throws his hands into the air. "Really? You think it's a big secret? Your father talked to my mother about it all the time, about how Viktor Malikov was the ringleader for a Brotherhood — a group of twisted vigilante thieves — and how he needed to stop him before it was too late. The only way we escape is to align ourselves with the head of the snake. Since Viktor's not around anymore, his kids are the next best thing."

"Yeah, except we're not exactly free and clear of the Brotherhood, either," I mutter.

My mind trips back to the day at my parents' house when Luka found evidence of the Brotherhood 7 in my dad's office. The details were sketchy at best, since nobody seemed to know much about the group and their activities other than the members themselves — members who were all coincidentally missing in action. But as time went on, my brothers have uncovered more and more. So even though it's no surprise my dad was living some secret life as an underworld tormentor king, doing hits on people including his own "brothers" who stood in the way of his plans to take over the planet, hearing it still makes my heart clench.

And I'll never know the truth because he's gone. Then again, based on who and what he was, this revelation doesn't shock me at all. Guilt swirls in my gut when the thought grabs hold of my mind. But it doesn't outweigh the disappointment and anger that festers deep inside of me since I know in my heart of hearts he was responsible for Valentina's disappearance.

"He's right," Gregor says. "If Kosovich tells us to fuck off, we'll be exposed. News will travel that we have nothing. And you'll never get the Princess Bride, or her piece of the kingdom, if her brothers have anything to say about it."

I twist a strand of hair between my fingers and tug it hard. Our sham marriage was supposed to be a business transaction — my hand in exchange for a piece of the Malikov pie. But that arrangement only worked when I was the bargaining chip.

"You're not gonna gamble with her life," Gregor says. "Dangling Tori in front of her brothers with the threat of her death would have gotten you into the fortress. But once they know the truth, that we have no network, no backing, and no money, you'll look like fucking Swiss cheese when they're done with you. Kosovich is the only shot we have to regain some credibility and influence. It's the only way we can protect ourselves and get back in with the Malikovs. A deal with Kosovich makes us valuable to them. And since we need a new bargaining chip..." He nods his head toward me and I flip him off.

Konstantin runs a hand down his stubbled chin. "Fine. But only if I go alone. G, you and Julian are gonna stay here with Tori. I don't want her moved from this place. There's plenty of security roaming around, and we can keep her on lockdown until I make the deal." He looks at Julian. "Let Kosovich know. Don't tell him I'm coming by myself, though. Let him think I'm coming with an army just in case he gets any stupid ideas."

Julian nods. "You're doing the right thing. This is how we rebuild. We can still take back what's ours, but we have to start somewhere."

I chew the end of my pen, trying not to listen to the rest of the conversation. I heard way more than I wanted to already. With a small sigh, I look back at the page and scribble the last line of the scene. I close the cover of the notebook and lie back on the fluffy pillows. My eyes float closed and I'm suddenly transported into my dark and deviant story. Only it isn't my fictional characters starring in my pulse-pounding fantasies. It's me and Konstantin — on the bed, against the wall, on the balcony of the hotel room, in the shower, on the hood of the car. Forward, backward, sideways, upside down. Every which way.

Because he's the true inspiration for my rejuvenated creative spark.

In the deep recesses of my mind, a slamming sound rattles my ears. I sit up with a start sometime later, my eyes heavy with sleep. I must have dozed off while the guys were still meeting. Daylight has fallen to dusk, the soft glow of the horizon hitting the tips of my toes. I run a hand through my hair and look around the dim room until I see him.

His hulking body hunches over the side of the bar set up in the corner of the room. He walks toward me holding a glass of some clear liquid.

My eyes fall to his other hand as he inches closer to the bed. I shift under his fiery glare.

Oh, damn...

"You've got one chance to answer my questions. One fucking chance before I take shit into my own hands." He drains the liquid from the glass before slamming it on the glass-top nightstand next to me. Then he shakes the notebook in front of my face. "Who the fuck is Jake? And is this all the shit you want him to do to you?"

CHAPTER 22
Konstantin

Fury bubbles in my chest as I hold her shocked gaze captive. I'm pissed as hell, not that it stops the raging hard-on from straining against my pants. How could she fantasize about some other guy while it's me touching her? While it's me fucking her?

With a low roar, I fling the notebook against the wall. It opens somewhere in the middle, the pages rumpled. Good. It's crap anyway.

"I really hate writing on wrinkled paper," Tori murmurs.

"Oh, so only smooth paper works when you use me as a stand-in for Jakey boy?" I yell.

"You're really being a little over the top right now," she says in a calm voice. And it only fires me up more.

"Am I? How the fuck would you feel if your fiancée was writing her sex fantasies about another guy?"

"If my fiancé was writing sex scenes about another guy," she says, her fingers creeping over one of my clenched hands, "then we might have a problem."

"Well, I'm not you, and we still have a big fucking problem."

She lifts an eyebrow, the corner of her lip twitching like she's trying not to laugh. Blood rushes between my ears. But it's not even anger. It's worse.

Tori's got me by the balls...and by the heart. But what stings more is that she doesn't realize it, or simply doesn't care. Either way, I'm at her mercy and that infuriates me most of all.

"Let me get this straight," she says, rising up to her knees so that her face inches closer to mine. "While I slept, you took my notebook and read my most personal, private thoughts. And because you didn't like what you saw, now you're upset with me."

"Upset doesn't even begin to describe it," I grunt.

"You don't have the urge to flip me over and punish me for what I did?" she asks, gazing up at me with blue eyes that glow with white-hot fire.

"And give you more material to feed your dickhead boyfriend? Fuck no." I pull my hands away from her and twist around before stalking toward the bar. I grab another glass, fill it with ice, and pour a double shot of vodka for myself.

I guzzle it down, the smooth liquid landing in my empty stomach. It wrenches with the knowledge that Tori wants to do those things with someone else. After pouring another double and sucking that one down, I'm calm. Calmer, anyway.

There's only one thing to do now. I'm gonna find this asshole Jake and kill him. It's a simple solution. Tori will get over him eventually. But there's no way I'm marrying her while I'm competing with another cock.

I glower at her. She's mine. All mine.

"Have I told you lately that you have some serious control issues?"

"They're not the only issues I have, sweetheart. But there isn't enough time in the world to unpack that shit." I slam my glass on the bar and stalk back toward her. "I'm gonna tell you this one time. Forget Jake. You're never gonna see him again."

She cocks her head to the side. "I think I will."

"The fuck you will," I bellow. I swing out my arm, sending the lamp on the night table crashing to the floor.

"You are insane," she shouts.

"Yeah, baby," I grunt, my eyes narrowing to slits. "Fucking crazy. You know it."

"That was a nice lamp, too." She frowns at the thick wedges of glass scattered on the floor.

"Fuck the lamp!"

"Why are you so out of your mind over this? Is it just because you think I'm in love with another guy? Is that what bothers you so much? The competition?"

I clench my fists, my lungs tight.

Competition. It's a fucking ugly word, one I've wrestled with my whole life. I never needed to be the best, and that pissed my father off to no end. He wanted a protégé who was a vicious, bloodsucking viper like him. And he let me know every fucking day what a disappointment I was to him. That's why he tried over and over again to hammer me into the ground...with my business, my fiancée, with everything in my life. I found out the hard way that I'd never be the best unless I destroyed the competition.

And that's exactly what I did to my father, my biggest competitor.

But the wounds never heal when you do shit you're not proud of. I never got the closure I needed. Yeah, I beat my father, but in the end, he still won. I lost everything. Things turned out exactly the way he would have wanted them to, especially after I let him get shot up by Malikov.

It was his final revenge ploy.

That bastard.

My vision floods with red as I glare at Tori. "Don't pretend to understand anything about me because you don't and you fucking *can't*."

Tori rolls her eyes. "Well, one thing I know for sure is that you look like you're going to pop a gasket right now."

I grab her by the wrist and pull her toward me. "My future wife will only fantasize about *me*."

"Do nightmares count?"

Flames roar deep in my chest. I've never met a sexier, more infuriating woman in my life. "If you want me to punish you so badly, why don't you just ask for it?" I seethe.

She flashes a toothy grin. "This way is *much* more fun."

"When I'm finished with you, you won't even remember Jake the Snake."

"Promises, promises," she says in a teasing tone.

"I'm serious," I growl.

"Show me," she whispers, puffing out her chest in a T-shirt I had sent up from the gift shop earlier. Her legs fall open. "That you're not all talk."

I drop my gaze to her panties, courtesy of a recent shopping trip Isabella did. My fingertips tingle with the urge to tear them off so I can taste that sweet pussy. My dick strains against my pants. He doesn't give a damn that he's just a replacement cock for Jake. I grit my teeth. How the fuck didn't I know about him? I never saw her with any guy but who knows? He might live out of state or be in prison for all I know.

I should fight what she's dangling in front of me. Why the fuck should I give in to what she obviously wants? She's looking to get off since her boyfriend isn't around, and my dick is as good as any.

Screw her. Screw him, too. I can be strong. I can resist the temptation.

I back away from the bed. A flicker of surprise flashes across her face when I don't take the bait. Her lips part the slightest bit, like she wants to say something. That's a fucking shocker, since she always finds something to say, and it's usually biting.

But instead of talking, her lips curl into a seductive smirk and her hand slides down the front of her T-shirt. The hairs on the back of my neck prickle. She grabs hold of my hungry gaze as her fingers rub against the silky panties. With a low, needy moan, her eyes flutter closed. Her fingers rub harder, and my cock throbs in response. I swallow hard, licking my lips when Tori slides the fabric to the side and plunges her fingers into her cunt.

Pent-up lust courses through me with each thrust of her hips against her hand. She writhes, her back arched, her pussy glistening with her juices. She alternates between flicking her clit and driving her fingers deep.

Be strong, motherfucker. Don't you dare touch her.

Yeah, but who says I can't touch myself?

My pulse slams against my neck. I yank open my pants and dip my hand into my boxer briefs. I grasp my cock, stroking it hard as Tori rides her own fingers. Her body quakes and quivers, her sharp cries piercing the air.

I rub harder and knead my aching blue balls as cum rushes to the tip of my cock. Sparks fire in my groin, blasting through me. I squeeze my eyes shut. The orgasm rumbles like a slow explosion, ready to erupt.

Then something soft, wet, and hot blankets my cock. My eyes fly open to see Tori's head bobbing up and down between my legs. Her lips close tight around my shaft, sucking me hard and taking me so deep, the tip hits the back of her throat.

I dig my fingers into her hair, tangling them in the soft strands. She sucks and pulls and tugs on my cock with her mouth, licking me up and down like she's a starving woman and I'm her next meal.

Fuck. Me.

I grab the back of her head, thrusting my hips against her greedy mouth. I fuck her face, my cock pulsating from the force of the orgasm. I drop my hands from her head and clutch her shoulders, tremors shuddering my body as a bolt of lightning zaps every cell in my body. My knees buckle, my chest heaves, and my toes curl.

Just because I watched her finger-fuck herself.

She pulls away, a satisfied smirk on her gorgeous face. Her lips glisten with drops of my cum, and I think it's the hottest fucking thing I've seen in my life. She sweeps her tongue over her lips and licks it off.

"You're not using that move on Jake," I grunt when I can breathe without panting.

"Really," she says, rising from her knees. She slides herself up the front of my chest, rubbing her tits against me like the bad girl she is. "Well, guess what? You're not the boss of me. I'm an independent woman, if you haven't already figured that out."

"You're making me angry...again," I hiss.

"I think I'm making you hot. Am I right?" She runs her fingers up the sides of my neck, then around the back of my head. They creep higher, tangling in my hair

My heart pounds fiercely against my chest, words lodging in my throat. I dig my fingertips into her hips.

Tori's defiant gaze makes me half-hard again. She pushes her hips against mine, grinding her pussy into my cock. "Say it," she breathes. "Tell me how I make you feel."

"It doesn't fucking matter. This is over." I grab a fistful of her hair and tug her head backward. "The wedding is fucking off."

CHAPTER 23
Viktorya

"It's what you want anyway," he growls, rooting me to the spot with his fiery glare. "You've been fighting it and me all along. And you're obviously saving yourself for someone else."

It takes me a few seconds to find words since the sudden shock of his announcement clouded my brain. And then I can't resist but to goad him a little more because I'm a bitch like that. "Wait, so you've held me hostage for a week, tying me up, violating me every chance you got, and all I needed to do was tell you about Jake, and you'd have let me go? Just like that?"

Anger shadows his chiseled features, disgust flaring in his expression. "It was never supposed to be about you. It was always only supposed to be about revenge and money."

"So something obviously changed," I press. "You've admitted that it has. Why can't you tell me what it is? Why are you so angry about this? Are you jealous? Of Jake? Make me understand why it matters to you who I secretly pine for if you get what you want from my family."

He averts his murderous gaze, storms to the bar, and grabs the bottle of vodka before sucking back a mouthful, and then a second one. He slams the bottle on the bar while I watch the cuts of muscle on his back tense and tighten, a tickling sensation on the tip of my tongue because I want so badly to lick each one.

"I don't want to fucking talk about Jackass Jake anymore."

"I asked you a lot of questions and you haven't answered a single one. You don't get to make the rules here," I say, walking toward him. "And I say the conversation isn't over yet."

"The fuck it's not. I'm going to take a shower," Konstantin growls, pushing me aside as he stalks into the bathroom. His heels dig into the carpet, his anger evident in the heavy footsteps.

"You're going to leave me out here alone?" I ask, sticking my hands on my hips. "Aren't you afraid I'm going to bolt?"

He stops with his back to me, his hand clenched tight around the door handle. "Do whatever you want. Leave, don't leave. I don't give a damn. I'll come up with a new plan. Don't think you ruined me, Tori."

"It, right?" I shoot back. "Don't you mean ruined *it*?"

He slowly turns, his forehead creased, his pained expression catching me completely off-guard. It flabbergasts me to the point where I don't even know how to respond. He must not know how either because he flips around without a word, slams the door shut, and seconds later, turns on the water.

My jaw damn near hits the carpet. That reaction was unexpected on so many levels. I practically handed myself to him on a silver platter and he rejected me, choosing to touch himself instead.

It's all about control. He wouldn't lay a finger on me because doing so would relinquish his power. Keeping his hands on himself helped preserve that. Him walking away and not taking what I put in front of him? That was punishment for me changing his rules. I made a move to take what I wanted, pulling that control away from him.

And then there's the glaring fact that he is green with jealousy over a figment of my imagination. I knew he was possessive, but wow. This is a whole new level of alpha.

I let out a sigh, my shoulders sagging. My gaze travels around the room until it hits the door. Like he said, I could walk away right now. I could escape, just like I tried earlier tonight. Nothing is keeping me holed up in this room anymore.

Nothing, except for the feelings that have inconveniently developed since he kidnapped me. I'd love to lie and say they're strictly of the carnal variety, but I can't. He blasted through the barbed wire wrapped around my heart with no concern about getting stuck, scratched, or sliced up. He barreled through, consequences be damned, shattering my perception of "his type."

Because while that "type" is still made up of dangerous, criminal thugs with no morals and Konstantin is so much like them, including my brothers, he also is so very different at the same time. He's been hurt, broken, and beaten down. But his first instinct isn't to kill. It's not to maim. It isn't even about taking revenge. His goal is to put the pieces back together. To make himself whole again, despite what others have done or taken from him.

In that way, we're a lot alike.

And maybe I've let him in because I sensed that likeness between us, a deeper connection than I ever thought would be possible with my sex-crazed captor.

I walk over to the door and place my hand on the white painted wood. A smile lifts my lips. I've never wanted to let someone in on my biggest secret more than I do right now.

I pull my hand away from the door and cross the room. I twist the bathroom door handle and push it open. A gasp nearly chokes me when I walk into the steam-filled room. Konstantin stands in the middle of the fogged-up, partial glass enclosure, his soapy, ripped muscles making my eyes bulge. Even through the steam cloud, his god-like body makes my knees wobble like Jell-O.

I pull off my T-shirt, strip off my panties, and drop both on the cool tile floor before taking a few steps toward him. His back is to me. I bite down hard on my lower lip, unable to drag my eyes away from his tight, perfectly rounded ass. My God, I want to bite it so badly...

I inch toward the open space, stepping under the hot spray. Water rushes down the sides of my face and my back, the heat singeing my prickled skin. I reach out and run my hands down the sides of his torso. He jerks around, startled. Then his eyes narrow.

"You needed some new inspiration?" he snaps, turning away from me.

"Yes," I say, trailing soft kisses down his spine.

"I'm not interested. Find someone else to help your creative muse." His voice is taut and gruff. It makes me smile to know he's this affected by me even though he clearly hates that I've made this kind of an impact on him. He's so fucking green right now, from the ends of his hair to the tips of his toes.

Tingles dance in my core at his nearness, and even though he's angry, he doesn't move away from me. He takes a step back, closing the space between us. I slide my hands around to the fronts of his thighs, massaging the tense muscles as I graze the sides of his balls. I slide closer to him, pressing my chest to his back. Water cascades down his spine, raining onto my face as I lick each cut, indentation, and swirl of tattoo ink.

He stiffens. My hands roam upward toward his pecs, then down over his washboard abs as I nestle my head against him. He shifts suddenly, twisting around with a death glare firing daggers of anger at me.

"Why are you here?"

"Because someone needs to set you straight." I run my fingertips down his arms, blinking fast as water droplets cling to my eyelashes. "You need to hear something."

"I hope you're not thinking of reciting that notebook shit out loud to me," he grouses.

"I think it could be really hot if I did that," I say. "But maybe later. There's something else I want to tell you."

He lifts an eyebrow expectantly but says nothing.

Because even though I want to tell him the truth about Jake, there's something I need to say first. I rest my palm against his heart. The steady thrum of the beat vibrates, fast and furious.

"But before I do, I just want to get something straight. I'm not a fucking yo-yo, okay? You kidnapped me, told me you were getting back at my family for fucking with you, then announce that you're going to marry me so you can get your hands on their money...money I have only a *fraction* of, so bad planning on your part." I stroke his soaked skin. "Then you renege and tell me I can go, that you'll find another way to get what you want."

"Yeah, so?"

I roll my eyes. He sounds so petulant. "So, if you're going to do something stupid that's going to hurt my family, I'm staying."

"That's what you really want?" He makes a face. "What'll Jake say when he finds out you chose to marry me instead of going back to him?"

A smile plays at my lips, and I step back a bit to get out of the path of the spray. "He'd understand that family always comes first. But Jake isn't going to be a threat to you."

"After I kill him, you mean?"

"You can't kill him."

"Why? Was he cursed to walk the Earth for eternity or some shit like that?" Konstantin scoffs.

"No, you can't kill him because he isn't real."

He narrows his eyes and follows me out of the shower spray. "What the hell does that mean?"

"I made him up. He's a fictional character. He doesn't exist in real life." I reach for Konstantin's hands and lace his fingers with mine. "What's written in that notebook isn't for the benefit of some elusive boyfriend of mine. I wrote it for you. For us. Because this thing that's happening between us, as crazy and deranged as it is, makes me very, *very* hot. It makes me feel things I've never experienced or imagined. It makes me want to do things...dirty, sexy things...with you. And I needed to write about it all because that's what I do."

I pause for a second, squeezing his hands. "I'm a romance author. You inspired me to write about us. So you don't have to feel threatened by Jake anymore, Konstantin. Because *you're* Jake."

CHAPTER 24
Konstantin

Tori just hurled a whole lot of words at me and processing them takes a hell of a lot longer than my cock likes. Because he's damn ready to accept just about anything she says, as long as he gets to bury himself inside that sweet pussy.

But my mind isn't nearly as forgiving. Or trusting.

"You do know what I'll do to you if I find out you're lying," I growl, grabbing her by the arms. I stare at her, searching for any hint that she's fucking with me.

A hint of a smile tugs at her lips, streams of water drizzling down the sides of her face. "Oh, I know. And part of me kind of wishes I was lying so you could deliver on that threat."

"Knowing you, you'll come up with another reason damn quickly."

Her eyes twinkle. "I'm already plotting ideas."

I let go of her arms, reach behind me and shut off the shower spray. Then I grab a towel from the brass bar hanging on the wall and drape it around her shuddering shoulders.

She pulls it tight around her, eyes sweeping over me with a look that says she wants to fuck the writing and start acting out the fantasies. I can't say I don't feel the same way. "No towel for you?" Tori asks. "I might get distracted."

"I'm your muse, right? Inspiration, at your service," I say curtly.

With a chuckle, she takes a step toward me. Her foot slips in a puddle of water and she yelps, skidding into my arms.

"See?" she murmurs, melting against my rigid body. "It's already happening."

"Why didn't you tell me the truth?" I ask, fighting with everything in me not to tear off that towel and fuck her against the shower wall.

"Because I was angry," she snaps. "You pulled me away from my life and didn't give a damn about what I'd left behind. You were angry and you wanted to make yourself whole again. Besides, it's not like you ever cared enough to ask what I did for work. You just assumed my life was worthless, didn't you? That I was some mafia princess who didn't have any aspirations of her own outside of the criminal underworld I live in? And oh yeah, that I look exactly like the woman who publicly ass-rammed you by leaving you for your dad?"

Ouch. I want to punish her for shooting off that mouth again, but I can't because everything she just said is true.

"You're right," I grudgingly admit. "I didn't care what your life was before I showed up in Miami. I had a beef with your family and I wanted to bring them to their knees however I could to get what I wanted. And I hurt you because you were a constant reminder of what broke me."

"You took every opportunity to let me know how much you despised me." She lifts an eyebrow. "Why should I have opened up and told you a secret that I've never admitted to another person other than my sister? You didn't deserve to hear it."

I furrow my brow. "Secret? Why would you keep that a secret? You don't want your family to know you write smut?"

She pulls away with a gasp and smacks me on the front of the chest. "Fuck off. It's not smut." Her cheeks turn pink. "I mean, what I've published isn't smut."

"What I've read sure as fuck is." I can't help the grin from creeping across my face, especially now that I know it's my sexual prowess making her pussy quake. "And anyway, why would you tell me? Why now?"

"Because you brought this out of me. This whole dark and dirty side I never knew existed. I always associated it with your kind but–"

"Whoa. What the hell does that mean? *My kind*?"

Tori expels a sharp, frustrated breath. "Look, you're not my type, okay? I always tried to stay away from guys like you. I thought mafia guys were always cut from the same cloth and that you were all vicious, vengeful criminals. Just like my brothers and my father. And I didn't want that. I didn't want to be part of that life. Bad enough I was born into it without a choice. I didn't want it to be my future, too."

"So why didn't you leave when I gave you the chance?" I narrow my eyes. The vein in my throat throbs. "I told you to leave."

"Yeah, but did you really want me to go?"

"Doesn't matter. I don't want someone who doesn't want me back, someone who thinks I'm some lowlife scumbag that isn't worthy of her. I went through that once. I'm not doing it again. I'd rather you go."

"Well, maybe I'd rather stay."

"Why? Because of what I'll do to your family?" I roll my eyes and hold up my hand so that it faces her. "Fuck it. I don't even give a shit about getting revenge anymore. I don't need them. I don't need anyone except myself. And I'll rise up because I always fucking do. So if you're here because you're scared of what'll happen if you leave," I grunt, "then just get out. I don't need to hear any more about how I'm beneath you and what you had planned for your future."

I grab another towel from the rack and wrap it around myself before stalking out of the bathroom.

"You are unbelievable," she yells, stomping out of the bathroom behind me. "Cutting me off like that before I even got to finish. You are such a stubborn ass."

"I've been called worse, sweetheart," I bark. "Way fucking worse. So if that was supposed to sting, you're gonna need to try much harder." I dig around in the gift shop bag for a pair of shorts. Since it's the Ritz, my best options make me look like a dorky, preppy fucker who's about to meet Brett and Poppy for a Bellini at the lobby bar. Khakis and madras. Fucking awesome.

"You know what? Just forget I even said anything," Tori shouts. "If you're going to act like a spoiled dickhead brat, you don't need to hear another word."

She storms back into the bathroom, bends down to pick up the T-shirt and panties she left on the floor and storms back into the bedroom. With lightning speed, Tori dresses, a grimace twisting her face. Whirling around, she spots the pair of shorts I got her and pulls those on.

"It actually felt good to want to tell someone this secret, but shame on me for thinking you'd care." Her nostrils flare. "I was stupid for saying anything. You just stand there and figure out how you're going to get your hands on money that doesn't belong to you. I'm getting the fuck out of here and away from you and the toxic cloud that surrounds you."

I grit my teeth, clutching the obnoxiously colored shorts in one fist as she slips on flip-flops. "How far do you think you're gonna get? Whoever tried to kill you will find you. And without me, what chance do you think you have to survive?"

She whirls around, her eyes open wide with shock. "Are you kidding me? I saved my damn self from that asshat. And I can easily do it again. No weapon? No fucking problem. So save your whole white knight routine for a real damsel."

I want her to stay. I need her to go.

She reaches for the doorknob and twists it. The door opens. I pull on the shorts.

Don't let her go...

My mind screams the words but my body stays put. The struggle for control is constant whenever she's in my airspace.

It isn't until she's in the hallway that I finally speak.

"Stop," I say in a sharp voice, crossing the room with a couple of long strides. I catch the door in my hand before it slams shut, but Tori is already headed for the elevator at the end of the hall. I slide a shoe against the door to hold it open. Then I jog down the hallway. I easily catch up to her and slam my hand over the Down button.

"You're not leaving."

"You don't own me. Snatch someone else you can use to get off," she sneers.

"You think this whole thing is about getting off?" I grab her by the shoulders and push her against the wall next to the elevator. "Is that why you think we're here right now?"

"I think you believe that if anything happens to me, my brothers will fuck your shit up beyond recognition. And that's why you're protecting me. You're really protecting your own ass because that's all you care about," she seethes.

I close my fingers tight around her arms. "You're wrong."

"You're a liar," she sneers, trying to shrug off my grip. But I won't let her. I have her now and I'm not letting her go ever again.

"I told you, Tori. You're mine."

"Yeah, until you get your ass in a twist because you don't like it when someone else has the upper hand. So fuck you, fuck your wedding plans, fuck your life. I'm out."

CHAPTER 25
Konstantin

"The hell you are," I growl at Tori, my chest plastered against hers. "You're not going anywhere without me."

The elevator dings and the doors creep open. A couple steps out into the hallway. The woman stops short to gape at us. Her husband grabs her hand and pulls her down the hallway. She keeps tossing glances at us over her shoulder.

"I'm not marrying you. I'm taking back my life. And you have nobody to blame but yourself. You offered it up to me." Tori's eyes glow with ire. "Get your hands off me and step away, Konstantin. Because I have full use of my legs right now and I will launch an attack if you don't get out of my way."

I drop my hands and move backward, my pulse throbbing against my throat. Tori pushes past me and hits the Down button. This time, I let her.

She watches the floor numbers light up above the elevator. I watch her.

The elevator dings again and the doors open. Her shoulders squared, she walks into the elevator car. The doors start to close. I jump in between them, forcing them back open.

"Don't go," I say, my voice thick.

"Why?" She folds her arms over her chest. "I don't want to be here with you. I don't want to be anywhere with you."

The doors start to close again, then pop back open when they graze the sides of my shoulders.

"I want to hear your story." I stare into her eyes.

"Maybe I don't want to tell it anymore," she snips. She sticks out one hip, her defiant glare making me want to bend her over my knee and punish her with my hand.

"Don't make a stupid mistake by leaving. You got lucky against that guy, but you might not the next time around."

"Is that really why you want me to stay? You think I need protection?"

I take in a sharp breath because I can't bring myself to tell her the whole truth. "Yeah." Let's just leave it at protection for now.

The elevator doors try to close again. This time, she shoves me backward before they hit my shoulders. Then she follows me into the hallway. With a death glare, she turns on her heel and walks stiffly back to our room. She pushes open the door and kicks my shoe out of her path. I walk inside behind her. The door closes.

Tori turns around, an expectant look on her face. "Convince me. Tell me why I should even bother wasting my breath on you."

"Because I care," I say through clenched teeth. "I wouldn't have gone after you if I didn't."

"You let me leave in the first place. You told me to leave."

My temples throb. She really is fucking impossible. "Tell me," I choke out. "Goddammit, I want to know."

She stares at me for a long minute. I guess she's evaluating the reasons for and against telling me anything about her personal life. It's true. I didn't ask. But that was more because I was afraid of getting caught in the net she has no idea she even cast over me. Keeping her at arm's length protected me from falling harder.

Except it happened anyway.

"I've kept this secret for years," she finally says. "And there's a good reason why nobody knows about my writing career. I don't expect you to understand, but I hate my life. Hate it with a passion. For years, we've always had to keep a set of eyes in the back of our heads because of some enemy with a vendetta. And as much as I hate constantly having to keep looking over my shoulder, I knew I needed to protect myself by learning self-defense."

"So that explains why you're such a brutal bitch."

She flips me off. "Something you learned the hard way, plenty of times."

"Yeah, and? So you grew up mafia. What'd you think your life was gonna be? Champagne and roses? Hell no. It would always be fucking machetes and ice picks, princess."

"I hated that," she says through gritted teeth. "And what I hated more was that there was nothing I could do to escape it. My friends all knew. Their parents knew. I never said anything to anyone, but I didn't have to. It was like wearing a scarlet letter. My father...everyone was afraid of him. They didn't respect him. They were scared shitless anytime he was around."

She walks over to the couch and sinks onto the cushion. "I was always the bratva boss's daughter. I lost so many friends because of it. And guys..." She looks up with a shake of her head. "The ones I was interested in steered very clear. The only ones who dared come close were the thugs my brothers hung out with, guys who were all wrong for what I wanted out of life."

"And I'm one of those thugs," I say curtly.

"I thought so when we first met," she says, tracing her finger over the edge of the coffee table in front of her. "And that's why I resisted you so hard. I mean, obviously because you kidnapped me and almost choked me to death. Those were pretty glaring red flags."

"Is that it? You wanted to escape your life? That's why you decided to write?" I rub the back of my neck, the stress knot growing at warp speed now that it looks like I might need another way to keep myself liquid. And drowning in vodka isn't the optimum solution.

She nods. "Kind of. Awhile back, I dated this guy. I really liked him. Loved him, even. He was perfect, or so I thought. He came from a great family, his dad owned some big corporation. He was sweet and respectful and caring. Everything I wanted. Nothing like the greasy fuckers I was trying to escape."

"So what happened?" I pick up a pen from the dresser and twirl it around my fingers. "Why didn't you marry Prince Charming?"

A pained expression shadows her face, anger alive in her eyes. "Because his mother was the mirror image of Maleficent. We'd kept our relationship under wraps for a while. And one day, we ran into his parents while we were at the movies. His mother called me soon afterward when my boyfriend was at work. Said she wanted to meet for coffee. But she didn't want coffee. She wanted me to know that she was never going to allow my boyfriend to keep seeing me."

I stop twirling the pen, capturing it in my fingers. "What'd he do?"

"He told me it was over," she says in a dejected voice. "In a fucking text."

"Bastard," I hiss.

She nods. "Being a Malikov is like having a perpetual black cloud hanging over my head. People saw what they wanted to see. They didn't care about who I was on the inside, only what I was on the outside. So I started writing as a way to create my own fantasy world, a place where I could live vicariously through my characters and have the life I dreamed about." A faraway look glimmers in her eyes. "I know it probably sounds stupid, but it helped me. I write sweet, small-town romance novels because they made me feel happy, warm, and tingly. And safe."

I pull out my phone and put Tori's name into the Google search bar. "I don't see any books associated with your name."

"That's because I use a pen name, genius. If people knew what I wrote, nobody would read it because of who I am. How could a bratva princess possibly know about happily ever afters?"

"Okay then. What's the pen name?"

She hesitates for a second. "Savannah Rose," she finally says.

My jaw drops once I hit the search button for Savannah Rose. "Holy fuck," I mutter, scrolling through the pages and pages of search results. "*USA Today* bestseller, *New York Times* bestseller, *Wall Street Journal* bestseller." I look at her. "You're fucking major."

Tori shrugs. "Maybe because people want to escape into my world as much as I do."

I peer at the screen, gaping at the words I read. "Wait, you've got a movie deal, too?"

She stands up from the couch like a pole was shoved straight up her ass. "I did. I got the call right before you snatched me. And this was the week I was supposed to meet with the Netflix executives about the details and terms," she says in an accusatory tone. "So thanks for that."

"Fuck," I mutter, tossing my phone onto the dresser. I rake a hand through my hair. "You should have said something."

"I figured I had bigger fish to fry, what with getting kidnapped and then ordered to marry a thug criminal."

"I'm gonna ignore that comment." I take a few steps toward her. "I'd have flown you to California. Is it too late? Who do you need to call?"

"My life is kind of upside down right now what with the people who want to kill me on my ass. I think the movie deal may need to take a back seat."

"Fuck that. Listen, Tor, I spent so much time trying to make myself whole any way I could. I'm not proud of everything I did, but I own it. I don't want to be responsible for breaking anyone else." My lips stretch into a tight line. "You need to make that deal. Take it. You earned it."

"Oh, so now you decide to play the part of the supportive fiancé? Don't you have other things to focus on right now, like this gala and the people hunting us?"

"We've both always had targets on our backs, Tor. That's not gonna end today. But the question is, do you want to stop living because of it?" I move closer, the tension in the air thick enough to stab. "Because I sure as hell don't. And if I'm gonna be dodging bullets and knives, I want to do it with you."

"Because I'm so good at it?"

I snicker. "Partly. But mainly because I like you."

"You like me."

I nod. "A lot."

"Really."

"Yeah, maybe more than a lot. Maybe I love you-like you."

"How romantic. I'm going to use that exact line in my next book, okay?"

"As long as I get to keep testing out these scenes with you, then yeah. Go for it."

Her face glows brighter than I've ever seen it. She brings a hand to my face. It's warm against my skin. Heat floods my body, blood rushing straight for my groin. "I think I love you-like you, too. It's weird feeling this way. I'm so used to hating you."

"I know. Same. And prepare yourself, I'm about to give you a whole chapter of material to work from." I dip my head, capturing her lips in a deep kiss. Our tongues coil with white-hot heat and hunger. I shove my shorts to my ankles and kick them off before pulling hers off.

I lift her into my arms. The tip of my cock grazes her wet slit. I back her against the wall and thrust into her pussy. She claws at my back, lancing the skin as I fuck her with hard, deep strokes. I pound into her relentlessly. The wall shudders and shakes from the force of our bodies slapping together. Her cries pierce the air, my heart hammering to the point of exploding.

"Konstantin!" A pounding on the room door follows.

What the—?

I pull away, breathless. "Julian?" I rasp.

"Open the fucking door," he yells.

I slide out of Tori and toss her the shorts. I put mine back on and jog over to the door. I twist the knob and pull it open. He pushes past me, gasping for breath.

"Julian, what the hell happened?"

He collapses against the wall next to the door, hunched over like he's been kicked in the gut. "Shit, I can't believe…we let that happen. Kosta…" he pants. "I'm so fucking sorry. We led them right here. Right to us."

Blood turns to ice in my veins. "Led who here? And where the fuck is G?"

CHAPTER 26
Konstantin

"You need to be prepared, Kosta," Julian says. "They're coming."

Bang! Bang! Bang!

Tori and I exchange a look.

"Let us the fuck in, Romanov," a deep voice growls from the hallway. "Or we blow your brother's pea-sized brain out."

Sonofabitch.

Tori's shoulders relax slightly. "Oh, thank God," she mutters.

"Really?" I snap at her.

"Well, yeah. Nobody is here to kill *me*," she says.

I roll my eyes, stalking over to the door and flinging it open.

"Did you really think you were gonna get away with it, asshole?" Nik bellows, lunging for me. He grips my shoulders and drives me backward into the room. Alek and Luka follow him inside with Gregor sandwiched between them.

Nik launches his arm out, his eyes flashing with rage. I duck around his fist, spin around, and grab my gun from the dresser.

I point the gun at him. "Took you guys long enough to find me. If these two idiots," I nod toward Julian and Gregor, "had kept their goddamn eyes open, you'd have never been able to figure out where we'd gone."

"They tailed us," Gregor grumbles. "All because Julian needed fucking coffee."

"Trust me, we're happy they're such idiots," Nik spews. "Because now we're gonna fuck all three of you up."

I glare past Nik at Alek. "What's the matter, Sev? You didn't want to get messy outside the restaurant the other night? You had my guys tailed so these fucking lunatics could do the job you were too much of a pussy to do?"

Alek's face hardens, his eyes dripping with malice. "I did my job. I made you fucking cockroaches scatter. This is on you. You led us right to you, Romanov."

"And now that we have you, we're ending you." Luka steps toward me. "We're taking Tori and we're going to kill all three of you bastards. You're a lying sack of shit, and now you're gonna pay."

"Luka–"

"Shut up, Tor." Luka holds up a hand to his sister. "This doesn't have anything to do with you."

"I'm the one who was kidnapped. It has everything to do with me. Besides, you can't commit a murder here, much less three murders. It's the Ritz fucking Carlton. How do you expect to get away with it?"

"You let me worry about that." Luka's eyes narrow to slits. "He made stupid moves against us, so now he's gonna have shit pie shoved down his throat. It's gonna choke him hard."

Tori smacks Luka's hand away. "Excuse me, but I don't remember saying I needed a protector. I can handle him just fine on my own."

Luka glowers at her. "So well you couldn't even make a break for it?"

"I had a chance," she says, her eyes flickering toward me. "I didn't take it."

"Why the fuck not?" Nik asks, pulling out his gun and waving it in my direction. "Not that it matters now. We're taking you with us."

"You know, I'm not some fucking rag doll that gets passed around like a scorching case of herpes in a nursing home. I can make my own decisions."

"Sorry, but do I need to remind you that you were kidnapped?" Luka grimaces. "If you can take such great care of yourself, how the hell did you let that happen?"

Tori's cheeks blaze. "I was caught off-guard," she says in a sheepish voice.

"That's a fucking first," Luka sneers. "Because I've heard over and over again for years about how you don't need anyone to protect you. I guess you shit the bed on that one, huh?"

Tori rolls her eyes. "I can say the same for you dumbasses. You worked with the guy for months and had no idea he had a vendetta against you?"

Luka's jaw tenses. "Don't challenge me, Tor. This asshole put me in the hospital because he was so hell-bent on taking down our family."

Tori recoils. "What do you mean? The La Gioia bomb put you in the hospital. The bomb Kenzie and her family planted because her uncle was paid to hit us."

"Her uncle was paid by *this fucking guy* to take us out." Nik stomps toward me and sticks the barrel of his gun into my chest. "That's what we found out the night of the wedding, right before you were taken. He was the one who put the hit on our family. It was a whole big takedown plot, one that got foiled when we beat those jackasses. So are you still gonna choose to stay with him, Tor? Knowing he's a lying scumbag who used us to get close, and then snatched you to take control of our organization?"

Tori looks at me. "Is that true?" she asks in a disbelieving voice.

"No," I say as Nik twists the barrel against my skin. "Not entirely."

"How the hell can you believe anything that comes out of his mouth?" Nik yells.

"Why did you do it?" Tori asks, pushing Nik's guns away

from me. "Was it all part of your plan to hurt my family? Is that why you changed your name?"

"I changed my name because Viktor Malikov killed my father and effectively crushed my livelihood. Nobody would work with me when they found out we were hit by the Malikov Bratva." I give Nik's shoulder a hard shove. "And you can blame yourselves for letting this happen. You didn't dig deep enough into my past. That's on *you*. I beat you assholes. I got inside."

Luka leaps at me, shoving me backward against the wall. "You better be talking about our *organization*, Romanov."

I flash a nasty smirk. "I'm sure I have a highlight reel somewhere if you wanna check out what I really mean."

Tori lets out an exasperated gasp. "Can you all please stop acting like stubborn children?"

"The only way this asswad marries you is if you're standing on my grave when you say your 'I dos,'" Luka growls.

"That can be arranged," I hiss. "I almost got you once. Don't think I'll miss the second time."

"Enough," Tori groans. "All this dick swinging is giving me a headache and a massive case of whiplash." She turns to look at me, her gaze cold as ice. "And even though I am livid with you right now for keeping all that from me, you need to tell them about what happened earlier."

"Sev here didn't connect the dots," I grunt. "He didn't know my real name was Mikhail Federov when he gave you my alias. And he didn't know my father was working against the Brotherhood 7 with a guy named Arseny Siderov to take out the head of the Ukranian mafia. Olek Moroz was hit in that attack. He wasn't the target your father and the Brotherhood were aiming for, though."

I push Luka away from me and rake a hand through my hair. "Viktor had my father killed because of his betrayal, but Arseny wasn't satisfied with the real target getting away. He came to me hoping I was pissed off enough to go after your family as part of a grand retribution plan. He didn't know I already had a strategy in place to get back what I lost after my father was killed. And he didn't like it when I got inside the fortress and left him outside in the goddamn cold."

"What's your point?" Nik says. "Why should we give a damn about Siderov? He's your enemy."

"Not anymore. Siderov tried to kill us tonight. Planted a bomb in Julian's trunk. He drove the car back to my house and the thing detonated, taking out all the weapons inventory and cash I had stored there. My business, up in smoke. And when Tori saw an opportunity to escape in the confusion, she took it. But some guy grabbed her before she could get away. He had a gun. Tried to kill her." My lips press together.

"He could never," Tori interjects.

"Maybe not that time," I say. "But we both know that's not the end of it. Not by a longshot." I turn away from Tori and look at Luka. "My plan was to invade your organization by marrying Tori and stealing back what I'm owed. Things didn't work out the way I wanted. Other threats surfaced, threats I didn't anticipate." I rub the back of my head, capturing Tori's gaze. "This past week opened my eyes to a lot — things I wasn't prepared to handle. I didn't anticipate that things would work out the way they did. But I'm not giving up what I have. I don't give a damn what you say or do about it."

"What the hell does that mean?" Nik asks. "And before you answer, just know that I've got a knife as well as this gun, and I will fillet your ass if I don't like what you say."

"I'm not letting Tori go. If you thought you were coming here to take her back, fuck off because she's not going anywhere."

"My sister isn't gonna let some pathetic loser with a grudge call the shots for her life," Luka growls. "And we won't let that happen either."

"It's not up to you," Tori says in a quiet voice, walking over to Luka.

His eyes nearly pop out of his skull. "Are you kidding me,

Tor? Why would you throw your whole life away for this scumbag?"

"I did what I had to do to help my family," I say. "And you'd have done the same thing in my position."

"I'd have made sure to collect," Luka spews. "You just fuck up at every turn. And you think using my sister is gonna get you closer to our money? Think again, asswipe."

"I don't care about the money right now. I care about Tori. That's why we're in hiding now. It's also why Tori isn't going to leave my side, no matter what you guys think, say, or do. Someone wants us both dead. And my guess is that they're coming for you all next." I pick up the bottle of vodka and hold it out to Luka. "So how do you think your empire's gonna stack up against that threat?"

CHAPTER 27
Konstantin

"And you think you'd do a better job of keeping Tori safe from this enemy?" Nik scoffs.

"I do. I'm not gonna let anything happen to her." My eyes dart in her direction. She stares back at me, her nostrils flaring. She's definitely pissed, maybe enough to tell me to fuck off. But I had reasons for doing what I did to her family, and I stand by them, no matter what.

"You've got no money, no influence, no network, nothing. How the hell are you gonna hold off this enemy, Romanov?" Luka rolls his eyes. "Or whatever the hell your real name is."

"I did a pretty good job of convincing you that I was a contender, didn't I?" I snap. "You guys bought it. Maybe I'm just *that* good."

Nik steps toward me. He's got nothing on me as far as height and muscle, but he's brimming with rage. I won't cower to him, though.

Fuck that.

For six months, I had them eating out of my hand so they could grow their weapons empire, all because they were too stupid to investigate my background. How's that my fault?

"You're not keeping her." The words spew from his mouth like hot lava.

"Excuse me, but before you guys negotiate my future, let me just tell you to step the fuck back. Nobody dictates my future but me, understand?" Tori's spine stiffens when she looks from Nik to me. And when she stalks over to me and smacks me across the face, I don't stop her.

I deserve it.

"You deserve much worse," she seethes, almost as if she could hear my own internal thought. "And I hate you for keeping that from me."

"You may hate me, but you know you'd have done the same thing in the name of revenge." I turn to look at Luka and Alek. "Any of you would have. So don't give me your high and mighty bullshit. When it comes to protecting your family and livelihood, there are no-holds-barred. If you say I'm wrong, you're fucking liars."

Alek doesn't say anything. He just stands against the wall, his legs folded at the knee, his icy glare chilling my bones because I know he's not finished with me. He's not the least bit intimidated by anything I can say or do. I'm tall, but he's a fucking monster at seven feet. And he's not just a monster in physical form, either.

He might not have known much about me before he gave my name to Nik, but I did my research on him. And I know he pretty much singlehandedly took down Sofia Rojas, the head of a Colombian drug cartel, after invading a trafficking auction she'd been hosting. I've also heard the story of how he killed one of Sofia's lieutenant's at a Monaco restaurant using nothing but a fork.

So was I stupid for calling him out the way I did? Fuck, yeah. But it's a risk I had to take. I won't crumble in front of these assholes. I'm acting like I've got nothing to lose...even though now I do have something...*someone*.

"You're alive, aren't you?" I snap at Luka. Then I turn to Nik.

"And *your* fiancée and her family accidentally detonated that bomb early. So don't blame me for their fuck up."

"You've got some pair of balls for bringing Kenzie into this," he grunts. He launches a fist at me again and I block his massive arm with my own.

"Third time's the charm?" I say, glowering at him.

"Third time I shoot you between the eyes," he growls.

Tori grabs the sides of her head and lets out a frustrated groan. "There are very real enemies who want us dead. Can we just sweep this crap under the rug for a little while and figure out how to divert the next attack?"

"You expect us to work with this guy after everything he did to us?" Luka's eyes blaze as he stalks over to the window and takes a look outside.

"How the hell are we supposed to trust them?" Gregor snaps at me. "How do you know they won't fucking shoot us in the back of the head when they get the chance?"

"Because they have a lot to lose." I stare Luka down. "Not just Tori, but the rest of their family and their organization, which if you remember, was easy enough to penetrate. Vaska, Torres." I lift an eyebrow. "I had them coming in their pants for a chance to make some cash by selling you guys out. You think nobody else in your organization is gonna fold the way they did? Think again, *boss*," I say to Luka.

He turns away from the window. "So what the hell are you proposing?" he asks. "Because if you're looking for my guys to save your ass—"

"I've done a good job of covering my own ass, thanks. But we have an opportunity to hit Arseny and end him." I kick at a dust ball on the carpet. "He's coming for all of us. But we win if we take him out first."

"How are we supposed to find him?" Nik asks. "Or maybe we just wait for Dipshit One and Dipshit Two to lead him back here?"

"Fuck you, Malikov," Gregor sneers. "Vaska and Torres were

your guys, weren't they? Part of your trusted crew? You still wanna go with calling *us* the dipshits?"

"Enough," I say, putting my hand up to stop Gregor from talking. "I know where Arseny is gonna be tomorrow night. A guy we're doing a weapons deal with, Remi Kosovich, is hosting a gala. He wants me there to meet in person before we secure the terms of the sale. Julian brokered the deal, but he wants me there."

"Sounds like a trap to me," Luka grumbles.

"Exactly. It's no coincidence that Arseny will be there. But he doesn't know you guys will back me up going in. We get inside, find him, and ice him. Threat destroyed for good."

My gaze tangles with Tori's. "He thinks Tori and I are getting married. She's guilty by association to me and your father. He wants revenge and will do anything to get it. And if he's tied up with Kosovich, they both have skin in the weapons game. Crushing you all clears their path to the top. We need to launch a surprise attack. If we don't do this at the gala, we're all fucked."

"What about the weapons deal? We need that money, especially since you're giving up your plan to take down the Malikov family," Gregor says with a roll of his eyes.

"As if he'd have ever gotten a piece," Nik grumbles. He picks up a pen from a nearby table and flings it at the wall in frustration.

"I'm planning to kill two birds with one stone."

"Of course. Because you never go big with anything you do," Julian says, sarcasm dripping from his lips.

We all glare at each other, tense silence hanging over us like a poisonous cloud. Alek finally steps away from the wall and speaks up.

"The Malikovs are part of Red Ladro. That means they have the syndicate's protection." He narrows his eyes at me. "You don't."

"I don't need your boys' club to have my back," I shoot back. "But if the Malikovs are part of your little dark superhero team, guess what? Arseny will open fire on your asses, too. There won't be a limit to the damage he does. He's coming and he'll get rid of anyone in his way. He's proven it before."

Alek's eyes spit white flames. If he has a gun, I fully expect to see it in his hand and pointed at me very fucking soon.

"Do you have a death wish?" Tori hisses under her breath so that only I can hear it.

I shrug. "He'll respect me for bringing up a fair point. One he needs to think about."

Tori lets out a snort.

"The prick is right," Luka says to Alek. "We don't know who Arseny may have on his payroll, either. We have to be the ones to cut the head off the snake so we can preserve our organization."

"At the gala," I nod.

Gregor shoots me a look, and Julian mutters something under his breath.

"You guys have something to say? I ask.

"Fuck it," Gregor says, throwing his hands up. "Like you ever listen to anyone anyway."

"That's right. Alek, Luka, Nik — are we in this together or what?" I walk in Alek's direction. Luka may be the boss of the Malikov family, but Alek calls the shots for Red Ladro. If Luka wants Alek's support, he's gonna have to wait for Alek to give the green light.

And I know for damn sure that Alek isn't gonna make a bad business decision this time around.

Alek strokes his beard, his cold gaze making my skin crawl. I stop when I'm in front of him. Stupid ballsy move, but he needs to know that I'm not–

Before I can blink, he's got one of my arms around my back, twisted so tight that if I make even the smallest move, it'll snap in two. He throws me backward on the carpet, my arm wedged under me against the floor. He then digs his knee into my chest, using his weight to hold me in place. With one hand, he slaps my tattooed hand onto the floor next to my head so that the phoenix is displayed. Then with his other hand, he pulls a Zippo lighter from his jacket.

With the flip of his thumb, the orange flame glows at the tip. I struggle in his grip, but I'm paralyzed under his massive body. He holds the flame against my skin long enough to make it bubble and blister, searing the flesh.

"Get the fuck off me, you psychotic motherfucker," I bellow.

"You're young and stupid," he seethes. "This is a lesson. Learn from it, or a hell of a lot more of your body parts will be charred just like that bird."

His jaw tightens. I bite back another scream. Finally, he pulls the lighter away from my hand. "That's to remind you how quickly you'll turn back to ash. And trust me, I'll make sure you'll never rise again." His voice is dark and gruff, tinged with promise.

I asked for this. More than once. And I'm sure Luka or Nik wouldn't have stopped at the hand if they'd have thought of this mode of torture first.

After struggling to my feet, I shake my hand out and stare at the charred phoenix image. Alek's a fucking sadistic bastard who doesn't like his ego being dented, even if it's with the truth. Well, fuck him if he thinks this is gonna silence me. I grit my teeth just as a loud knock at the door interrupts the scathing words I want to spew.

"Yeah?" I ask, the hairs on the back of my neck jumping to attention.

"Mr. Romanov," a female voice calls out. "This is Cassie from Concierge. I'm just dropping off the tuxedo you had delivered."

What the—?

I twist around, furrowing my brow at my brother and Julian. They both shake their heads. A quick peek through the peephole confirms it's a woman dressed as a hotel employee. I squint at her name tag.

Cassie.

"You can just leave it. I'll grab it in a minute," I say.

"Of course. Please contact us if you need anything else."

"What the fuck is that?" Luka mutters, dragging a hand through his hair.

"Is it another bomb?" Tori asks, crossing the room and stopping next to me.

I pace in front of the door, my hand on the back of my neck. "Get back. I'm gonna open the door."

"Are you sure that's a good idea?" She puts her hand on my arm and winces at my burnt flesh.

"No. I'm definitely not sure of that. But I'm gonna do it anyway. All of you, get into the bathroom and close the door, just in case."

"Shouldn't we just leave?" Julian asks, a doubtful expression on his face. "How is that bathroom door gonna protect us?"

"If you wanna go, then go. But if the purpose was to get us to scatter, then good luck trying to escape whatever the fuck might be waiting downstairs."

Julian hangs his head, his lips tight. Gregor shoves him toward the bathroom. "Pussy," he mutters.

I give Tori a gentle shove toward them. "Go. Just to be safe."

She bites down on her lower lip. "I want to stay. This involves me, too."

"No risks," I murmur, stroking the side of her face. "Besides, if shit goes down, someone needs to be left standing so she can avenge us."

"Get in the bathroom, Tor," Luka orders.

She hesitates, then grits her teeth and follows Julian and Gregor.

Alek, Luka, and Nik all stare at me. I pull the door open and look left and right. The hallway is clear and quiet. I drop my gaze to the floor. A large white box sits innocently in front of the door.

Goosebumps pop up along my skin. I bend down to grab it, ignoring the stinging sensation that explodes over my inked hand. I pick it up and take it inside. The door slams closed behind me.

"Watch out," I say, pushing past the guys. I place the box on the dresser. "It's light. Really light. I don't think it's a bomb."

"What the hell could it be? Someone who knows you need a tux sent it up here," Nik says. "How is that even possible unless Arseny found out you were going to the gala? And if that's the case, your plan is fucked...and so are we."

I suck in a breath and pull off the lid, my heart pounding hard as the seconds pass. I lift the pieces of tissue paper until I finally see it.

Blood turns to ice in my veins, my insides submerged in a deep freeze. My temples throb. I press my fingers to them and take a step away from the box.

"Sonofabitch. She's the target," I choke out.

Luka shoves me aside. "What the fuck are you—?" His voice trails off.

Arseny's not coming for me. He didn't show up until I made my move against the Malikovs and snatched Tori. He could have killed me any time after I told him to stick his proposal up his ass months ago. But I'm still alive.

It's because he doesn't give a shit about me.

He's coming for Tori.

CHAPTER 28
Viktorya

"Nothing has blown up." I press my ear against the door, but only hear a faint murmur of low voices through the thick wood. "I think it's safe for us to go out."

"We should wait for Konstantin to give us the okay," Julian says, rubbing the back of his neck.

Gregor gives him a shove. "Jesus Christ, dude. Did you leave your balls in the glove compartment again?"

Julian glares at him. "Fuck you. Some people might say I'm smart to be cautious with all the shit that's happened in the past week."

"Some people might have plenty of other things to say, too," Gregor mutters.

I roll my eyes. "You guys can hole up in here. I'm not waiting anymore." Pushing the door open, I take a deep breath, my heart wedged in my throat. It's a good thing that there was no explosion. But something bad is looming in the air. I can feel it. And the fact that nobody has come to get us confirms that feeling.

Alek, Luka, Nik, and Konstantin all look up when I gingerly walk out of the bathroom. Luka's normally tanned face is pale, Konstantin's is red with rage. Nik's jaw is taut to the point where it might crack. Alek just stares at me, his dark eyebrows knitted together. He's the one who wordlessly drops the lid back onto the box.

As if I'd miss that sleight of hand.

"What's in the box?" I ask. My pulse hammers hard, my fingertips numb from clenching and unclenching my fists.

"Nothing for you to worry about," Luka says with a quick peek over his shoulder.

I look at Alek as I close the space between myself and whatever that package contains. "You covered it when I came out of the bathroom. Why?"

"Because it isn't important for you to see it," he says evenly, never averting his eyes.

"Why don't you let me be the judge of that? Don't treat me like I'm some frail and fragile piece of crystal that's going to shatter. I'm not Julian." I turn to look at Gregor. "My balls are always with me. Never in the glove compartment."

He smirks and winks at me. "Damn right, princess. You're a badass."

"Hey," Julian says defensively. "Leave me the hell out of this. It's bad enough I have the enemies of these fucking guys breathing down my neck because I'm guilty by association. I don't need yours, too."

With a snort, I storm toward the box. The guys form a human barrier, blocking me from grabbing the lid. "You've all seen what I can do to you if you don't move away from that damn box," I yell, balling my hands into tight fists.

"Tor," Nik says, pulling me by the arm. "It's important that you let us handle this now. We've got a plan and we're gonna take care of the people who want to hurt–"

"Nik, shut the fuck up," Konstantin grunts.

I whirl around. "Want to hurt *who*? *Me*? They can fucking bring it because I'm not going to hide, dammit." My heart beats wildly. I'm pretty sure my blood pressure is high enough to blast through the stratosphere.

Luka grabs the box and darts around Alek, heading for the

door. I play the damsel for a split second and let out a defeated sigh, my shoulders slumping. It's just enough of a show that Alek shifts slightly, convinced I'm not going to make a run for that box.

Dumb fuck.

He'll make better choices next time. I slip through the space between him and Konstantin, lunge for Luka, and tackle him to the floor once he has his hand on the doorknob. He pulls the box close to his chest so I can't grab it, but he obviously doesn't give me the credit I deserve because there's no way in hell he gets out of here without me seeing what's in the box.

I wrestle it from his tight grip. My fingers lock around the lid. He tries to pull the box away, but I knock off the top. Then I elbow him and punch it out of his hands. It lands a few feet away, near the bar. I scramble over to it, but Luka grabs my ankles to stop me. I pitch forward onto the carpet, kicking my way out of his grip, in pursuit of the box.

"Tori, stop," Konstantin says, his voice tight. I glare up at him, my hands clutching the white cardboard.

"Never," I hiss before dropping my eyes to the contents. I pull out sheet upon sheet of crumpled tissue paper. A yelp escapes my lips and my hand freezes in mid-air. "Holy shit..."

I grip the bridal veil by the crystal-encrusted headpiece and hold it up in front of my disbelieving eyes. My mouth falls open. It's beautiful. Soft white tulle edged with the same tiny crystals as on the headpiece. The stones are also woven into the fabric so that the bride would sparkle every time the light catches the facets.

But that's not why the strained sound erupts from my chest.

Fresh blood stains the innocuous-looking fabric, as well as my fingertips.

"Was there a message?" I gasp, still staring at the veil.

"I think the message is pretty damn clear," Alek mutters.

I drop the veil like it's just erupted into flames, my bright red fingers suspended in mid-air. "He wants to kill me."

Konstantin drops to his knees beside me and pulls me close to him. "He's not going to get near you, babe. I swear on my life I won't let him hurt you."

"You got in close," I murmur, still focused on my fingertips. "Remember? You figured out what people wanted, what they'd do in exchange for money. Everyone has a price, right?" I twist around to look at my brothers. "We know this. It's ingrained in our minds. We're always good until we're not. Until someone comes along waving lots of bills and making promises. Then, we're fucked."

"Not this time," Luka growls, kneeling on my other side. "Nobody will get close, Tori."

I shake my head. "You can't guarantee that."

Luka, Alek, and Nik exchange a glance with Konstantin.

They all know I'm right. If someone is willing to die, they can make the kill. The question is, how willing is Arseny to rely on someone else to carry out his work?

Or will he be the one to do the hit? Is this going to be his way to get back at my father for fucking up his plans?

"I've never been the target before," I mutter, dropping my hand into my lap.

Konstantin strokes the back of my head. But I don't want to be comforted. I swipe his hand away, pulling away from him. I jump to my feet and kick the box away.

"No, don't coddle me," I growl. "None of you dare do that. There is no fucking way that bastard is getting away with my murder. Hell fucking no. I will torture him within an inch of his pathetic life. And when he's begging me to just pull the trigger and end his excruciating misery, I will torment him more. And worse than any nightmare he has ever had."

"You'll have complete protection—" Nik starts.

"No protection," I shout. "I don't need it. Save it for someone who does."

"Don't be difficult, Tori," Luka says. "Or stupid. We all need it. All the time."

"Well then, keep it for yourselves. I'm not crying. I'm not cowering. And I'm sure as hell not hiding."

"You won't have to do any of those things," Konstantin says, rising to his feet. "I'm going to take care of him. This doesn't change the plan at all. And trust me, I'll get the bastard."

He looks at the other guys. "You know he won't show his face unless he's got plenty of his own protection surrounding him. We don't know his endgame. But we do know he's going to make a move. That's the message he's sending. He's trying to lure us into his trap. Except we're gonna set one of our own first."

"Don't you think we should try to find him tonight, before the gala?" Julian asks. "It seems pretty risky to let him live when he's made these threats against us. Besides, you don't know that the veil is meant for Tori. It could have just been a way for him to incite you and get you running."

Gregor nods. "He's actually right. We don't know that Tori is his primary target." He looks at her with a shrug and a half-smirk. "Sorry, I know you have lots of lethal plans for him."

"If he ends up caught in my crosshairs, he's gonna suffer, regardless of who his real target is. I don't take chances." My lips curl like I've just tasted poison, my gut wrenching like it's a piece of taffy being stretched, pulled, and twisted relentlessly.

"He's obviously tracking us," Konstantin says. "He knew Julian's car would eventually make it back to our house. He knew to send the package up here, which is a huge fucking security gap that the hotel is gonna hear about."

"Curious," Nik says, narrowing his eyes at Konstantin's shorts. "Madras? I never took you for that guy."

"Options were limited," Konstantin says curtly.

"That's a familiar theme of the day," Luka says darkly.

"What are we supposed to do until the gala?" Julian asks. "Sit around with our dicks in our hands? I feel like we need to do something. Now."

"Patience, Julian." Alek gives him a look. "Let him come to us. We're in control that way. You go running off, you immediately put yourself on the defensive. Sit tight, be prepared. That's how we win."

Julian frowns and stares out the window.

"We'll get rooms here," Nik says. "Better for us to be in the same spot."

Konstantin looks at Gregor and Julian. "You guys want to stay, too?"

Julian shakes his head. "I can't leave my mom at the apartment. Maybe we should go and get her, bring her back here with Lev? You need security on site if you're going to stay. And the Ritz has proven that they're a little loose with protection."

"Good idea," Konstantin says. "I'll make the arrangements."

I pace the room until everyone leaves. When the door finally closes for the last time, I look at Konstantin, ire knotting in the back of my throat.

"He's fucking dead," I hiss, balling my fists against my thighs. "And I won't need any help making that happen."

"Easy, Black Widow," he says, referring to one of my favorite badass Marvel comic characters. I'm Russian and damn destructive. How could I not idolize her?

"Easy, my ass. He called me out when he sent that veil. And I'm coming to play."

"Your safety is more important than revenge." He sweeps a hand through my hair. "I gave you my word. You need to trust me."

"I know, I just–"

The blaring ring of the hotel room phone interrupts my next thought.

Konstantin narrows his eyes, walks over to the phone, and stabs the speaker button. "Hello?"

"Mikhail, did you and your fiancée like the gift?" a deep, accented voice asks.

"Arseny," he hisses. "You motherfucker."

"You had your chance to work with me. You told me to fuck myself. Remember? I believe those are the words you used."

"You're dead," Konstantin growls. "Do you understand me?"

"You're so full of empty threats, aren't you? I got you twice. You can't run. You can't hide. You, Tori, or the rest of the Malikovs." He pauses. "Now, take care of that veil. It's Tori's something new to her, but also old and something borrowed since it belonged to one of my ex-wives."

My heart clenches. He's forgetting something.

Or is he?

"She needs something else, though. Something...blue." Arseny chuckles. It's a dark, ominous sound that has my skin crawling with dread. "*Blue.* Tell me, Mikhail. Doesn't it make you wonder *whose* blood is on that veil?"

CHAPTER 29
Konstantin

"A lot of bad things can happen at weddings." Arseny's voice takes on a demonic tone. "I'm sure your fiancée would agree. She knows exactly what wedding I'm talking about."

"You fucking bastard," Tori seethes, pushing past me and dropping to her knees next to the speakerphone. "If you did anything to my sister...if you hurt her at all...I will kill you with my bare hands. Do you understand me? You have never experienced the kind of pain and torture I will inflict on you if I find out–"

"Tori Malikov," Arseny says. "I didn't realize I had such a captive audience. Pun intended, of course."

"Tell me where she is," Tori seethes, her voice shaking with anger. "Tell me now, you sonofabitch."

"That's the thing about being in control, Tori. I don't have to take your orders. And your bullshit threats don't scare me. If I wanted you dead, you'd already be in a box. Maybe I've got bigger plans for you and your family. Maybe I'm about to execute them." He stops and laughs. A chill slithers over my skin. "Execute. Sounds about right."

Tori slowly turns her head toward me, her rage-filled expression screaming for revenge. She holds my gaze as she speaks tersely into the speaker. "I'm going to make you a promise, scumbag. Right here and right now. If I find out you had anything to do with Valentina's disappearance, I will cut your balls off and shove them down your throat until you choke on them. But I won't let you die. I'll save you, slice off your pencil dick with a steak knife, gouge out your eyes so you won't see what's coming next, and then I will slowly dissolve your body in a tub of acid from your feet to your head."

Jesus, she's descriptive. And I know she'll make good on each and every torture-tinged promise, too.

"You have a big imagination," Arseny says. "How well will it serve you once I take a machete to that pretty neck of yours?"

I grip the edge of the table, my knuckles turning white. "You had your chance to beat Viktor Malikov and you fucked it up. You trusted the wrong guy, motherfucker."

"Did I?" Arseny asks. "I'm not so sure I chose wrong. I guess we'll have to wait and see how things pan out. Are you getting excited? We're almost at the climax of this story. And I love a good climax, especially the big twist at the end. The one you never see coming. That's always my favorite part. Makes reading the book and watching the movie worth the time you spend."

"We're coming for you," Tori says, her teeth clenched. Red spots pop in her cheeks, a stark contrast to the suddenly pale skin surrounding them. "You won't be able to hide. We will find you. And we will–"

"The only thing you will do is suffer, just like I've suffered," Arseny grunts. "That is the one thing all of you can count on."

Click.

A strangled gasp slips from Tori's mouth. "Fuck," she whispers. "He has to know about Val. All of that bullshit about bad things happening at weddings, the blood, the 'something blue'..." She jumps up from the floor and runs to the room door. "He has her. Or he's...hurt her. We need to find her, now."

I grab my cell phone and follow her out the door and down

the hallway. She stops outside Nik and Luka's room, which they were lucky enough to get on our floor, and pounds on the door. "Guys. Let us in."

Nik pulls the door open a few seconds later. We walk inside.

"What the hell is up?" he asks.

Tori relays the details of the conversation, and Arseny's insinuations about their missing sister Valentina. "That blood might be hers. We have to do something. She could be right here in Sarasota."

Luka folds his arms over his chest. "Alek's guy wasn't able to find a damn thing out about her, and he's traced the entire world over. How would he have missed that she's right here in Florida, after all this time?"

I lift an eyebrow. "Alek has been known to fall short when it comes to researching a target. How do you know this guy is even legit? I mean, for fuck's sake, I slipped under his radar. Yours, too." And just as I say the words, a sharp pain slices through my burnt hand. It's like the fucking sicko is here in spirit instead of next door in his own room.

"He wants us to scatter. That was why he set off the bomb at Konstantin's house. We came here and he found us, taunting me with all that talk about bad things happening at weddings." Tori wrings her hands together as she stares out the window. "He's watching. He wants us to make a move. He has to have Val. She would be his leverage, right? He wants to hurt us, so using her to lure us is a perfect plan."

Nik punches the wall. "We have to find this guy. Now."

"I think you guys are chasing a ghost," Luka says flatly. "It's not about her."

"How can you say that?" Tori screams, running over to him and pounding her fists against his chest. "Don't you dare give up on her."

"I'm not giving up," Luka says. "I'm just saying she's been gone without a word or a trace for more than six months since her last call to me, and we've had people actively searching for her. If someone found her and snatched her, it would be the worst-kept secret ever with our network and reach. She's either in hiding somewhere or..."

The rest of his words don't need to be spoken. They hang in the air like a poisonous cloud, slowly killing all remaining shreds of hope for Valentina's whereabouts.

"She's not dead," Tori says. "She can't be."

"So how the fuck do we find out for sure what this cocksucker has up his sleeve?" Nik growls. "Whether or not he has Val, he's still coming in hot. We don't know why, we don't know how, and we sure as fuck don't know where or when." He turns to look at me. "I think the gala is bullshit."

A pounding at the door follows. Nik stalks toward it and flings it open. Alek glowers at us from his position in the doorway.

"Why does it look like you're about to give us bad news?" Nik asks.

"Because I am." Alek steps into the room and holds up his phone. "For shits and giggles, I had my tech guys hack into the security and phone systems here to track the deliveries and phone calls that came in today. I wanted to see if we could make a connection that would give us a location for Arseny."

"And?" I ask. Dread licks the hairs on the back of my neck.

"The security feeds came up empty. They didn't get anything using their facial recognition software. But I was just on with them, and they traced an incoming call to your room a few minutes ago. The phone number was registered to Remi Kosovich."

"Fuck," I breathe. "So Kosovich is working with Arseny to trap us or..."

"He's dead." Alek puts his phone into the pocket of his pants. "Because Arseny doesn't need him anymore."

I dial Julian's number. It rings once...twice...three times. "Sonofabitch," I mutter when it goes to voicemail. I get the same thing when I dial Gregor. "Where the hell are those guys? They should be back at Lev's apartment by now."

Questions pop between my ears like exploding bullets. I don't even know who I'm running from anymore. And the one guy who can lead me to Kosovich isn't answering his damn phone.

"Alek, see if your guys can get a location for Kosovich. Maybe they can ping a GPS signal or something. If he's not dead, he can lead us to Arseny."

A sudden blaring sound rings out. We run over to the window overlooking the parking lot. Cop cars and ambulances swarm the front of the hotel.

"What the hell is happening down there?" Tori mutters.

My blood runs cold. There's been so much talk of traps that it never occurred to me that we might not need to be lured anywhere. For all we know, just being here plunged us right into a quagmire of evil.

"I'm going down to check it out." I walk toward the door.

Tori grabs one of my arms, the one with the untorched hand attached to it. "I'm coming with you."

I turn and place my hands on her shoulders. "You are going to stay right here, do you understand? We have no idea what's happening, and if shit's gonna go sideways down there, the last thing I want is for you to be in the middle of it." I bring a hand to the side of her face and quickly brush my lips against hers. "I told you I'd protect you. Now it's your turn to trust me."

Her eyebrows furrow. "I hate that you're doing this alone."

"I used to think I could do shit like this because I had nothing to lose. No amount of risk bothered me." I drop my voice so only she can hear. "But I have something now. Something to keep safe. Something to love. I'll be fine if I have you to come back to."

Her lips pull into a quivery smile and she nods. "Be careful."

Nik walks over to us and hands me a gun with a roll of his eyes. "I don't need to see or hear any of the other shit, just so we're clear."

"Then it's a good thing you guys got a room down the hall," I say, grasping for a sliver of humor.

But the tension in the air assures me it's completely out of reach.

A few minutes later, I'm downstairs in the lobby. Groups of hotel personnel, cops, and EMTs gather in areas of the large, brightly lit space. I slip through the crowd, trying to listen to the conversations happening around me. That's when I see a few EMTs wheel out a gurney with a black body bag strapped to the mattress.

My chest tightens. The sound of a choked sob jolts me. I turn to see a young girl talking in hushed tones to an officer. He's making notes as she gives a statement. I move closer to them, straining my ears to hear what she has to say.

"She'd gone on her break and never came back," the girl weeps. "So I called her a couple of times. But her cell phone was under the concierge desk. An hour passed and nothing. I called her parents at home and they hadn't heard from her either." Another sob shudders her body and voice. "Please find the people who did this. Cassie was my best friend."

Cassie. As in Cassie the Concierge.

Motherfucker. Arseny had that poor kid killed.

If I didn't already have a million reasons to skewer his ass, now I have a million and one.

My phone buzzes against my leg. I pull it out of my pocket and let out a relieved breath. Gregor. Thank fuck.

"G, listen. We've got some big problems, and I need you guys to get back here as soon as–"

"Hold that thought." Gregor interrupts me, his voice grave. "Because we have worse problems than you can fucking imagine. And one of them is the blood on that veil."

CHAPTER 30
Viktorya

"Where is he?" I fist the sides of my hair, my heart speeding up like a race car engine with each second that ticks past.

A knock at the door sends me about five feet into the air. I lunge for the door handle, careful to press my eye against the peephole before I twist the brass knob.

"Oh my God," I gasp. I fling open the door and throw my arms around my brother Taras.

He holds me tight for a long minute. I breathe in his signature scent of Versace Eros. He's not usually the huggable type. He's more the throat-slitting type, if I'm being honest. But while I'm not used to shows of emotion on his part, it feels really good to have him here with us.

Especially with what we're about to face. We need Taras's brand of lethal and sadistic for what comes next in this very sinister story.

"What are you doing here?" I ask, reluctantly breaking away.

He nods toward Nik and Luka. "They called and told us about the gala. There was no way I was letting them have all the fun with the motherfuckers hunting you. Death? Dismemberment? Not necessarily in that order? I'm here for it."

I turn to my other brothers with a questioning look. "Is it safe for Mom to be home with Zak and Danil? Did you guys arrange for extra security since we're all here?"

"It's all covered," Luka says. "And Alek has some of his local guys keeping watch, too. They'll be fine. And so will we."

I nod, then turn back to Taras. "Did you see Konstantin downstairs?"

A flicker of disgust settles into his expression. "If I'd have seen that fuckhead, I'd have pummeled his ass into the ground." He narrows his eyes at me. "The guys filled me in on what's been going on with you two. Don't think that's gonna stop me from beating him to a bloody pulp."

I cock my head to the side. "Maybe in the next chapter? Because we kind of have a lot of other stuff to focus on right now, and I think it should be all hands on deck."

Taras rolls his eyes. "I'll think about it. But anyway, if he was downstairs, I'd have never found him. There's a mess of people down there, cops, emergency techs, ambulances, you name it. I saw a body bag, too."

My jaw drops. "Oh my God. Where the hell could Konstantin be?"

Taras looks at Luka and Nik. "Is it bad to say I wish it was him in the body bag?"

Nik snickers. "I think we've all had that wish plenty of times in the past week."

"I feel like a caged animal right now." I rub my hands down the sides of my arms. Goosebumps pebble my skin. "Can we turn up the air?"

"Tor, it's seventy-four in here." Luka points to the thermostat.

"Fuck," I mutter. I don't rattle easily, but then again, I've never been the star of a psycho killer's show before either. And knowing that Konstantin is in the line of fire makes me even more unsettled. I can't have his blood on my hands, too. I slam my fists against my sides. "We need to do something. Why are we just sitting around and not looking for this guy?"

"My guys are trying to find Kosovich," Alek says. "He'll lead us to Arseny."

I fill Taras in on the phone call we received and what we know about Remi Kosovich.

"I've heard of him," Taras says, grabbing a can of soda from the mini bar and popping open the top. "Billionaire who travels with an armored human wall surrounding him. I was surprised to hear he was hosting a gala. He's not the type to put himself in the spotlight."

I let out a frustrated groan. "We can't wait until tomorrow night, holed up in these rooms like hamsters spinning on wheels. We have to find him no–"

Knock, knock!

I dart past Taras. A quick glance out the peephole relaxes me for a split second...until I open the door.

Konstantin's forehead pinches, his expression dark as he stalks through the doorway. "I just got a call from Gregor. When he and Julian got back to my security guy Lev's apartment, they found the place trashed and Lev dead." The vein in his forehead throbs. "And Isabella was gone."

"No." A horrified gasp slips out of my mouth. "Not Isabella."

Konstantin nods. "No note, no leads, no trace. She's been the closest thing I've had to a mother for years. And I couldn't protect her."

My mind trips back to Arseny's comment about "something blue."

Dead. Lev. Possibly Isabella.

"It's not your fault." I snake an arm around his waist and lean into his side. "You couldn't have anticipated that she'd have been targeted, too." My throat tightens. "What the hell is this guy's game? Is he after us or you guys?" I ask Konstantin. "Because my head is spinning like a damn top right now, and I can't make sense of any of this."

"I think it's safe to say he's got a vested interest in both of our families." Konstantin looks at Alek. "You have anything on Kosovich's location?"

Alek shakes his head. "Nothing is coming up."

"The reason why the cops are downstairs is because one of the girls who worked at the concierge desk was found dead." Konstantin's lips pull into a tight line. "Her name was Cassie. Arseny must have had the poor kid killed after she dropped the box off to make sure nobody tracked that delivery."

"Scumbag," I mutter.

"I still don't get why he surfaced when we got back to Sarasota," Konstantin grumbles. "He had so much time to launch whatever attack he was planning after I told him to shove his proposal up his ass. Why did he decide to wait until now?"

"I wouldn't think he'd wait until the gala to take you out," I say. "Not when he's had so many chances before now."

"That's what doesn't make sense. But I'm done sitting around with my thumb up my ass. Arseny is out there, and he's making these moves to lure me out, too. So fuck it, I'm going. I'm not playing according to his rules anymore. I'm making my own rules."

"I'm going, too," Nik says, grabbing his gun and sticking it into his waistband.

Luka, Alek, and Taras do the same thing. They make up a small but deadly army of crime kings ready for battle, like a group of dark vigilante superheroes. For as much as they may hate Konstantin for lying to them, kidnapping me, and wreaking havoc on my entire family, they have his back. And he has theirs.

It's oddly heartwarming.

"Okay, so where are we going?" Luka asks. "Since we don't have a clue as to where the fuck these guys are?"

"If I'm right, we won't have far to go. Arseny knows we're here. And you'd better believe he's watching and tracking our every move."

"So we're just supposed to drive around and hope he comes

after us so we can fight him off?" I make a face. "Doesn't seem like the smartest strategy to me."

Konstantin lets out a sharp breath and grits his teeth. "We don't have a choi–" Then he stops. "Wait." He grabs his phone and stabs the screen. "I installed GPS trackers on all of our phones when we got the latest versions. If Isa has her phone with her, I can track her location."

"You really think they'd be stupid enough to let her take her phone?" Nik asks.

"If she had it in a pocket and they didn't check her before taking her, then maybe. It's worth a shot." Konstantin peers at the screen, and a hair of a second later, a notification bleeps.

With a grave look on his face, he looks up from the screen. "I found the phone. It's in Sarasota Bay."

"Shit," Luka mutters. "They found it and dumped it. Or they dumped her along with it."

"I'm gonna bet she's not with the phone. She'd be more useful to them alive than dead," Konstantin says. "We can go to Lev's place. He's got security cameras at his apartment. If we can get into the system and grab images, maybe we can use facial recognition to identify the fuckers and somehow track them. But we have to move. I can't stay here like a rat in a cage anymore."

"Tori doesn't have a gun," Taras says, putting down the can of soda.

I glower at him. "I'm probably the one of you who doesn't need one. Besides, there aren't many places for me to hide it, anyway. I'm practically in pajamas."

"Good point," Taras says, pointing his own gun at Konstantin. "And don't think I'm done with you, asshat. We've got shit to settle. Later."

"Great, like there aren't enough people out there who want me dead," Konstantin mutters, walking toward the door. He pulls it open, checks to his left and right, then leads the way into the hallway. Nik and Luka's room is close to the elevator, and since it happens to be on its way to our floor, the doors open almost immediately once Konstantin hits the Down button.

We pile into the car, a strange sense of camaraderie weaving us together. Despite the mistrust and ill feelings harbored by my brothers, we all have a lot to protect right now. And working together is the only way we'll win this twisted and deranged game of Arseny's.

The elevator doors open to the crowded lobby. A complete zoo of people swarms the space, holding up phones and recording the melee. It's a complete social media circus, and I'm sure the Ritz management is flipping the fuck out over the situation.

Yellow crime scene tape blocks off an area off to the left where I guess the girl's body was found. I shake my head. Another senseless death. My blood curdles as I remember all of the things I said I'd do to Arseny once I found him.

And hell, yes. I'm going to execute each and every one.

"Come on, let's take the side entrance. We're parked in that lot anyway, and it'll take us ten years to fight through the hordes of rubberneckers out front," Luka says, leading the way to the exit.

With one hand on the gun under his jacket, Luka pushes open the door. He jerks his head left and right before taking a step. "Holy fuck," he says, shoving it open all the way. He pulls his gun, holding it in his outstretched hand.

I push through my brothers, following Luka's gaze. My jaw hits the pavement. Some beefy guy has his arms wrapped around a screaming, struggling girl in leggings and a sports bra about fifty feet away from us.

A blonde girl.

A girl who looks exactly like me.

It's Mischa. Konstantin's bitch ex...and my doppelgänger.

Reality blasts me like a rush of frigid air.

They think they just kidnapped *me*.

Holy shit, it's true. I *am* the target...

CHAPTER 31
Viktorya

"Fuck me. She's Tor's identical twin," Taras says. "That's bad news for us. And worse news for the woman they grabbed."

"They think she's Tori. We need to stop them. They can lead us to Arseny." Konstantin grabs his gun and runs past us toward the dark blue Honda Accord across the parking lot. The masked guy shoves a screaming Mischa in the back seat, and before he can even close his door, the driver peels out of the spot and heads for the exit.

Taras pulls out his gun and darts across the side road. He points his gun at the tires of the Accord as it careens around the empty stalls. He fires off a few shots to stop the car, but by then it's too far away. He pulls his keys out. "Come on. We can't let them get away. My rental is close."

We all follow Taras to a nearby red Dodge Durango and pile inside. It feels like hours before we start moving, even though barely a couple of minutes have passed. I dig my fingers into the sides of the leather seat where I sit wedged between Luka and the door.

"This thing is a glorified minivan," Nik grumbles. "How the hell are we supposed to catch them?"

"I got it. Besides, they're driving a Honda, not a Lambo." Taras floors the gas pedal. He spins the steering wheel and corners like a race car driver. The Durango responds surprisingly well around the turns. Palm trees whizz past. When we get to the end of the private road leading into the resort, Taras doesn't hesitate before swinging the wheel to the left.

"Why the hell did you go left?" Luka yells from next to me in the back seat. "Maybe we should have gone right."

"Sorry, there wasn't time for a fucking conference," Taras grumbles. "My gut said go left, so I did." The engine roars, the truck getting the workout of a lifetime with Taras's heavy foot at the helm. I squeeze my eyes shut, now clinging to the "oh, shit" bar.

"He planned the whole fucking thing as a distraction," Konstantin grouses, scraping a hand over his chin. "Finding that body, calling the cops, the media circus. It was the perfect chance to grab their target."

"You mean the one they *think* is their target," I mutter. "And if we don't move any faster, our hopes of catching those guys will disappear like a magician in a cloud of smoke."

"I see something up ahead," Konstantin says a few seconds later, pointing at something in front of us. I peer through the windshield at the dark dot from my spot behind him.

"Can this thing go any faster?" I ask Taras, clutching the sides of Konstantin's headrest. We've advanced to warp speed and my stomach knots like a pretzel, but we're still too far behind the Accord.

"I'm a little afraid it might just explode if I push any harder. But fuck it." Taras stomps the gas again and the truck shudders slightly before gathering speed.

Konstantin opens the window as we close the space between us and the Accord. A gust of warm Bay air rushes at my face, blowing my hair around my face and blocking my view. He points his gun at the car's tires and fires. Once, twice, and finally, he catches the rear right tire.

The Accord skids across the asphalt and crashes into the brush lining the side of the road. The doors fly open, and two guys scramble out with guns in their hands. Taras doesn't try to avoid the line of fire. He drives straight into it.

"What the hell are you doing?" I yell, ducking behind the headrest.

Just before he crashes into the car, Konstantin lands a shot, and Taras wrenches the steering wheel to the left to avoid a collision. The Durango screeches to a stop, half in the road, half on the gravel.

The injured guy collapses to the ground, his face riddled with pain, his yells piercing the air. The second guy, the driver, jumps back into the car. He hits the gas. The tires squeal and smoke as the Accord juts out of the tall grasses. The car practically does a donut once the tires hit the road. Then it blasts off like a damn rocket while the guy on the ground keeps shooting at us, covering the escapee and keeping us at bay.

Bullets pepper the metal and the windshield of the Durango.

"Sonofabitch," Konstantin yells, firing off shot after shot at the guy on the ground who jerks left and right, his gun-toting arm now riddled with bullet holes. The gun slips from his hand. Deep red blossoms spread over the fabric of his shirt.

Konstantin and Taras jump out of the truck and run toward him. I push the back door open, my heart swelling to the point where it just might burst. My knees shake, threatening to buckle. But I push forward, powered by adrenaline and fury, and storm through the grasses. I drop to my knees next to Konstantin.

The guy flounders against Konstantin's tight grip around his neck, rasping for air.

"Tell me where he's taking her," Konstantin growls.

"F-fuck you." The kidnapper claws at Konstantin's scalded hand with his one good one, digging his nails into his raw, blistered skin. His eyes dart left and right, widening when he sees me. "Wait...what the hell?"

"That's right, asshole," I snap. "You grabbed the wrong girl.

What do you think your boss is gonna do to you when he finds out? May as well tell us where to find him so we can take care of him before he takes care of you for fucking up."

The guy lets go of Konstantin's hand and flips me off.

Konstantin's jaw clenches. He presses his hand tighter around the guy's neck. Dickhead kicks his one good leg out, a gurgling sound lodged in his throat. His eyes glass over and his movements slow, the life draining from his body like helium from a slashed balloon.

A flash of black catches my eye when the guy grabs for the gun on the ground next to him with his last sliver of strength.

"Gun," I shout, hitting Konstantin's shoulder.

Crack! Pop!

Two bullet holes puncture the guy's forehead. He goes limp in Konstantin's grip.

I gasp, twisting my head around in the direction of the shots. Alek drops the hand with the gun in it as he walks in our direction.

"What the fuck, Sev?" Konstantin yells. "We don't have a location on Arseny. This guy was gonna give it to us."

"Like hell he was. Get back in the truck. We're wasting time. The Accord can't have gotten far on that flat tire, and even if it did..." Alek holds up his phone. "I got a picture of the license plate and sent it to my data team. I gave them a description of the car and our location. They're tracking it now."

Konstantin drops the guy and we run back to the Durango and climb inside. A buzzing sound grabs my attention. Alek stabs something on the screen and speaks into his phone.

"The Accord is heading north on Tamiami Trail, in the direction of May Lane."

"How the fuck is that car still drivable?" Nik mutters. "They're hauling ass, even if the tires are zero pressure run-flats."

Alek continues feeding Taras the Accord's movements like he's morphed into a 3D version of the Waze app. We wind around what feels like all of Sarasota until we reach an industrial park.

Bright white buildings surround us, lined by a perimeter of tall, swaying palm trees.

"The Accord is in here somewhere," Alek says.

"What the hell is this place?" Taras asks.

"There's a warehouse around the corner registered to Remi Kosovich," Alek says, his voice taut. "Number six eighteen."

Taras drives cautiously around the side of the buildings until we find the one we're looking for. And the Accord is parked right outside the loading bay. We pull past the warehouse and stop around the corner before piling out of the truck.

Konstantin jumps out of the front seat. His phone vibrates and he stabs the Accept button. "G, Arseny's guys showed up at the hotel to snatch Tori. We tailed them to Kosovich's–"

Bang! Crack! Pop!

I scream as a hail of bullets rains hellfire on the truck. My brothers and Alek scramble out of the truck, shooting at the faceless assailants strategically hidden around the perimeter.

"Do not fucking move, Tor," Luka yells.

I clutch the sides of my head, my fingers tugging at my hair as bullets lodge themselves in the doors, hood, and roof of the truck. The explosion of shots rattles my brain. I peer through the windows facing the direction of the attack, trying to pick out some figure, but all I see is a sea of white.

A final shot fires. An eerie silence falls over the place. My ears ring, my temples throb. A sharp pain assaults my chest. I slowly push open the door. I slip off the running board and tumble out of the truck. I slam into the concrete, my shoulder taking the full impact of my fall.

I hit the ground right next to Konstantin. He's on his side, a pool of blood spreading under his right shoulder.

A strangled scream catches in my throat as I reach for him.

"Mikhail was always too reckless for his own good. I've got bigger plans for you and your family, Viktorya. And a much bigger vendetta to carry out."

I recoil and squint at the figure hovering over us to find a gun barrel pointed straight at me. Bile shoots up the back of my throat, angry tears springing to my eyes. "*You*. You fucking evil backstabbing traitor."

My insides plunge into a sudden deep freeze.

Isabella's lips curl into a demonic smile. Her hand never wavers, that gun still pointed right between my eyes. "Now, Tori," she hisses. "Is that any way to talk to your future mother-in-law?"

CHAPTER 32
Konstantin

A skull-splitting pain explodes down the right side of my head. I open my eyes a crack, just in time to see Isabella waving a Glock 19 in front of Tori's horror-stricken face. I roll over onto my back, another scorching jolt of agony shooting down my right arm.

Bringing a hand above my eyes to shield myself from the brutally bright sun, I slowly sit up. A wave of dizziness assaults me. I fall back onto my hands, bits of gravel digging into the flesh.

"What the hell are you doing with that gun, Isa?" My mouth twists as I look at the woman who has cared for my family for as long as I can remember.

Everyone has a price...

"I'm here to make sure that I get what I'm due, Mikhail," she says in her typical soothing tone, a harsh contrast to the cynical words tumbling from her mouth. I'd found it comforting that she never raised her voice. She was always easygoing and eager to keep the peace between our family members. It was nice to have a quiet, calming force in our otherwise volatile lives.

But tranquil is the last thing I feel right now. Betrayal slices through my heart with the jagged edge of a dagger.

"Now get up. You, too, princess," Isabella says to us. I stagger to my feet with Tori's help. A group of men with guns surround the Durango. We drove right into a fucking ambush...an ambush that Gregor tried to prevent.

Gregor. Fuck.

"Where's G?" I grunt, wincing when I try to move my arm. One of those fuckers clipped me in the shoulder and it burns like it's being torched. "What did you do to him?"

"Nothing yet," Isabella responds coolly. "But what happens next is entirely up to you. So be very careful what moves you choose. A lot of lives depend on them."

Alek, Luka, Nik, and Taras walk around to our side of the truck, their hands behind their heads. Tori's arm tightens around my waist.

"My God, what the fuck is happening?" she whispers.

"You're about to find out." Isabella grabs her and sticks the gun to Tori's temple. "Don't be a hero, sweetheart. Otherwise, they'll all have matching bullets in their heads."

Isabella pushes Tori forward. "Bring the rest of them inside," she says to her thug crew. "We can't take any more risks today, and the princess is key to everything."

Sonofabitch. She knows none of us will make a move while she's got Tori in her grip. And Tori knows we're all dead if she tries to escape. The most death-defying group of people I know, at this traitorous bitch's mercy.

We walk deep into the unknown with gun barrels pointed at the backs of our heads. Splotches of memories color my scrambled mind.

The phone call. Gregor's panicked voice. His ominous warning.

My temples throb; the banging sound reverberates between my ears. I clutch the side of my head to stop the pounding force so I can think, but it's useless. I can't form a solid coherent thought.

The warehouse is large and bright white. I stop short once we're inside, and the thug with the gun to my skull shoves me forward. "Move it, asshole," he mutters.

I grit my teeth. He's the first one I'm gonna kill. A quick glance to my right shows a stack of wooden crates lined up against the wall. I catch Alek's eye and he gives a small nod.

I don't know what's in those crates, but it just may be the exit strategy we need.

A shrill scream shatters the air, and another memory blasts through my mind.

Mischa.

"Mikhail, tell them they have the wrong girl," she cries out when she sees me, struggling against the chair she's tied to. "I'm not supposed to be here. I have a photoshoot. This is a big mistake!"

"Photoshoot," Isabella says with a soft laugh. "Who do you think set up your fictitious photoshoot, Mischa? You are exactly where you're supposed to be. Right where I want you. Now keep quiet or I'll tape your mouth shut."

"Fuck you, Isabella," Mischa shrieks. "I always hated you, you bitch."

Isabella's lips curl upward. She takes a few steps toward Mischa and stops. "So beautiful. Always turning heads and stealing men from others," she murmurs. With the side of the gun, she strokes the side of Mischa's face. Then she swings her arm out and smashes the gun against Mischa's cheek. Mischa screams again, a stream of blood trickling down the side of her face. An angry red mark spreads over her fair skin.

"Not so beautiful anymore," Isabella says, pointing the gun upward from its spot under Mischa's chin. Her lips quiver, her eyes wide open with pure, unadulterated fear. "When I get through with you, nobody will think you're beautiful ever again."

"What the fuck is going on, Isa?" I yell.

"You don't talk unless she says so." The guy behind me yanks on the collar of my shirt, flips me around, and swings his arm in the direction of my face. I block his punch with my bad arm, yelping like a bitch as his fist collides with my bullet wound. Then

I give him an elbow to the throat with my good arm. He doubles over, clutching his neck.

I turn to glare at Isabella. "You betrayed us? After everything we've done for you and Julian?"

She lets out a tight laugh. "Everything you've done for me? What about everything you've taken from me?"

"What the hell are you talking about?" I roar. "Who's taken anything from you?"

Isabella takes a few steps toward me, the gun still pointed at my head. "You killed him, Kosta. You killed your father. He begged you to protect him, and you just let him die. He was going to drop Mischa and take us away from all of the terror and the threats of death and destruction. He wanted to save me, to save his sons." She pauses, her dark eyes blazing with fury. "He wanted to give us a new life, a real chance at happiness. But you ruined it. And you turned your brother into a pawn for your own gain."

I hear the words she's saying but they make zero sense to me. "Gregor has always been an equal partner–"

Isabella waves her hand in the air. "Not Gregor. Julian."

Fuck *me*.

"Do you know how hard it was for me to sit back and watch you treat him like some errand boy?" She shakes her head, circling me like a predator. "It was always your show, and we were just props to you. Your plans, your brilliant ideas. Julian ended up doing all the work and getting nothing in return. So I have my own plan now. Julian will marry Tori. And I am finally going to get what I deserve."

"I don't give a flying fuck what you say or do, there's no way in hell I'm marrying that pussy bitch son of yours," Tori screams.

Isabella smiles at her. "It's good to have an opinion, darling. Just be careful about who you share it with unless you want me to become a monster-in-law."

Crack!

Tori crumples to the ground with a scream. Blood soaks the thin fabric of her T-shirt. I pull off my polo and fall to my knees next to her, pressing it against her wound. She grits her teeth and glares up at Isabella.

"Like this is supposed to stop me? A fucking flesh wound?" she snaps, pressing my shirt against the deep-red stain spreading over her shirt.

"It wasn't meant to stop you. It was meant to stop them." Isabella nods her head at the Malikov brothers. "She doesn't have long, gentlemen. We'll have to move quickly if you don't want the princess to bleed out."

"You crazy fucking bitch," Nik yells, rushing for Isabella.

She points the gun at him. "Don't think I won't pull the trigger, Nikolai. Because I will."

"What's the fucking play here, Isabella?" I growl. "What do you want?"

"Not just what Isabella wants. What *I* want."

My eyes dart in the direction of footsteps clicking over the concrete floor. Arseny Siderov walks into the room like he owns the fucking place, a shit-eating grin on his tan face. He's dressed in an expensive tux and looks like he's on his way to a gala.

Kosovich's gala.

"You think that Armani tux can hide what a shit stain you are?" I say through clenched teeth.

"I think it'll do," he says with a smirk. "Don't be bitter that I beat you at your own game, Mikhail."

"The fuck you did." I stagger to my feet. "You didn't win a damn thing."

"Didn't I, though? You're all here, surrounded by the threat of death. And I am about to get exactly what I want, what I've planned for months. Retribution."

Arseny pauses and looks at Luka. "When Mikhail came up with his ridiculous plan to infiltrate your family, I never thought he'd get away with it. I figured you and your brothers would be smart enough to stop him. But you weren't. You invited him into your bed with no clue who he really was and what he really wanted. Now look at you. All of you. Powerless to stop what comes next."

He turns and exchanges a knowing look with Isabella. "And trust me, what comes next is going to hurt like the worst pain you can ever imagine."

CHAPTER 33
Konstantin

My eyes tangle with Tori's. Her face pales more and more with each second that passes. She needs a doctor, now. The question is, how the hell am I supposed to get her to one with all of these goddamn guns pointed at me?

"I was disappointed that you turned down my proposal," Arseny says to me. "But I found a willing partner. And as it so happens, it's turned out to be a win-win for both of us."

"Where the hell is Gregor?" I yell. "What have you done to him?"

"Gregor is leverage," Arseny says. "Uncooperative leverage but leverage just the same. If you're not careful, he'll end the same way Lev did."

"Was it Lev's blood on that veil?" I bellow. "You twisted fuck!"

"He shouldn't have tried to fight me so hard. I was willing to spare him but he was too damn stubborn." Arseny walks over to me and holds up his phone. Gregor stands on his tiptoes at the edge of a table, a noose looped around his neck and his wrists tied behind his back. "Back to Gregor. You make a move, the table goes flying."

My chest tightens. The room G is in has the same white walls as the ones surrounding us. But this place is a maze. If shit goes sideways, how the hell am I going to get to him in time?

An impossible fucking situation.

Who lives and who dies?

And how the hell do I choose?

I slant Luka a look. The guy's supposed to be a master assassin. How the hell are these assholes around us still standing with guns in their hands, for Christ's sake?

But I know exactly why. Tori. She's the reason why we're all standing here with our dicks in our hands. And they all know it, too.

"Where's Kosovich? Did you kill him?" My jaw tightens. I want to know exactly how deep these cracks go. And how we were set up like fucking chess pieces.

Arseny smiles. "He was critical to my plan. He led me to Julian and Isabella. Of course I had to gain his trust. And then once I did, I cut his throat."

"If you brought us here to kill us, why are we still alive?" I ask.

"That's a good point," Arseny says. "There really is no good reason. When you kidnapped Viktorya, you brought sweet revenge play right to my doorstep. The heads of the Malikov Bratva and Red Ladro right in front of me. Helpless. Hopeless." He snickers and shakes his head. "You finally did something right, Mikhail. So now that I have what I want, I really don't need you anymore."

"What do you want from *us*?" Luka's voice spews disgust and disdain.

"Your father fucked me, and as the head of your family, you're going to suffer the consequences of his actions. I don't give a damn about your money. I have more than I could spend in ten lifetimes. The money is for Isabella. But even in death, I want Viktor Malikov to know that his legacy is about to turn to ash. That his all-powerful empire is about to go up in flames. And that all of his sons, the backbone of his organization, are about to take their places next to him. In hell."

All of his sons...what the *hell*?

"Leaving Tori as the sole heir to the Malikov fortune," Isabella finishes. "She will marry Julian, and all of it will be ours."

"You people are fucking insane!" Mischa screams, slamming the legs of the chair into the floor. "Oh my God, somebody help me, please! Why am I even here?"

Isabella turns to look at her. "Because you are a cheating, lying, dirty whore. You lured Mikhail's father away from me. And for that, you're going to die, too."

Mischa chokes on a sob, her face bruised, bloody, and tear streaked. Circumstances aren't ideal, but I can't say I don't love the display of anguish.

"What the fuck, Mom?" Julian's angry voice fills the room as he stalks toward us. "You're not killing her. You said I could keep her."

"Julian," Isabella hisses. "Stay out of this."

"The hell I will. We made a deal. I marry Tori, we kill her, and then I get to keep Mischa." He turns to look at Mischa, who couldn't look more shocked if she'd just stuck a wet finger into an electrical socket. "I've waited for her for too long. I love her. She's going to be mine, and you're not taking her away from me, Mom."

Holy hell. Are we seriously the main characters in this shit show?

"After all this time, you still haven't learned to keep your damn mouth shut," Isabella shouts, for probably the first time ever. "She is a dirty slut who deserves to die, just like the rest of them. You'll be richer than you've ever dreamed. You can have any woman you want. Let her go."

"I want her," Julian says. "If she dies, I'm out. And then you can pick up the pieces by yourself."

"Goddammit," Isabella yells. "No wonder your father always passed you over. You couldn't manage your way out of a paper bag. Do not ruin this for me. I finally have a chance to live the life I was meant to. Nobody will stand in my way, do you understand me?"

Mischa's jaw is on the floor as she looks between Julian and Isabella. "Fuck my life," she whimpers.

"Enough of this soap opera bullshit. Isabella, you have Tori. I don't give a fuck what you do with her." Arseny nods at one of his guys. "I have a gala to host, now that my business partner is indisposed. We've been here for too long. Take the Malikovs out. Line them up against the wall."

Gregor is literally hanging onto his life right now somewhere in the depths of this hellhole. And Tori could be bleeding to death. If there was ever a time to rise...

Fuck *yes*.

I have no weapon, but maybe I don't need one.

"Hey, is there any fucking way to rise from *these* ashes, Sev?" I yell. Alek looks at me, his eyes narrowed. I jerk my head toward the crates behind me. He gives a slight nod.

One of the guys grabs Luka by the back of the neck and shoves him forward. Luka stumbles, one hand on the ground. With his other hand, he grabs a hidden knife from an ankle strap. He jumps up and drives the tip into the guy's jugular. He pulls it out, twists around and jabs another guy in the eye.

Nik and Taras lunge for two other guys, ducking around their guns and wrestling them to the ground. Shots fire, bullets ricocheting off the concrete walls.

Isabella screams, firing into the air. "You are not doing this to me. It's my time!"

Mischa kicks her legs out, sweeping Isabella's. She trips, tumbling to the ground. "You little bitch. Let's see how much modeling work you get with a bullet hole between your eyes!"

Shots erupt into the air.

Mischa's chair flies backward, the wooden chair breaking once it hits the ground. More gunfire follows, the sound of exploding bullets deafening. Bodies hit the ground. Screams reverberate between the walls.

Alek tosses his Zippo lighter at me. I catch it and flip open the top. Tori hands me my bloody polo with shaky, clammy hands. I hold the fabric to the flame, light it up, and toss it at the crates, praying there's something flammable in them.

Flames roar, the noxious smell of burning wood and plastic choking me. I loop an arm around Tori and hoist her up. "I have to get you out of here," I rasp, holding her against me as we dart away from the firefight. I glance over my shoulder. Smoke billows from the crates. "I don't know how much time we ha–"

"None, Mikhail. Your time is up." Arseny grabs me by the arm. My bloody, dead arm. "I told you what would happen if you tried anything stupid," he hisses, holding up his phone. "Hang the bastard," he shouts into the speaker. "*Now.*"

CHAPTER 34
Viktorya

I wince, my body jolted by Arseny's sudden tug of Konstantin's arm. I keep my hand pressed tight over the bullet wound in my side as Arseny pulls him away from me. I hope like fuck there's an exit wound. I have to believe Isabella didn't actually want to kill me since that would keep her from her alleged fortune.

"What the fuck is in those crates?" Julian roars at Arseny. "You didn't think to ask before you iced the fucking guy?"

Smoke billows from the blaze, but nothing has exploded.

Yet.

"I had other things on my mind, you little prick," Arseny growls, still staring death daggers at Konstantin. He pulls out a silver pistol and waves it in front of Konstantin's face. "Like beating *you*. Which I'm about to do."

"Your fucking old ass isn't gonna be beating anything but your dick," Konstantin snarls, struggling in Arseny's grasp.

My chest heaves. I drag in long, deep breaths. Each one hurts worse than the last. I sneak a look at the gash. Blood stains my hands. If I don't put some real pressure on this wound, I'll be over.

I back up to a wall, keeping my hand pressed to my side as all hell breaks loose around me. Nik, Taras, Luka, and Alek are surrounded by slain bodies, thanks to Luka's knife and their collective will to kill and destroy. Isabella screams when Luka grabs hold of Julian and presses the tip of his knife to Julian's jugular.

"Just pull the trigger, bitch," he growls. "Because I really want to gut him right here while you watch. Your cash cow is gonna bleed out right in front of you."

Isabella screams and she lunges for Julian.

Crack!

She flies backward and crashes to the floor next to an unconscious Mischa and her broken chair, the barrel of the gun in Nik's hand smoking. Luka tightens his grip on Julian. "If you wanna be next, make a move. Please make a fucking move. Give me an excuse to end you, fucker."

I grit my teeth, searching for a weapon. Any kind of a weapon. The only thing I see is, ironically, a fire extinguisher hanging on the wall nearby. I creep along the wall and pull it off the hooks. The weight of the canister in my arms sends a ripple of anguish down my right side.

He needs me. I have to do this.

I inch forward, cringing with each step. Konstantin drives a fist into the side of Arseny's head, ducking when the pistol comes swinging around to his temple. He rushes at Arseny, a loud roar erupting from his throat. Then he gives him a hard shove backward into the flaming crates.

Arseny screams like a little bitch, engulfed in an orange inferno. Konstantin kicks his gun-toting hand and the pistol flies across the floor.

I hunch over and drop the red canister, the sound of clanging cymbals thundering between my ears. Taras runs over to me. He pulls off his shirt, balls it up, and sticks it against my wound.

"Hold it there for a second," he mutters, pulling off his belt next. Then he wraps it over the shirt and tightens it to the point where I choke out a cough. "That'll help keep the pressure on the wound. But we need to get you out of here."

"No," I gasp. "Gregor is here. Arseny just ordered the guy with him to kill him." I shake my head. "We can't leave him."

Taras glares at Konstantin over his shoulder. "Fucking guy," he mutters. "I should let him get iced for everything he's done. Him and his family."

I clap a hand over my nose and mouth. "We need to get away from these crates."

"Would have been good for him to find out what the hell is in them before setting them on fire," Taras says with a roll of his eyes.

A sudden spray of cold water blasts from the overhead ceiling sprinklers, courtesy of the clouds of thick smoke spreading through the air. Konstantin runs over to us. "Taras, get her to a hospital. I need to find my brother. He's here somewhere."

"No way," I say, clutching his arm. "I can help."

"You need to get to a hospital." Konstantin runs a hand over the side of my face. "Please go. I need to know you'll be safe."

"Safe, my fucking ass," Julian yells, barreling toward us with what looks like some kind of rifle. "You killed my mother. You killed Mischa. Now you all die!"

He points the weapon at us and pulls the trigger, not expecting the powerful recoil. He stumbles backward, and Taras fires off two shots to the chest. Julian crumples to the ground. Deep red stains appear over his white shirt, spreading until they've completely soaked through the fabric. Julian throws a hand over his chest, blood drizzling from the sides of his mouth.

"H-he was my father and he fucked me over, too," he rasps as Konstantin falls to his knees next to him. "None of us deserved his abuse. And he didn't deserve to have us as his family."

"You asshole," Konstantin mutters. "How could you do this? Why did you betray us?"

Julian shakes his head. "I only wanted to be with Mischa. Mom promised I'd have her. She's all I wanted. I didn't care about money."

"What about us?" Konstantin asks. "You didn't give a shit about us?"

"I was always on my own." Julian's chest shudders, his voice shaking. "Always separate. On the outside. I wanted Mischa because I wanted to be part of something I'd never had before." He gasps for air. "I just didn't want to be alone any...any..." His voice drifts off, his eyes floating closed.

Konstantin jumps up from the floor and kicks over a nearby table. "Motherfucker," he roars. "Even from the goddamn grave, my father is ruining fucking lives."

A small movement catches my eye. Arseny leans forward, his face bright red and blistered from the flames that engulfed him before the sprinklers brought him unwarranted mercy.

"You bastards are finished. All of you. Right fucking now!" Arseny grabs the rifle and fires it at us at the same time Luka blows a hole right into his skull. He collapses back against the crates, the rifle clattering to the floor.

A loud crash assaults my ears. A tortured, garbled scream follows. I choke out a strangled cry and stagger toward Konstantin. "Gregor. He's here."

Konstantin runs toward the side hallway where Arseny made his appearance a little while ago. I follow not too close behind. Taras wraps an arm around my waist and drags me along.

"Tor, you need to see a doctor," he hisses. "This is fucking stupid. I'm not losing you, too."

"No. Not until we get to Gregor. Please," I rasp. "Just help me. I'll be fine."

"Stubborn bitch." Taras grits his teeth but hangs onto me.

Konstantin tears down the hallway, weaving in and out of rooms when he stops short in one of the doorways.

"Fuck," he mutters, darting into the room.

More white walls surround us, the stench of death heavy in the air.

I clutch my midsection, my stomach twisted like a lanyard when I raise my eyes upward.

We're too late.

The wooden table lies under Gregor in pieces. Two guys point their guns at us. An eruption of gunfire follows. I fall to the ground. Nik, Luka, and Alek rush in behind us, peppering the wall and the guys with bullets.

Konstantin grabs a chair and leaps onto the seat. Luka tosses him the knife, and Konstantin slices the rope slung around Gregor's throat. He crashes to the floor, landing hard on the concrete. Konstantin jumps off the chair and presses an ear to his chest, his fingers searching for a pulse in Gregor's neck.

I lie still on the floor, my breaths short and shallow. A wave of numbness snakes down my right side. Icy fingers wrap tight around my insides.

Konstantin rolls Gregor onto his back and opens his mouth before starting chest compressions. I blink fast, my vision blurring slightly.

Please wake up. Please don't die...

He dips his head to give two rescue breaths before starting the chest compressions again.

"Come on, goddammit. Breathe," Konstantin yells.

But his voice sounds thick and muffled, like my head is submerged in water.

He looks up at me, his eyes red, his mouth quivering. He shakes his head.

No...please no...

I reach for him. My lifeline. The one I never knew I wanted... or needed.

But he's too far away. Or maybe I'm too far away.

I struggle to sit up, but my body doesn't respond. I float upward like my body is being carried away on a fluffy cloud. The white walls fade to black, blunting my pain. My eyes float closed after one final, stifled breath.

Then darkness swallows me whole like the demon I've tried to avoid my whole life but am finally forced to succumb to.

CHAPTER 35
Konstantin

"They kidnapped my brother and fucking hung him," I growl at the police officer as he scribbles on his little notepad. "How many different ways do I need to say it?"

"Look, I can appreciate the fact that you're upset, but it's important that I get all the details." The cop's eyebrows knit together. "We're talking about a multiple homicide in an area where people pay a lot of money to not ever have to hear the word 'murder.'"

"It was self-motherfucking-defense." I ball my fists, ignoring the sting of pain that follows when the burned skin on my hand tightens. "I got the call about his location and brought my friends for backup. We got there, and the bastards opened fire. My girlfriend was hit, too. For Christ's sake, they kidnapped an innocent woman from the Ritz-Carlton parking lot and dragged her to that warehouse while all you yahoos were running around the place holding your dicks trying to find the person who killed that kid in concierge."

"And both women were also with you in the warehouse?" he asks, his pen working furiously to record every word I spew.

"You want me to give you an attendance list?" I roll my eyes. "I've told you everything you need to know."

"The weapons you and your, ah, friends had on your person? They're all registered?"

I clutch the sides of my head. "No disrespect, Officer. But right now, you've got a warehouse full of dead bodies. Lowlife criminals who committed murders and kidnappings and arson. There's more than enough at that industrial park for you to investigate and clean up before the virgin ears of your 'people' hear words they won't like."

He's losing patience with me, but I don't give a shit. I have bigger problems right now than potential incarceration for being an uncooperative witness.

"How's your brother?" he suddenly asks, finally looking up from the pad.

"If you're finished blasting me with questions, I'd like to find out." I glare at him, my chest tight.

One minute I'd actually thought everything was miraculously going to be okay. I'd been able to revive Gregor at the warehouse before the EMTs showed up. He was awake, responsive, and alert.

Then we got here and the shit storm blew in right behind us. I got swept right into the eye of it and can't seem to claw my way out.

The officer nods and holds up the pad. "I'll be hanging around here for a little while. If I have any other questions, I'll find you."

I grit my teeth to keep the words I really want to say from slipping out and push past him without another look.

Alek meets me by the red double doors. "How's your arm?"

I shrug. "It's pretty numb right now. Like the rest of me." The bullet only clipped me, so damage was minimal. The doctor shot me up with some pretty powerful shit before he sewed up the bullet hole and stuck my arm in a sling.

Ironic that all of my actions leading up to today resulted in a bullshit injury for me, and near-death for the two people I love.

"I'm sorry about what happened with Julian and his mother. I know that kind of betrayal cuts way down deep. And even though you're a little prick bastard, you didn't deserve it."

"Thanks, that makes me feel so much better." Sarcasm drips from my words. My chest feels hollow, like a sledgehammer was swung right into the center of it, leaving a gaping hole in its wake.

"Life is full of shitty surprises, Romanov. If you wanna survive them, you need to be on your guard at all times."

"Is that what you told Luka and Nik when I snatched Tori?" I sneer.

"I can end you right now, you little cocksucker. Don't forget that." His dark eyes narrow, his tone menacing.

"Look, I appreciate your little pep talk, or whatever the hell this is, but I'm not okay with it. With any of it." My lips twist. "I fucking put my brother here. I put Tori here. I made them targets because I couldn't protect them from the enemies living under my goddamn roof."

"If you're gonna win at this life, you're gonna need to pick yourself up, dust yourself off, and move forward. Do you know how many times I've made my family and my wife targets?"

"With your charming personality? I can't believe it." I roll my eyes.

Alek grabs me by the scrubs one of the nurses gave me when I ran into the Emergency Room without a shirt on. He tugs the fabric tight and pulls me close. "Keep your friends close," he hisses. "But never fucking take your eyes off your enemies. Always assume they're lurking and ready to strike. And when they do, be ready. That's how you win."

He lets go of me and gives me a little shove backward. "Tori's done. That's what I came to tell you. Luka, Taras, and Nik are in with her now, but she wants to see you. Your fucking pity party is over." Alek claps me on the back. "I'll be out here."

"Okay. I'm going in to get an update on G first." I push through the door with my good arm. My sneakers squeak along the polished tile floor. A burst of anger erupts from my gut like a raging bonfire. This isn't a pity party. It's a goddamn train wreck, and it's all on me — the deaths, the betrayal, the lies, the deceit.

My jaw tightens at the sight of the pale blue walls on either side of me. Another fucking aggravating color. How is it possible that a color can quell emotions? May as well paint the damn walls bright red and unleash the emotion. Open Pandora's box and let people fucking feel.

I dig my heels into the floor harder and harder with each step I take toward the nurses' station.

Darkness permeates my mind and poisons my memories. Years of lies wind around my heart and squeeze it like a vise.

I was so focused on building myself up from the goddamn ashes that I let everything around me go up in smoke. I did things out of spite, I hurt innocent people, and I brought harm to the people I care about most.

"Mr. Romanov," a crisp female voice calls out, interrupting my self-beratement.

I twist around, my stomach wrenching like an invisible hand has just punched a hole in it.

A petite woman with red hair and freckles greets me. "I'm Dr. Cavanaugh, Gregor's attending physician. I just wanted to give you an update on his condition." Her eyebrows furrow as she scans the pages of a chart in her hands. "As you already know, upon arrival, he was drowsy and restless. We immediately ran blood tests to check for oxygen levels, and then took chest and spine X-rays to determine the extent of damage from the noose. Fortunately for Gregor, you arrived just in time and cut him down before any major injury was sustained. And you were smart to perform CPR right away. A few seconds delay could have resulted in a very different outcome for him."

"So…" I swallow hard. "Does that mean he's going to be okay?"

She pulls down her surgical mask, a smile lifting her lips. "Yes. He is."

I fist the sides of my head and lean backward against the wall, a sigh of relief slumping my shoulders. "Thank God," I mutter.

"We're going to keep him for observation for the rest of the day, just to make sure there is not a delayed reaction to the trauma. And if everything looks good, you'll be able to take him home."

"When can I see him?"

"I'll have someone get you in a couple of minutes once he's settled." She smiles again. "I imagine you want to see Viktorya Malikov now? I was told by her brothers that she wants to see you."

"Yes, can you tell me which room she's in?"

Dr. Cavanaugh points to a room down the hall on the left. "Room 8."

I jog toward the open doorway when a voice floats into the hall.

"Mikhail?"

It stops me dead. I back up slightly and peer into the room just before Tori's.

Mischa flashes a weak smile at me. "Come in."

My eyes tangle with hers, but I don't move from my spot in the doorway. "I don't think we have anything else to say to each other. I'm pretty sure we said it all the other night."

She nods. "I don't blame you for feeling the way you do. But I do have something more to say to you. A few things, actually. Please? All I'm asking for is a minute."

I square my shoulders and slowly approach the bed. "How are you feeling?"

"Well, I'm alive, so there's that." Her shoulders slump, a defeated look on her face. Her skin is paler than normal, and the mischievous sparkle has gone out of her eyes. I guess that happens when the threat of death hangs over you like a guillotine blade. She raises a hand to the back of her head. "The doctor said the concussion isn't too severe, and I'll probably be out of here in a few hours."

"Okay."

"How's Gregor?"

"Out of the woods, thank fuck. They're moving him for observation, but he's good. Gonna make a full recovery."

"I'm really happy to hear that," she says, her voice breaking. A loud sniffle follows. "I'm sorry. I don't want to keep you, I know you're worried about your friend...your fiancée, I mean."

"Yeah."

"Mikhail, I just wanted to tell you I'm so sorry for everything. What I did was horrible, and I can't ever take it back."

"Is that all?"

She lets out a deep sigh. "I've been going through a really rough time since we broke up. I was dragged into the ditches by your father before he died, thrown into the mess between him and your mother. He cheated on me, too, by the way. My modeling career plummeted. That's why I'm here. When that bitch Isabella said she baited me with the photoshoot, I realized it was my own fault that I was forced to look death in the face and acknowledge all of my past mistakes, and believe me, there are more than I care to count." Mischa shakes her head. "I escaped death and a lifetime of hell with Julian by the skin of my teeth, all because of your friends."

I lift an eyebrow. "I'm glad the near-death experience helped you get all introspective and shit. Well, I've gotta go."

"I get it. I'd want to get away from me, too." She turns a sad gaze up at me. "I hope your fiancée knows what a good guy she's getting. I definitely do."

I back away from the bed. "Take care of yourself, Mischa."

Tori caught my eye months ago because of her resemblance to Mischa. I projected so much hatred for Mischa and my father onto Tori, and in the end, I fell harder for her than I'd ever imagined was possible. And now, with each step I take toward her room, I release the full weight of the disgust and disdain that's plagued me ever since I walked in on my father and Mischa together.

I'm finally free.

CHAPTER 36
Konstantin

Tori waves me inside the room when I appear in her doorway. "How's Gregor?" she asks.

I slide a hand down the side of her face. "Good. The doctor is going to let me know when I can see him."

"I'm so happy to hear that," she says with a squeeze of my hand.

"How are you feeling?" I ask.

"Like new." She smirks. "I knew that crackerjack crazy bitch didn't want me dead. Although if I did become her daughter-in-law, that end might have come quicker than not."

"You're the most agreeable, even-keeled, tranquil person I know," I joke. "How could you possibly piss off anyone to the point where they'd want you dead?"

Tori giggles. "People who live in glass houses shouldn't throw stones."

"Glass houses are overrated, especially here in Florida. Hurricane season will tear the shit out of them."

"Not to interrupt all this cutesy bullshit you've got going on with my sister here, but this thing between us isn't over," Taras growls. "If you think you're just gonna get away with everything you pulled because Tori doesn't want to kill you anymore, doesn't mean there aren't plenty of others who will gladly do the job for her."

"Yeah, this isn't over," Nik says, standing from his spot on the window ledge. "And I think I'd like to pick up where Alek left off in the hotel room. I've got a Zippo, too. And I'll happily burn off every tattoo on your fucking body."

I lace my fingers with Tori's. "If that's what it'll take to get your blessing, then fine. Torch me."

"Blessing for fucking what?" Luka glares at me like he's trying to fry me like bacon in a pan using only his eyes.

"I want to marry Tori. I want her to be my wife."

"Are you insane?" Nik yells. "You kidnapped her and almost got her killed. You almost got us *all* killed, you asshat."

"It doesn't change how I feel about her."

Dots of pink color Tori's cheeks and she grins at me.

"You mean the way you love me-like me?" she asks with a knowing glint in her gaze.

"Love you-like you, my fucking ass," Taras grumbles.

"Love you-love you," I murmur. "I love you, Tor. From the second I put my hands around your throat."

"How fucking romantic." Taras rolls his eyes. "I should've shot you at the warehouse when I had the chance."

"But you didn't. So that's on you," I say, my eyes never leaving Tori's face. "And your fuck up is my gain."

"I love you, too, Jake," she says with a wink.

"Jake? Is that your real name?" Nik roars.

Tori bites down on her lower lip. "No," she says. "Let's just say it's kind of my pet name for him."

"Jesus Christ," Taras mutters. He looks at Luka. "You're just gonna let this happen? After he almost killed you?"

"I'm fucking invincible, Taras," he says. "And I think fucked-up love stories seem to run in this family. Who am I to tell Tori she can't be happy with that dickhead? Look at me and Natasha and Nik and Kenzie. Twisted fairy tale shit, yeah?"

"How the hell are you gonna allow someone we can't trust into the family?"

"Not for nothing, but I don't trust you guys, either," I snap.

A light knock on the door stops Taras from spewing more hate. Dr. Cavanaugh pops her head into the room. "Mr. Romanov, Gregor has been moved to the second floor and is in room 206. You can stop in whenever you're ready."

"Thank you, Doc," I say.

"I'm coming with you," Tori says, gingerly shifting herself toward the edge of the bed. She winces. "Help me out. And don't even think about stopping me."

"You don't have to come. Stay here and rest–"

"No," she says. "He's going to be my family." With a look over her shoulder at her brothers, she smiles. "That's right. I'm marrying Konstantin. Or whoever he is. Because I love him."

Luka smirks. "As if there was anything we could say to stop it from happening."

"The only smart one in the bunch," Tori says. "That's why you're the boss." She looks up at me. "Let's go."

A few minutes and a wheelchair ride later, Tori and I step off the elevator on the second floor. I wheel her down the hallway to room 206. Gregor is leaning back against a pile of white pillows, a lazy smile on his face while a gorgeous brunette fawns all over him.

When she finally leaves, I wheel Tori closer to the bed and bend down to give him a half-hug while cradling my bad arm.

"You scared the shit out of me," I say. "When I ran in and saw you hanging there...fuck. I thought it was over."

"Thanks for saving my life." He grins. "And thanks for taking a little bit too long to get to me so that I could spend the next few hours with Nurse Emma. Maybe she'll give me a sponge bath before I leave. I feel really dirty."

Tori chuckles and immediately lets out a groan. Her hand flies to her side. "Fuck, that hurts," she gasps. "And you're a sick and twisted puppy, G."

"Sick and twisted, yeah. Must be in the blood." He looks up at me. "By the way, speaking of sick and twisted, I think I was in pretty bad shape at the warehouse. Must have been hallucinating because I imagined that your whore ex-fiancée Mischa was loaded into one of those ambulances."

"You weren't hallucinating." I quickly fill him in on our run-in at the Ritz, how Isabella lured her here under the guise of a modeling job, and how Julian had held a torch for her all this time and wanted to keep her for himself.

"Sonofabitch," he mutters. "That makes so much sense now. I always thought he had a thing for her."

"Since when?" I ask.

"Since I walked in on him jacking off to one of her lingerie ads." Gregor waggles his eyebrows at both of us. "Sick and twisted all the way. Just like his mother. And just like his father, too."

"Yeah." I bring a hand to the back of my neck and massage my strained muscles. "Who the hell could have ever predicted any of that to happen?"

"He was our brother," Gregor mutters. "And crazier than a shithouse rat."

"Grape doesn't fall far from the vine."

"Which grape? The mother or the father?" Tori asks me.

"Both," Gregor and I answer together.

"I'll take cold-blooded killers any day over those psychotic bitches," I mutter.

Tori kisses the top of my gauze-wrapped hand. When the nurse stitched up my arm, she treated my hand, too. "Sounds like the perfect happily ever after to me."

CHAPTER 37
Viktorya

"Where are we going?" I stare out the window at the rows of eucalyptus trees lining Los Gatos Boulevard.

"To celebrate," Konstantin says as he turns left onto Blossom Hill Road. "Big news deserves big surprises."

"Good surprises, I hope." I flash him a grin, the same one that has been plastered across my face since signing the contracts at Netflix headquarters earlier this morning.

"Only the best for you." He reaches over and gives my hand a little squeeze.

"Something tells me you're going to want me to write about what happens next, am I right?" I tease.

Konstantin catches my eye and winks. "Maybe. We'll see how inspired you get."

"I can't wait." I do a little shimmy in my seat, letting out a gleeful whoop. "Babe, can you believe this is happening? *Small Town Superman* is going to be made into a movie. *My* book. *My* story." I clasp my hands together as he drives through the entrance for Vasona Lake State Park. "How is this real freaking life?"

A couple of hours ago, I signed contracts that officially make me a writer for the movie adaptation of my bestselling book. I'll be one of the producers, I'll have a say in the casting, and I'll get to walk the red carpet at the premiere.

With Konstantin by my side.

Yes, Konstantin. Whoever he was is in the past, and Konstantin Romanov is the guy I want in my future.

And maybe my future as an author will take a new turn when I publish our dark and spicy romance. I still haven't figured out the ending, which in my eyes, is actually our new beginning.

Our story isn't exactly the pixie-dusted fairy tale I thought I wanted. It began with a kidnapping and a near-strangulation, which, off the bat, kind of defy the rules for romance. And instead of the upstanding, chivalrous, and honorable hero sweeping me off my feet, it stars his dark and deviant alter ego getting me on my back, bent over the couch, against the window of the hotel...anywhere and everywhere.

He's everything I never knew I wanted...or needed.

My real-life romantic muse.

The proof is in the offer I just got from one of the big publishing houses back home on the East Coast. I sent Sheila the partial manuscript for my dark romance, the one sparked by the filthy threats, dirty promises, and sinfully salacious punishments delivered by Konstantin's hand. I figured it would be a hard sell since it's so off-brand for my pen name, but people clamored for it. And with a six-figure deal in hand, Savannah Rose is about to branch off into the darkness.

"It's only gonna get better," Konstantin murmurs, driving down a quiet road. The rippling waters of Vasona Lake glitter in the early afternoon sunshine.

"My God, this place is gorgeous. How did you find it?"

"I did some research. Found some of my own inspiration." He pulls off the asphalt and heads down a gravel-lined trail. The truck bounces a bit over the uneven road. Tall trees with hanging overhead branches create a trellis of sorts. We drive deeper into the brush until we reach a clearing right on the shore. The Range Rover rolls to a stop next to a thicket of bushes.

Konstantin puts the truck in Park, turns off the engine, and gets out. He jogs around to my side and pulls open my door before offering me a hand. I lace my fingers with his and step onto the ground, gravel crunching under my feet.

"There's something so familiar about this place," I muse, looking around. I feel like I've been here before, which is so odd because I've never been out to California in my life. But the view of the lake, the smell of eucalyptus, the crispness in the air. I feel like I've been smacked with sudden déjà vu.

"Well, this is part one of the surprise," he says. Then he reaches into his back pocket and pulls out a black scarf.

"Kinky," I say, running a finger down the front of his white T-shirt. "Is that for my wrists or my ankles?"

"Your eyes," he says with a grin.

"Oohh. Okay, I'll play." He ties the scarf over my eyes, takes my hand, and guides me forward. I move with ginger steps since the ground is uneven. Birds chirp. A cool breeze whispers against my skin and flutters through the leaves.

"We're here," Konstantin says, stopping. I stand still next to him, anticipation making goosebumps pop up along my arms and legs. He slowly unties the scarf. I blink fast to adjust my eyes to the light. Then a disbelieving gasp escapes my lips.

"Konstantin..." I clap a hand over my mouth as the exact scene I've written about comes to life before my eyes.

Vases of brightly colored sprays of star-gazer lilies surround a large yellow blanket. Lit candles line each edge. In the center stands a bucket of Veuve Cliquot champagne bottles, two crystal flutes, and a large brown wicker picnic basket. A platter of strawberries and chocolates sits just beside the basket, along with bowls of brown sugar and whipped cream.

Tears spring to my eyes. "You actually read it?" I whisper, a sob catching in my throat. The setting for my most famous scene from *Small Town Superman*. How did I not connect the dots as we drove through the park?

His lips curl upward. "Of course I read it. Don't you know the book is always better than the movie?"

A giggle-sob bursts from my chest. "This is amazing. The best surprise ever."

He shakes his head. "Not even close." He leads me onto the blanket and hands me a champagne flute. Then he picks up one of the bottles and pours us both a glass.

"We need something to toast to," I say with a sniffle.

He nods. "I agree. But first, I need to ask you a question."

My heart floats so high in my chest, I feel as if I'm being carried through the skies on a big fluffy cloud. I smile through the tears, my fingers trembling as I clutch the stem of the glass.

Konstantin places his flute on the ice, rises to one knee, and pulls a black velvet box from his pocket. He flips open the top, and a huge pink diamond ring sits in the center. I reach out to trace the edges of the glittering stone, the exact one Jake proposed to Karina with in *Small Town Superman*.

I raise my eyes toward Konstantin's, my lips quivering as he asks the question we both already know the answer to.

"Will you make me the happiest man in the world by becoming my wife?"

"Yes," I squeal, throwing my arms around his neck. Joyful tears spill down my cheeks.

I still can't believe the arc our story took. Talk about the craziest twists and turns imaginable. But the ending...the excitement of marrying someone I love and the idea of sharing forever together...it's perfect.

And I'm sure my mother will be thrilled to hear the news, that one of her daughters will finally get her happily ever after.

A tiny pang jolts my heart when the realization hits that our wedding will be missing someone incredibly important to me. Valentina would be so happy to stand by my side and witness Konstantin and me begin our forever together. I wish with everything in me that she'd gotten her own perfect ending and charmed future.

I pray there is a chance she still can. Someday.

When Konstantin's lips capture mine in the sweetest and most promising of kisses, I know that this moment couldn't possibly be any bit more beautiful than if I'd written it myself.

Which I did.

And our happily ever after?

Well, that's not something that could ever be told in one book. Ours will be the most epic of romance sagas, complete with twists, turns, and spice galore — all the ingredients for a sinfully sexy story that will have us flipping pages for a lifetime to come.

Epilogue
TARAS

"You missed the exit for the house," Tori calls to me from the back seat.

"Look, I'm a little hungry, okay?" I peer at her and Konstantin in the rearview mirror. "I waited at the airport for you guys for hours because of the storm that never hit. The least you can do is buy me some dinner." What I leave out is the fact that I'm bringing them to their surprise engagement dinner at Il Gabbiano, Tori's favorite restaurant on Biscayne Boulevard. It would have been nice to have it at La Gioia, but Konstantin fucked that up when he put a hit on the place.

"I guess we can wait a little while to get home," Konstantin murmurs against Tori's ear. "I hope you're not too jet-lagged."

She lets out a giggle and my stomach actually clenches. I wrap my fingers tight around the steering wheel, my lips twisting like I've just tasted dog shit. It's bad enough I just saw my sister getting felt up by some guy in the back of my brand-new gunmetal gray Dodge Charger Hellcat. But knowing said guy is becoming part of my family after almost destroying it is a jagged pill that scrapes the sides of my throat every time I try to swallow it.

I had no desire to be part of the decorating committee and

meet at the restaurant early, so I got stuck with the job of chauffeur instead.

"Romanov, the only reason why you're allowed in this car right now is because you're marrying my sister. But don't think that a wedding ring will keep you from getting choked if you step outta line," I growl.

"Taras, come on. You have to stop being such a prick to my fiancé." Tori pauses. "Otherwise, he won't let you be our baby's godfather," she finishes in a singsong voice. Another round of giggles follows.

I slam my foot on the brake as we approach a red light. "Baby? Nobody told me anything about a baby."

Tori and Konstantin exchange a knowing look.

"That's because you're the first one to hear it," Konstantin says.

It's the first time I've seen him smile and not wanted to carve his lips off his face with my stiletto knife.

"A baby," I say incredulously. "Holy fuck. I can't believe it. Congratulations, guys."

"We just found out this morning. It's super early, but we didn't want to wait anymore." Konstantin gives Tori a hug.

Even in the darkness, I can see them both glow like flaming Roman candles.

"You still hate me?" Konstantin asks.

The light turns green, but my foot stays pressed to the brake. I stare at the empty stretch of road, trying to process the news. My kid sister, having a kid. I shake my head. It's amazing how the news of a baby can make so much disgust and anger fade away like a fart in the wind. Not that I'm letting him off the hook that easily.

"I may need some time before I answer that. Like, maybe nine months." I try to keep a straight face, but now I've got baby on the brain and my lips betray me.

"Just don't say anything yet, okay? It's a night of lots of surprises!" Tori exclaims.

I let out a chuckle and shift gears before lifting my foot off the brake. "A fucking baby. I can't bel–"

"Taras," Tori yells. "Watch out!"

Blinding light flashes in my periphery. An SUV barrels through the red light, heading straight for the side of my car. I swing the steering wheel to the right to avoid the crushing impact, but my hands move like they're pushing through thick tar. Time slows to a screeching stop. Screams shatter the air as the Hellcat spins and skids across the pavement until the passenger side door crashes into a guardrail.

My body lurches forward, my head crashing against the steering wheel before falling backward. The noxious scent of seared metal and burning rubber assaults my nose.

"Guys," I mutter what feels like hours later when my mouth finally decides to work.

No response.

I slowly crane my neck, a sharp pain exploding down my left side. "Guys," I say again. "Can you hear–?"

My door opens. I fumble behind my back for my gun, but before I can grab it, I'm staring down the barrel of someone else's.

"Get out of the car now, Taras. You're coming with us."

I blink fast, squinting into the bright lights behind the man with the gun. "Who the fuck are you?"

He's wearing black sunglasses and a baseball cap pulled down low over his face. He steps backward, and three other guys point their guns at me.

"You're not in a position to ask questions. Make a stupid move and we open fire on your sister and her fiancé. And then we blow up Il Gabbiano. Now get the fuck out of the car."

"Why should I believe you're not gonna do any of that if I go with you?" My temples throb, vision blurring from the smack of my head against the steering wheel.

"Because I need leverage, Taras. If I take everything away from you now, you'll have no reason to cooperate with me. So get the fuck in my car, and your family will be spared. Resist and you all die, including your sister. And spoiler alert, I'm not talking about the one who's unconscious in your back seat." He pauses, a sinister grin lifting his lips. "I'm talking about Valentina."

Taras Is Up Next! Are You Ready For His Explosively Hot Enemies to Lovers Captive Romance?

Click here to read MERCILESS MONSTER on Amazon - Free On Kindle Unlimited—>

SNEAK PEEK OF MERCILESS MONSTER

TARAS

Alexis slides across the couch cushion, stopping when her leg grazes mine. Her lips curl into a slow smile. "I saw you talking to my dad. If anyone can drive someone to drink, it's him. He's pretty scary."

I lean back against the couch, my cock very aware of her nearness. "I don't scare easily."

"Good," she murmurs. "Because that would be a big turn-off."

I quirk an eyebrow. "Does that mean you're turned on?"

She bites down on her lower lip and traces a finger over the top of my hand. "You don't seem like the kind of guy who needs to ask."

"You don't seem like the kind of girl who needs to hear the answer."

Our gazes tangle. Lust sparks the air between us. My skin prickles as her deep blue stare sweeps over me.

I nod toward the setup on the dance floor of my nightclub. "All your fans would be really disappointed to know you're back here making a move on me."

Alexis shrugs. "Well, I had no choice since my father would have cut off your dick if you made one on me first."

"You think I'm afraid of him?"

She cocks her head to the side. "You're definitely afraid of one of us. Which one is it?"

"I'm trying to be respectful of my business partner. You don't shit where you eat."

"I have a few ideas about where you can eat. And *what* you can eat."

"Sounds like maybe your father should be more worried about you than any guy."

"He raised me to speak my mind and take what I want."

She closes the space between us. I catch a whiff of a heavy perfumed scent that screams of sex and sin. Alexis flips her hair over her shoulder and leans forward. I try hard to not stare at her bikini top but those tits taunt me, begging me for a look and a taste.

Fuuuuck. Why do I feel like I'm in some twisted version of *Punk'd* where Vlad is gonna leap out from a dark corner with an ice pick in his hand?

"He's gone," Alexis whispers, almost as if she read my mind.

"So you're afraid of him, too," I say with a chuckle.

She giggles and the head of my dick tingles. "No need to poke the sleeping bear, you know? Now how about you buy me that drink?"

Alexis slowly rises to her feet, giving me a full view of everything she has on display. And I'm loving every second of the show. I stand up and she gives me the same eye-fucking that I just treated her to.

"So, Karma, huh?" Alexis asks. "Not a bad choice for a night club name."

"Everything you do here comes back to you threefold."

"Sounds promising." She runs her hand down the side of my arm. "I'd like to see how that plays out."

We walk over to the bar. She grins at Lila, the bartender who looks more deflated than a flattened helium balloon.

"Can I get a Grey Goose martini? Dirty, please." Alexis looks up at me, making no effort to hide the hint of suggestion in her expression.

Lila shoots me a glare that tells me she is definitely gonna spit in my vodka and in Alexis's martini then turns around and stalks to the other end of the bar.

"So, Netflix, huh?" I say. "Did you ever think that was gonna happen once your business took off?"

"Never in a million years. But I always figured shamelessly promoting my motorcycle restorations by modeling with them while wearing teeny tiny bikinis would catch someone's attention."

"I think it's safe to say you've caught everyone's attention."

"Everyone?" she asks.

I open my mouth to answer but at that second, a bright flash of light catches my eye. Another damn camera flash from the dance floor blinds me. I furrow my brow as two guys approach one of the girls here with Alexis and smack her ass. She screams, shoving her hands at their chests. And the fuckers just laugh.

Alexis gasps. "What the hell?"

I clench my hands into tight fists and stalk toward the dance floor. "Get security," I snap at my brother Zak along my way. Then one of the guys shoves the blonde and yanks open his long black trench coat. He pulls out an AR-15 and fires it into the air. The glass chandelier shatters and crashes to the floor.

I stop short and grab the gun from my waistband. Screams reverberate between my ears.

Time slows. My legs feel like they're moving through the thickest tar. The other guy with the shooter pulls out his own AR and with a sinister chuckle, opens fire on the crowd. Bullets explode. People dive to the floor. Panic and fear are so thick in the air, I choke.

My brothers Luka and Nik run over, guns in hand. I squeeze off a few shots but one of the shooters takes off for the side door.

"Stop that bastard," I bellow to Ilya, one of our heads of security. "Don't let him get away."

"I've got the other one," Luka grunts, tearing after the first guy who opened fire.

I run after Ilya who has a head start because of his location.

"Get out of the way," I yell at Ilya before I tackle the shooter to the floor. I smash his head into the ground until his face is covered with blood. "Who the fuck do you work for?"

I yank the guy's head backward by his hair. Sick fuck actually smiles.

"You'll find out when he wants you to."

"What the fuck is that supposed to mean?" I slam him into the ground one more time to make absolutely sure I've broken his nose. Another round of gunfire erupts behind me. I roll off the guy, pointing my gun at the chaos.

"Taras!" A piercing female scream follows.

I drag myself to my feet, chest heaving. A sharp pain assaults my chest.

It's Kenzie, Nik's fiancé.

The shooter rolls away from me and darts toward the door.

I don't bother to go after him.

I can't.

"We all have targets on our backs."

Those words loop through my mind as I stagger toward Nik, my eyes rooted to the spot where he's sprawled near to the bar. Kenzie leans over him, her tears mixing with the blood stain spreading over the white fabric.

"You'd better be prepared, Taras."

No.

Not this time.

Not fucking again.

"This is what happens when you fuck up, Malikov," a deep voice growls from a few feet away.

My throat constricts, knotted by regret and rage when I turn my head. A thick arm holds Alexis captive, the other hand pressing a gun to her head. Her eyes are wide with terror.

"You gotta learn to pick your business partners better," the guy hisses. "Now everyone dies."

Click here to read MERCILESS MONSTER on Amazon - Free On Kindle Unlimited—>

Meet Kristen

Kristen Luciani is a *USA Today* bestselling author of steamy and suspense-filled romance. She's addicted to kickboxing, Starburst jelly beans, and swooning over dark, broken anti-heroes. Kristen is happily married to her own real-life hero of over 20 years.

In addition to penning spicy stories, she also has a part-time job as her three kids' personal Uber driver, which she manages to successfully juggle along with her other tasks: laundry, cleaning, laundry, cooking, laundry, and caring for her adorable Boston Terrier puppy. Mafia romance is her passion...and her poison.

Follow for Giveaways
http://on.fb.me/1Y87KjV

Private Reader Group

http://bit.ly/2iQBr5V

Complete Works On Amazon
https://amzn.to/3HgM5y1

VIP Newsletter
https://dl.bookfunnel.com/28e0amc80q

Feedback Or Suggestions For New Books?
Email Me! KRISTEN@KRISTENLUCIANI.COM

Want To Join My ARC Team?
https://www.facebook.com/groups/316777206096987

Want A FREE Book?
https://bit.ly/2Jubp8h

Instagram
http://instagram.com/kristen_luciani

BookBub
https://bit.ly/2FIcoP1

facebook.com/kristenlucianiauthor

twitter.com/kristen_luciani

instagram.com/kristen_luciani

CPSIA information can be obtained
at www.ICGtesting.com
Printed in the USA
LVHW080737261122
734074LV00053B/4369